A NOVEL

FLUX

JINWOO CHONG

MELVILLE HOUSE
BROOKLYN • LONDON

FLUX

First published in 2023 by Melville House

First Melville House Printing: January 2023

Melville House Publishing
46 John Street
Brooklyn, NY 11201

and

Melville House UK
Suite 2000
16/18 Woodford Road
London E7 0HA

mhpbooks.com
@melvillehouse

Library of Congress Control Number: 2022947913

Designed by Beste M. Doğan

ISBN: 978-1-68589-193-0
ISBN: 978-1-68589-035-3 (eBook)

A catalog record for this book is available from the Library of Congress

The authorized representative in the EU for product safety and compliance is Easy Access System Europe, Mustamäe tee 50, 10621 Tallinn, Estonia.
gpsr.requests@easproject.com

"It's a pleasure to encounter a work like Jinwoo Chong's debut novel, *Flux*, that offers a healthy dose of brain-bending pleasure without making it the whole point . . . *Flux* happily offers a moving appraisal of lives buffeted by personal and systemic traumas; a deep dive into the good, the bad and the ugly of self-serving corporate culture; and no shortage of 'wait, what the heck just happened?' thrills." —***New York Times Book Review***

"The narrative pleasures of *Flux* lie less in the big reveals than in watching Chong knit together genre tropes from sci-fi movies, speculative fiction, and thrillers to tell a story about how what we remember can imprison us . . . An imaginative exploration of how cultural memory and grief interact."

—***Washington Post***

"A smart and stylish addition to the tech thriller genre with interesting things to say about family, society and, indeed, reality itself."

—***Gary Shteyngart,* author of *Little Failure***

"Jinwoo Chong's engrossing debut braids three narratives—a boy in mourning, a whistleblower, and a laid-off media employee—to unspool a mystery examining pop culture and time." —***Vanity Fair***

"Jinwoo Chong's experimental debut brings to mind Charles Yu's similarly genre-bending novel *Interior Chinatown*: Both express a deep affection for Hollywood nostalgia, cut through with the bittersweet reckoning with their imperfect heroes who nonetheless made for unprecedented representation."

—***Literary Hub***

"*Flux* is brisk, stylish, and sexy, a high-stakes noir thriller that makes room for big philosophical ideas." —***Philadelphia Inquirer***

"As Chong's characters intersect through time and space, both style and substance pour out of the seams of this striking debut novel." —***Esquire***

"It's rare for an author's debut novel to gather a lot of buzz, but that only shows how intriguing *Flux* is . . . Jinwoo Chong has crafted a lavish mystery that's hanging-off-the-edge-of-your-seat good." **—*Cosmopolitan***

"A time-traveling noir and ambitious climate novel, *Flux* takes a close look at what happens when twenty-first-century egomaniacs bring their grifts to bear on the climate crisis. The result is a story that is equal parts wry and tender."
—*The Millions*

"A brilliant and enjoyable sci-fi tech thriller . . . "Flux" is haunting. I cannot begin to describe the plot without spoiling the joy of discovery. At its heart is a guy, trying to define himself even as he realizes that there's no box to describe everything he's experienced and everything he feels."
—*Pittsburgh Post-Gazette*

"Stunning . . . a profoundly moving story about grief, and about surviving in the hyper-capitalistic world of today . . . Chong knows how to boldly blend the boundaries of genres . . . an immensely rewarding read."
—*International Examiner*

"Mind-bending . . . Chong writes with such subtlety and skill that readers won't realize the true nature of the speculative mystery at play until they're already waist-deep in these interlocking narratives. The result is a gorgeous speculative gem." **—*Publishers Weekly*, starred review**

"Not yet 30, Chong bursts forth, Athena-like, with an impossible-to-simply-label masterpiece that melds various genres—from Bildungsroman to speculative fiction, coming-of-age drama to epic tragedy, crime documentary to noirish thriller—into an intricate literary mosaic."
—*Booklist*, starred review

For my father

The fact is that, insensibly, the absolute strangeness of everything, the sickly jarring and swaying of the machine, above all, the feeling of prolonged falling, had absolutely upset my nerves. I told myself that I could never stop, and with a gust of petulance I resolved to stop forthwith. Like an impatient fool, I lugged over the lever, and incontinently the thing went reeling over, and I was flung headlong through the air.

—H. G. Wells // *The Time Machine*

FL
UX

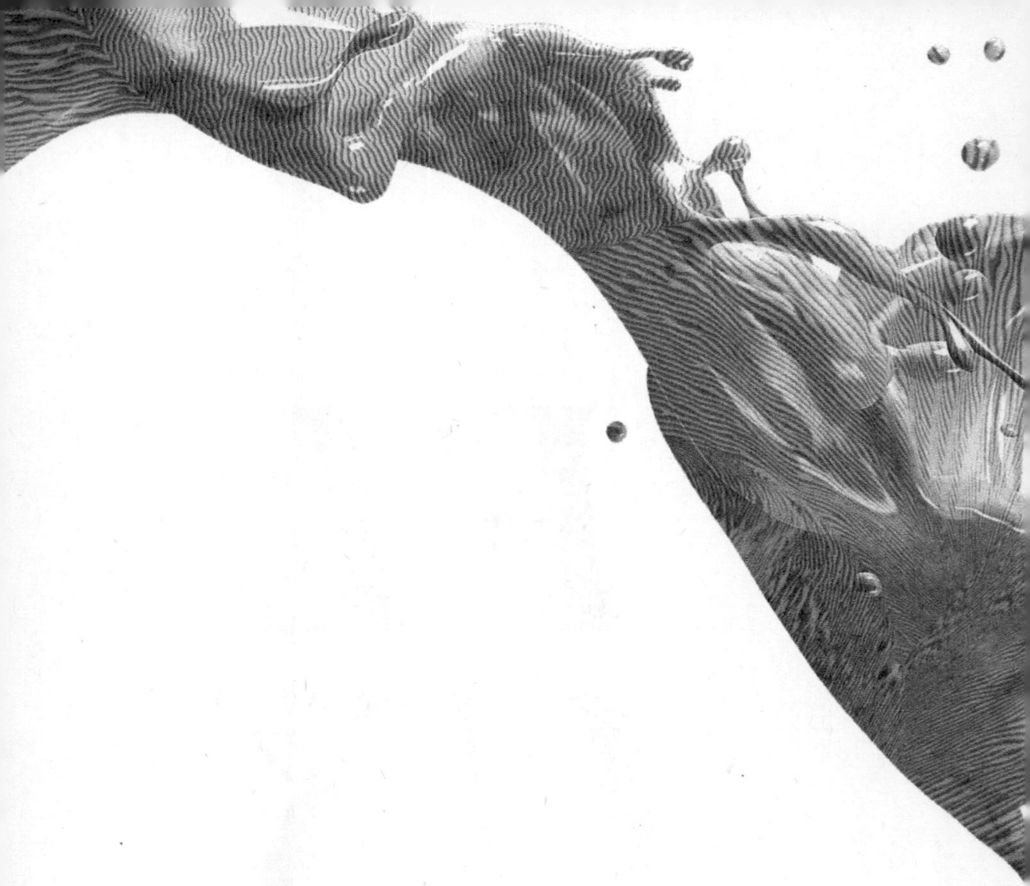

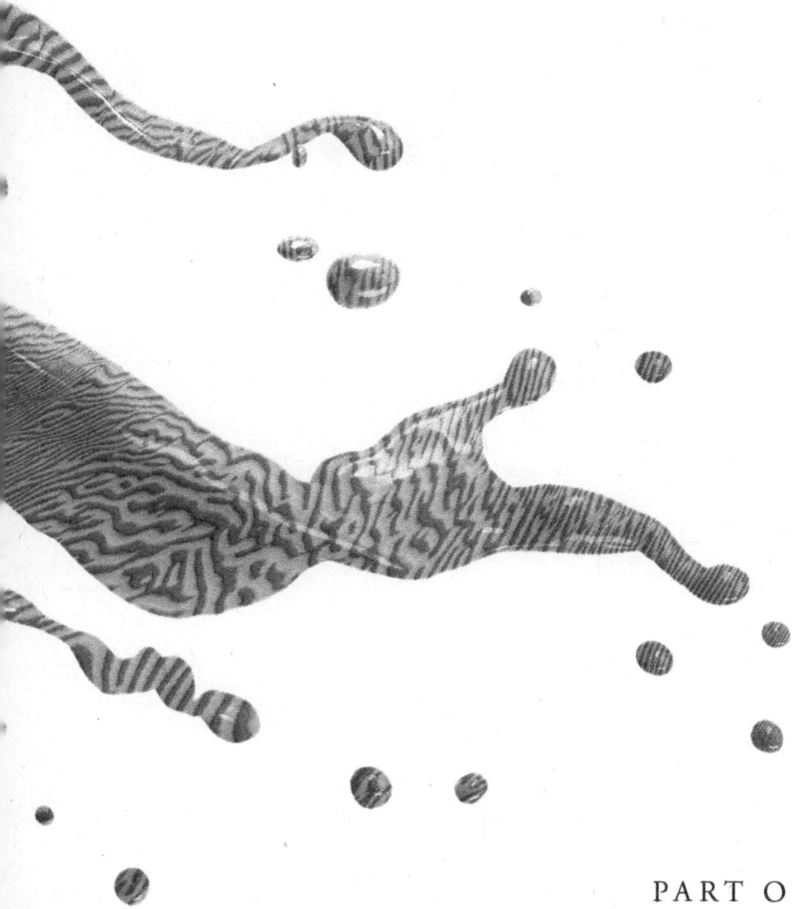

PART ONE

Severance

1

Your line was always: "give me a reason." Always. And forget the fact that it was and continues to be the cheesiest TV-pilot-gravel-voiced-detective-mystery catchphrase ever written. It was your thing, you were the guy who wanted everybody in the world to give you a reason, *the* reason, any reason, and for the most part, for most of the episodes through 1985 and 1986, people did. When you said it, the world was right. Your writers were genius. They kept us—kept me—coming back because, above all, we loved you too much to see you fail. That's why the show worked. After the rocky pilot and early yarns, you found your footing with the Little China episode (season 1, episode 14, "Fractures of the Heart"), after which you were unstoppable. They loved your chiseled face, your dark aura and hard eyes. You were handsome, cunning, young—one of the youngest detectives on the force, you fulfilled the legacy of your dead mother and father, killed in a home invasion when you were a child (retconned as such season 2, episode 4, "Anytime, Anyplace," from a house fire mentioned in the pilot). You got what you wanted, you nailed them, every time, you were a step ahead, a bar above. I loved you. For real, man, I loved you. I hate what's become of you, what they say about you, that you're derivative, that you're toxic, because none of it is your fault. Because every day after school I was the kid busting out the tapes and watching the scratchy reruns from the '80s until I was yelled at. I still have all the episodes, digitized and saved on a flash drive that I play on my laptop to fall asleep. My mother never liked the show, saying always it was too violent. She didn't like the guns and didn't understand that was just the way of your world like I did. You want a reason, Thomas Raider, *a* reason, *the* reason it all happened, and I'll give it to you. This pisses you off; you want answers now, I'm sure, and to that I'll say this: do yourself a favor, play a little pretend with me. It should be easy for you. You're not even real.

The dumbest part about the way they've been tearing you down lately is that they're all forgetting the fact that *Raider* defined an entire genre of television. Three years after *Hill Street Blues*, two after *Cagney & Lacey*, this was a show that played in the dark. You know why you only did two seasons? Your critics weren't ready for you, they couldn't take the blood and the bodies, too detailed, too ghastly for the 4:3 aspect ratio. Conservative pearl clutchers chided your drinking and sexing, the fact that you never smiled, not once, for forty-six episodes. Middle-aged nerds of today would've gone nuts for you, they would've dressed as you for Comic-Con and defended your abject womanizing to their wives and girlfriends. You dealt a rawness that couldn't be glossed, the hard edges of those alleyways, your filthy clothes, that fucking *jacket*. You know,

I'd kill for that leather jacket. You were a king when you wore it. Don't forget the fact that *Raider* was one of the only shows putting Asians on TV. By season two you were almost exclusively among us, the shopkeepers and immigrants. We said more than unsubtitled Cantonese, we played more than kung fu masters or dragon assassins. They even gave you a son, that six-year-old street urchin, Moto (season 2, episode 6, "Mercy for the Damned"), who you rescued from a drug ring. I used to think I looked like that little kid. I'd imagine I was him and you were my real father come to take me away. It's my favorite episode. It's the promo they show every time some history special mentions *Raider*. You, trenchcoated, half shadowed, holding that little Asian boy in your arms, staring into the dark rain falling all around you and straight into my soul.

And still, as it happened, two seasons was plenty enough for Antonin Haubert, the actor who played you. By the end, he had movie offers, endorsement deals. He didn't fight the network when there was cancel talk. He had a face that could play rough like he had on *Raider* but a mutability underneath that couldn't be taught. He could play the wholesome friend, sadistic politician, principled lord, gay wizard villain. Typecast proof. Antonin Haubert was dark and sexy and on his way to further greatness, and—history will show—the wall of film, television, music, theater, and exemplary Presidential Citizens awards hanging somewhere in his cliffside palace near Malibu are nothing to scoff at. Forty years later, you'd be hard-pressed to hear Antonin Haubert even mention the show anymore. The guy was so entwined with American pop culture despite not even being American that one could barely think of movies without picturing his godly, symmetrical face. Still, time will always bend forward. He was seventy-one this year. He got the ovations at award shows but belonged to the cadre of legends now, taken both more and less seriously by modern folk. He'd pop in for brief, pivotal guest spots on prestige television shows and promote his memoirs and his charities without doing much of anything, these days.

We all moved on. This month's cover of *Metropol* was a profile of Antonin's son, Hadrien, an arthouse twink with huge eyes, at only twenty-two years old already one of the biggest stars of our age for playing a baby-faced serial killer in a terrible movie called *Gorgeous Demons* last year. He won thirty awards for it and trended every time he tweeted. I saw the mockup of the *Metropol* cover last week in the office, hanging on the window wall near the art department. He looked a lot like you, Raider, the lips were the same, and so was the scraggly hair. He was wearing a jewel-embroidered Gucci corset that hugged his skeleton ribs and a shag blanket hanging off his shoulders. The editing had been done so as to accentuate the circles under his eyes and gold leaf in swirls on his cheeks. In slick white font around his head were the words *MAD ABOUT THE BOY.* It was the gayest thing I'd ever seen. It sort of worked. Sort of.

I was picturing the innocent slope of those lips when I woke, moved my head, turning to my right, found Gil still asleep and breathing his feathery breaths into my armpit. I wasn't much used to such close contact with him, at least without our dicks involved. I reminded myself that I did in fact like the way Gil made me laugh, also the way he paid for dinner. I didn't believe it was a power thing. In the pit of my heart I knew Gil just thought paying for dinner was a sweet thing to do, which it was, and I liked him so much better because I knew he thought like this when I never could. I moved my arm down, slowly, and his eyelids fluttered. For half a second he noticed me in front of him, then roused himself awake, shimmying up around my shoulder to rest his head next to mine.

"Too early. Go back to sleep," he mumbled.

You'd think he was sweet, too. I didn't know this for sure, of course. There were no queers on *Raider*, not that I remember. You were a gruff straight boy prone to violence and a single word doing the work of ten, so maybe you would have looked at us curled together in my bed and felt rage or fear—whatever it is that moves people like the founder of Chik-fil-A or the Alabama State Senate to argue extermination. But I hoped you wouldn't.

As though he'd been waiting for it, Gil propped himself on an elbow, squinting at me. He didn't look six years older than I was. We'd have had more problems if he did. There were minute but definitive differences between us: he'd always had big eyes, which he used often to convey meaning without fully realizing their devastating effects on people around him. Jewish, but on his dad's side. He picked and chose when to indulge his bacon-and-egg sandwiches, and he wasn't circumcised, either. His arms and legs were hairier, but I was in better shape.

"What?"

"You're not sleeping," Gil said, observing me.

I shrugged. The light was bright and violent through the window above us, all white because of the snow falling outside. First snow of the year and it had almost invited martial law as the lights went out, one by one. Nevertheless, if it stayed on the ground another two days, we'd have the first white Christmas in who knows how many years. The thought made me happy. I reached over his shoulder and found my phone. Almost nine. He watched me get out of bed and pick my clothes up from where we'd pooled them on the floor.

"You want any breakfast?" he asked me. I didn't answer him until I was dressed.

"I'll be late if we have breakfast."

Gil sat up, rubbing his eyes with the backs of his fists. ". . . About that," he began to say.

I wasn't listening. I glanced outside, judging the depth of the slush on the street, and dug a pair of Gil's boots from the closet across the room. We were supposed to be off for the holidays by now. It didn't matter much to me; I would go in and scroll my desktop Twitter feed, order lunch around eleven, same as I always did. The holiday party I'd gotten blasted at had been the past weekend. I still had my gym membership in the fancy place next to the office lobby. Should I bring shorts? Sneakers? Gil appeared in the bedroom doorway, where I had pushed our leftovers from last night out of the room.

"Just be late," he pleaded, simply, raking his back in a cat stretch with his fingertips.

I made a noise through my nostrils. He was being needy, and I didn't understand why. I didn't stick around any longer to find out. I opened the door and shut it behind me. Took the garbage out without looking back, into the hallway, then the snow.

You wouldn't exactly understand why. It's not something I'm proud of. I knew what Gil wanted from me. He seemed to ask it every time our eyes met these days. Questions like these weren't supposed to matter so much at my age, and it didn't make me feel good to imagine that they did for him. Did Gil want to marry me? Adopt kids? Coach little league?

When I liked Gil too much I thought about your jacket, the kind of no-shit, absolutely icy guy I'd be if I could wear something like that every day. There was an awesome replica of your jacket that I saw somebody selling out of a personal shop a couple months ago. I wanted seriously to cash my last paycheck to buy it. There was a cut in the left sleeve from the pilot, where you rip it open on a chain-link fence going after some coke runner through an industrial park in the opening scene. We never learn the perp's name, and the important part is that he gets away while you lose your footing and fall two stories onto a pile of woodchips. You look down at your jacket, feeling with your fingers the rip in the pleather. For a second the camera enters your perspective, staring up at the unfinished beams, at the white sky. It's only your second week on the detective bureau, nobody blames you. You wear that same jacket with the tear in the sleeve for forty-five more episodes. I've read that the costume department made over a hundred of them. I wondered briefly, zooming into the pictures of the replica, whether this was one of them. There would be production numbers somewhere, no tags if it were custom. I didn't buy it, before you ask. Gil would have said something mean about it; he didn't like my obsessions—any of them, especially mine for you.

After two stops, I exited the subway on the southwest side of the memorial park, on the other side of which towered the glass building that housed a realty firm, several computer systems fulfillment companies, a super-luxe mall in the lobby, and the high-gloss headquarters of the hundred-year-old newspaper company that owned *Metropol*, *Pointe*, *HollywoodNow*, and a raggedy collection of other dying magazine brands marching slowly into the ether. It was both good and bad to be a marketing guy at one of these companies. Perks like free subscriptions, the pristine Apple Store office that cost a billion dollars and change, run-ins with Clooney promoting an HBO miniseries in the twenty-fifth-floor video wing. All that for a job that amounted to very, very little. You know those little pieces of cardstock that fall out of the magazine when you're flipping through them at the airport? Let's think—'84, so *Rolling Stone*? *Newsweek?* You're flipping through one of those at the bodega next to the precinct. You have an hour off before you're due in court for arraignment, and that little slip of paper falls out from behind a page flashing *ALERT! ALERT! RENEW YOUR SUBSCRIPTION NOW AT 85% OFF!* That was me. Except I didn't even write the copy, we sourced that out to copywriters. We used an ancient system of keys and codes to split *Metropol*'s 3.4 million print subscribers into a hundred innocuous segments. Rich, poor, urban, rural, men, women, white, nonwhite. Something you might not know: it was massively effective to raise the low net-income segments up to twenty dollars more an issue each renewal period. Sure, you'll lose a few new next round of expirations, but an infinitesimally small margin of people—even those who might be doing their progeny a favor by saving that eighty-nine dollars a year—ever notice the money leaving their accounts each month and end up going through the gargantuan trouble of doing something about it. We made sure of that by keeping our customer service on a website that hasn't changed since 1998. Year over year it was about an extra ten million for the conglomerate.

I slapped my badge onto the turnstiles and pushed my way through to the elevators. Beyond the lobby I saw the shiny stainless opening of the gym I was planning on skipping out around three to get to. The elevator doors were about to close on me alone when they hiccupped, then groaned back open for a young woman who sat two rows of desks down from me to step inside. We gave each other small smiles as the car lurched upward.

"Happy holidays," she said to me.

"To you, too," I said. The words banged around my brain for a few seconds after, the way it sounded. *2 U 2 U2, You Two, too.*

"Doing anything fun this year?" she asked. Her name was maybe Lee?

"Staying around here," I said. I let a beat go before remembering: "How about you?"

"My husband and I are seeing my parents upstate," Lee(?) said, checking her watch. "It's our first Christmas together since we got married."

She showed me her ring, which I thought was pretty cute: the ring and the way she showed me, blushing, no doubt still getting used to its weight on her finger. I liked Lee(?). We didn't work on any of the same accounts and so had only ever messaged each other things like *hey is the PressWorx login working for you right now?* and *do you know what kind of soup they have downstairs for lunch?* Still, nice girl. I imagined her husband was the softest guy you could possibly imagine, and that it was her favorite thing about him.

"Congratulations," I told her. The doors slid open on the thirtieth floor, and we stepped out past the neon tubes arranged in artistic loops around the living wall decked with imported ivy. A tech aid was wheeling a big cart of old desktops out into the hallway in front of us.

"Any idea why they haven't called vacation yet?" Lee(?) asked me. I shrugged.

"Boss knows, wouldn't he?"

"I mean, it's a little irresponsible," Lee(?) said, "waiting this long. It's not like Christmas just happens whenever it wants with no notice."

We stayed silent until I turned off at my row, giving her a small wave as she continued on. My desk was cluttered with the papers I'd left there the previous Friday, little pages torn out of a notebook that I was using to count actualized totals for the past month. The owners tortured themselves letting a bunch of humanities majors do the accounting work instead of hiring professionals to do it for them. My digital clock, same as Gil's, was reading twelve midnight and blinking. I glanced at my phone and adjusted it. I glanced around the desks, each of our little digital clocks blinking midnight, on and off in imperfect unison. Pretty much the only sign around here that anything had even happened at all. I sat, eyeing the corner of my tabletop where an intern had dropped next week's pubs. They did this periodically, every desk in the office from the receptionist to the editors got free copies. It cost the conglomerate about a hundred thousand a year.

Hadrien Haubert sulked at me from the January *Metropol*. It was a good magazine, really. Not *Vanity Fair*, but respectable.

No, despite its absolutely communist name, it's not Russian, and has nothing to do with Russia. I know you'd like that, Raider. Half the baddies in the early yarns were Russian mobsters. The title's inception twenty-five years ago was the product of a branding meeting, one of the first ever that the conglomerate had built itself instead of bought from an indie owner. Mysterious, kind of sexy. Its masthead font liked to change every couple of seasons. They now threw an Oscar party near the LA office every year. The title covered strictly entertainment news for the first fifteen years but has since branched, along with most everybody else, into glossy fashion for the covers and horny think pieces about facets of politics that are palatable to young liberals. I flipped to the profile and picked a page at random. "What are you reading these days?" the interviewer had asked him. "*The Wanderer*, dark matter entropy, Rumi," said Hadrien Haubert, "*The Tale of Genji*. It's the first novel in history, did you know that? And written by a woman. Huge influence to my director and me last summer when we were making *Gorgeous Demons*. Huge."

"Motherfucker," I said under my breath, but continued skimming. The second half of the profile followed a weeklong shoot in Budapest for Saint Laurent resort and cruise wear in which Hadrien had taken his interviewer along to the public baths and started a small riot in the water when recognized. Several older guests went to the hospital for head trauma, I'd read about the commotion on Twitter. It mentioned twice that Hadrien held both French and American citizenship, having grown up between homes while his father divorced his mother over a three-year period, during which time he also made six films. It was mentioned that Hadrien and the elder Haubert are on good terms. "We did Christmas at his place. I hadn't been there in almost a decade." I stopped reading, turning the issue over in my hands. *MAD ABOUT THE BOY* was just vague enough to fit everybody in Hollywood, in case Hadrien had dropped out of the cover. You could see every single one of his ribs, chipped black polish on his fingers. He was going to host *SNL* early next year.

"Hey."

I looked up at him, laying his crossed arms over the chest-high lockers that flanked our bay of desks.

"Hey."

Gil was wearing the same suit I'd seen yesterday, no tie. He looked surprisingly alert. He looked around himself, as though surprised to find himself apprehensive.

"Let's . . . " He broke off. "Let's talk, huh?"

I glanced around at the empty desks. I stood up, followed him past the water fountains to his glass-doored office at the end of the hall. Gil took his place at his desk. I sat in front of him.

"Let me guess, you're unsatisfied with my work."

"Don't joke," Gil said. "You left before I could tell you."

"Tell me what?"

Gil opened his jacket, leaning back against his chair. I did not find myself in his office for many reasons. I was one in a team of twenty that reported to him. We were very careful. Still, it was the desk between us, or maybe his folded hands in front of him, that made him so suddenly a stranger that I felt a little coil of heat work its way up my spine.

"We were bought out yesterday," he said quickly. "That's why there was no vacation announcement. HR's scrambling to prepare the termination packages."

He seemed to want some time after saying this, the way he stared down at his hands, so I let him have it. Termination packages meant—termination. Obviously. I glanced at the clock above us. Nine-thirty. Running right on time, battery operated.

"So," I said finally, "all of us."

Gil nodded.

"All of us. It'll be announced today that they're putting *Metropol* and a couple other news titles for sale. Doesn't vibe with the new buyer's audience."

"The new—"

"They're called France. France Corp. They're based in the Midwest, they own every gardening and home decor title you can think of, plus a bunch of local television stations, which explains why they haven't completely dried up like we have."

"What the fuck kind of name is France Corp?"

Gil frowned at me.

"France," he repeated. "Francis? Francis Corporation? I could've sworn—"

He looked around his desk at nothing, to no avail.

"Sorry," he said. "I know it's tough, so close to Christmas."

"It *is* Christmas. It's three days from now. We're all supposed to be off for vacation and instead you've made us all come in to get fired."

"Yeah."

We let another ten seconds pass. Others had started filling the desks behind us. I expected Gil had a long day ahead of him.

"Just, how it happened," Gil said, placatingly. "Internal marketing's always one of the first departments to go, especially when they've got their own people. Can't really say what's going to happen to editorial. Might keep their jobs, though I suppose—that's up to the new buyer, whoever that's going to be."

It had dawned on me that I would lose my health insurance soon. My 401(k). How was I going to pay my rent? My shoebox uptown that I was very glad to leave abandoned for days at a time to sleep over at Gil's whenever I could. These were little objects that had orbited me without much notice but now, suddenly, could blink away and leave me destroyed.

I asked: "What's going to happen to the magazine until then?"

Gil glanced at the corner of his desk, where the face of Hadrien Haubert glared out at the ceiling. "Too early to say. It'll be in the interest of the buyer to keep it running until they can sell it, pretty sure. I imagine not much is going to change at all, on the outside. Still lost eight million on it last year. It's drowning."

He was looking very carefully at me. When I didn't say anything, he pulled out a drawer from his desk and placed a brown folder in front of me. I opened it, finding a packet of brochures, employment resources, and a letter—signed by Gil and our vice president of human resources—informing me that I was, how'd you say: fucked.

"They can give you eight weeks' severance," said Gil. "That's the envelope clipped to the front."

There it was. I opened it, finding a printed check and a paperclip inside. You'd imagine most people would be thinking of the future, faced with a moment such as this. You did it every day, thought a step ahead; it was the only way you stayed alive. It wasn't so different from police work for us laypeople. Categorized into columns were friends you'd confide in for comfort, family you'd tell if there were bills to pay, contacts you'd inform, perhaps with a request for "drinks sometime when we're both free." It seemed a luxury, to have that many people to think of.

"Aren't I supposed to be talking with somebody from HR?" I had the wherewithal to say.

"Half of them are already out," Gil said. "If it wasn't me, it would've been an email. You would've had to come back here on a weekend or something to get your things."

I spotted my desk behind me, over my shoulder. Farther away I could make out the back of Lee(?)'s head, bent low over something on her monitor. I nodded again and eased the little envelope containing my severance check out of the folder. Gil cleared his throat, gesturing to the letter, at the bottom of which was a line indicating my signature. He handed me a pen, and I signed, and it was over. Nice and quick, nothing to cry about.

Over the top of the paper I saw him reach a hand toward mine and lay his fingers delicately on top of my knuckles.

"I'm here," Gil tried. "You know . . . if you want to talk. Whatever you—"

"I'm good," I told him, smiling. "Really good."

I pulled my hand away. Gil nodded, cautiously. He kept his eyes on his door, at his view of the hallway beyond. I stood up, folding my check in half and crushing it into the bottom of my pants pocket. The last of the slush on my boots had evaporated to white crystals caking the underside of my soles that came off in flakes as I returned to my desk, aware vaguely of Gil craning his neck from his desk chair to look at me. From my top drawer I took the pens I'd been hoarding, my stapler. I left my badge on the corner of the tabletop. There were tons of papers I'd stuffed into the bottom drawers over the years. Old magazines, budget notes. For a time, I'd kept all the surplus from a sale we'd done involving some decorative plates celebrating the birth of some celebrity baby in my bottommost drawer. I was going to leave it all there.

"You're back soon," I heard behind me. Lee(?) was carrying an armful of binders. For a moment I imagined she was moving out of her desk, maybe she'd gotten an email like Gil had said. But she smiled, again, and I realized she didn't know.

"I'm back?" I repeated.

"No almond butter in the kitchen? What happened to those fancy clothes, by the way?"

I glanced around at myself. I was missing something. Lee(?) half-laughed, setting down her binders.

"They need to put out a schedule or something. I'm tired of walking down there and finding out they only have peanut butter."

"Yeah," I said, not hearing her. She shrugged. Her eyes went above me as the door to Gil's office opened again. I didn't want to turn around. I couldn't have told her, Raider. You made decisions like this all the time—ugly ones—and people respected you for it. If I stayed any longer I'd have to watch it happen all over again, you understand that, don't you? You would've nodded and said it was the only way, what I did, taking my pens, my stapler, jacket under my arm, walking past the desk bays and Lee(?) and Gil and everybody else to the elevators at the other end of the floor, and going down, all the way down.

—

I caught myself doing my wrist thing that my doctor had told me was terrible for my joints. There was a point, turning it clockwise, that I could get a small click that made me feel like I was accomplishing something. I'd learned how to do it as a teenager. I couldn't crack my fingers back the way I've seen chiropractors do to people in viral videos. It was the only thing I had. I could be forgiven today. This had been my first job out of college. At the time, I'd heard the words "digital," "subscription," and "consumer revenue" at about half-attention. I was only thinking of the salary. With the kind of money I'd be paid, I could afford to live in the city. I had higher intentions for myself in the city. I'd eat out and stay up all night and fuck everybody I met. I was twenty-two. Could you tell?

I passed the gym after the elevators let me off and continued across the marble to the shopping center, which opened out in front of me, a vault of glass showing me the sky, frosted over with snow. Several trees weighed down with fake crystals and lights scattered around the area. I felt like walking, like being someplace else. There were televisions on the far side of the atrium showing news reports, more injured admitted to hospitals from the eighteen trains that derailed during the blackout.

I'd noticed last night that Gil's oven was still blinking 12:00 because he hadn't reset it. And it made me think, briefly, that people never usually talked about the blackouts for as long as they seemed to be talking about this one.

I mean, think about it. Imagine for a second that at 8:45 p.m. the entire East Coast goes black for almost half an hour. Cars slip and crash on black ice when the streetlights go out, airborne planes take wild loops around the airports trying to contact their towers through the snowstorm, all of New York, Georgia, and North Carolina lose cell coverage. I heard there's still a couple suburbs without power. That's some shit, right? I was home, thank God. Can you fathom being stuck down in a subway car for an hour? After the lights came back on we got a press bite from the president—the outages would continue, everybody seemed to agree. It was not a matter of random catastrophe, a brief storm here, an earthquake every now and then, but one of structural inadequacy, the country's energy consumption butting up against the cap of our infrastructure, yadda yadda, best minds, energy secretary, emergency bill on the floor of the House as we speak. Gil had been on his way home with groceries, he told me later. I'd asked him what kind of psychopath hits the all-night mart for groceries at 11 p.m. on a Wednesday but he'd just laughed, and I'd forgiven him for doing it. He could do that to me sometimes, make me tolerate him.

The president's press secretary was running through the numbers on a pie chart decked in bright colors that pierced my eyes on the hi-fi screens. I turned sharply into the first opening I could find, an empty Italian boutique, and took my time among the shelves. There were three of us on the luxury carpeted show floor: an enormous suited man standing guard by the anti-theft detectors and a girl wearing all black folding cashmere by one of the far walls. And now me. Everything inside was painted white and gold, so many mirrors around that I could see at least three of me wherever I turned.

I wasn't going to sleep well for weeks. I didn't have a job anymore. I hadn't updated my resume in six years. I was a person prone to these kinds of petty hang-ups. You'd roll your eyes, wouldn't you? What did I have to lose sleep over, really? No more money to spend on eighteen-dollar cast-iron mac and cheese. No more dental coverage. Maybe even no more *Metropol*, a magazine whose print edition was more than fifty-percent advertisements and had still managed to run at a spectacular loss for the past four years. I felt my severance check crumple on itself in the pit of my pants pocket. Eight weeks would be up real soon, I was sure of that.

"Looking for something?"

The girl had come my way carrying a stack of silk scarves. I knew the brand. There was at least ten thousand dollars on her arm. She had a sheet of black hair that went past her shoulders and lines around her mouth as though she smiled a lot, which I thought was funny as she didn't look very happy to be here. I shook my head.

I saw her shoulders lower slightly. Maybe she'd been really busy and was dreading a difficult customer. I was a tourist, she must have thought, as I wasn't so shabby as to be mistaken for homeless.

"Let me know," she said. "I'm Min."

"Min," I said to her back when she turned around and took several steps away from me. She came back to me.

"What do you sell the most of here?"

She glanced around, surprising me, as she was genuinely thinking about it.

"We're known for our wallets," she said. "They're handmade in Italy. It's a leather-weaving form called intrecciato. Takes almost an entire day to make one. That's why it costs so much."

"How does it hold up? What kind of warranty would you put on a wallet like that?"

She dug a little black piece out of her back pocket, opening it for me.

"Had it eight years. It was my mother's for another twenty."

"That's impressive."

I wondered if she worked here because she'd seen that wallet in her mother's purse all her life. It was a nice story. I liked to believe something like that was true, or else she wouldn't have shown it to me in the first place. Min set down her scarves, wiping her hands.

"Do you want to see some of them? New collection's in, just last week."

"I think I need a bag," I told her, holding up my pens and stapler. She narrowed her eyes a fraction.

"Is that a joke? Did you come here to ask for a shopping bag?"

"No, a bag. Purse. Hand purse. Whatever it is for men."

She made an exaggerated nod, pausing to look me over.

"Are you Korean?"

"I—" A rush of blood came to my ears before I got the rest of the words out. "Yes. On my mother's side."

Min smiled at me, the creases around her mouth showed, along with a dimple on the left side. My ears were still pounding.

"You remind me of my dad, is why I asked."

She led me to a wall of bags and chose a small piece attached to a belt and buckle.

"Fanny pack," I said.

"Belt bag," she corrected. "You can wear it around your waist, but all the models do it over one shoulder, front or back. It's what everybody's doing now. It's a fashion thing."

"Will I look cool wearing it?"

She rolled her eyes, lifting it up for me. I slung it over one shoulder and followed her gestures to the nearest mirror. We stood side by side, looking at it.

"It's nice," she said, "fits your shoulders."

"Why this one?"

She looked at me through our reflection.

"It's wide enough for your stapler."

We smiled at that one. I took it off me.

"Do you take checks?"

They took checks. Min rung me up and scanned my ID. The cost of the bag came out to about a hundred dollars more than my entire eight-week severance, which I put on my debit. I stopped her wrapping it and cut the tags off with a pair of scissors she handed me. Slung over my shoulder with my stapler and pens inside, I looked like I had somewhere to be.

"This is helpful," I said. "Put your name or whatever on the sale if that gets you commission."

"Already did, thank you."

She slid my driver's license back over the glass countertop that separated us.

"Are you okay?" she asked me.

I nodded vacantly. "Yeah, why?"

She frowned and lightly tapped the check, with its big red *TERMINATION* stamped over the memo line.

"Severance check, right?"

"Yep."

Her eyes widened just slightly.

"I used my discount on a pair of boots here when my boyfriend broke up with me last year," she said. "Still cost me nine hundred dollars. Do you know what, though?"

"What?"

"It felt good for a minute, maybe. Then I went back to feeling like shit. I don't even like those boots."

It was the kind of thing you'd hear from somebody taking a long-winded route toward making fun of you, but somehow I didn't feel that way coming from her. I replaced my wallet in my pocket.

"I'm sorry your boyfriend broke up with you last year."

"Thanks."

"Do you want to get dinner with me tonight?"

She thought about it, I could tell. There was something catching in her throat as I asked her, and we spent a long time listening to the jazzy Christmas interpolations filtered in through the speakers until at last she blinked twice and told me: "no."

I moved my head up and down a couple times, then turned and walked out of the store. I didn't want to go home—*my* home, where I hadn't been in days, which would be cramped and dusty after my eyes adjusted from Gil's full-wall windows and grimeless countertops. I might walk around for a while, listen to the music. There was a cookie store somewhere on the fourth floor that baked them boulder-size and used peanut butter morsels in the batter. My phone buzzed for the first time that morning in my pocket and I fished it out of my pants. Gil was calling. I let it ring itself out and put it back in my pocket. I looked back only once on my way to the elevator. Min had stepped out into the doorway beside the security guard and was watching me with her arms crossed. I couldn't read the look on her face. I stopped at the doors and pressed the up arrow. We were a couple hundred feet apart now. Her face was foggy, a pinprick. The doors opened. I was still looking at her when I took my next step, watched her unfold her arms and put a hand up, thinking: what a strange thing to do, wave at me.

My foot sunk lower; I felt the air rush away as my leg dropped out under me, the dark insides of the elevator shaft swallowing Min, the mall, and the rest of the light up along with it. I was really doing it—I was really falling down an elevator shaft, at present. And it wasn't my job I was thinking of, and it wasn't Min, or Lee(?), or whether I would break my neck, or anything, really, that came to mind while I waited for the rest of my body to crumple and my weightlessness to come to a heavy stop somewhere at the pit of the shaft rising up around me. I was thinking about the words this morning, the first words I'd heard when Gil woke with his head in my armpit and moved himself higher up, as if to kiss me. The words "go back to sleep." I wished I'd listened to him. If I'd just listened to him I wouldn't be a hundred dollars indebted to my new handmade intrecciato belt bag and falling down an elevator shaft right about now. Too late. My head smashed against something hard. I couldn't tell if I'd closed my eyes on account of the darkness.

I know you get it. You've had your head smashed by worse, you've been tossed around alleyways into trash, over bars into expensive bottles of liquor stored label-out on shelves. The truth is, I haven't seen an episode of the show in about two weeks, not since the *Times* article in which myriad reputable sources stated that Antonin Haubert once broke his first wife's arm, nose, and index finger with a fire poker in an altercation on New Year's, 1994. Things moved quickly after that. He'd always invited chuckles around Hollywood for his intensity, but this was all too much. It spilled out in a matter of days: several other incidents along the way, at least ten costars, production assistants, casting directors, extras, men and women, shattered drinks, flipped tables, knives wedged in doors and walls. Statements from all but one were accounted for in the court documents, Hadrien's mother, who hadn't said a word to journalists and still lived near him in London. The *Metropol* issue had already gone to production by the time the news broke. Hadrien hadn't yet said a word about it. His people canceled most of his press in the meantime. It was early enough for those of us following the controversy not to be entirely sure how best to feel about the whole thing. I was mostly certain he was in the same boat. These things happened, didn't they?

Looking at it now, his face, your face, it was like looking at an alternate history that had been wiped clean save for a few instances of bizarre photographic evidence. They were saying Antonin Haubert would face prison time. He'd had both Oscars rescinded, the Medal of Freedom shortly after. His socials went dark after it had all come out, not a single statement. He was holed up in his Malibu palace with the blinds drawn so not even the drone paparazzi could get at him. And it made me angry. It made me angry to think of the way he'd treated you all these years, now this. He'd taken you and desecrated everything you stand for, and it was disgusting. Antonin Haubert was a fucking rat, he should die for what he'd done, but there was a piece of me that still loved him, because the same handsome face I saw was yours, forty years old now on the television screen. A piece of me that said, "why, why? Fuck!

FUCK! How could you do this to me? How the *FUCK* can you do this to me?" And it was selfish of me. I should let you go. I would if I could, which—I realized—was a very polite thing to say. Even if saying it hasn't helped anybody with anything, ever, and never will.

2

They were waiting for him at the freight entrance, around the back of a nondescript glass tower downtown: a young woman with a badge around her neck and a bottle of Fiji, as well as Tor, who had his in-ears switched on and was talking animatedly to the air. With a finger he swiped at something a foot from his face, then two more times. It seemed a P.A. hadn't sent him the right call sheet and was being roundly savaged for it over the phone. After a second more, Tor tapped the receiver in his left ear and hung up on her, glancing up.

"You're late."

Train got stopped on the way, Blue signed to the girl with the Fiji. She appeared flustered, looking his way, then Tor's, who was again too busy to respond.

"Oh—I'm—" she stammered, "I'm not—"

"Relax," Tor told her, "we haven't got an interpreter. We're sorting that out for you in a couple minutes anyway."

He snapped his fingers at the Fiji girl, who offered Blue the water. She gestured to the elevator doors—"Right here, Mr. Blue."

“Don’t call him that,” Tor said as they piled inside. “It’s not even his name.”

He got another ping and turned away from them. The elevator car rocketed upward, far faster than any of them expected, buckling all of their knees. Blue’s hands and toes were numb from the snow; he was grateful for the heat. It had been a weekslong journey toward this day, the signing of release forms, waivers, a contract that ensured his compensation for waiving his face rights as they would appear on air. He had been in what seemed like constant contact with Tor ever since the network had reached out the first time, all that while ago. Now this. He had been told that the next hour was what they called a display run, preliminary work before the shoot. He would meet the light and makeup teams, who would recreate the look they wanted when the program was filmed a few days from now. He would also be walked through several of the establishing shots: at home, cooking, getting on and off the subway, all against screens, as they would fill the rest in VR. Cheaper, he was told, than shooting on location. Besides, the software these days was seamless. Nine out of ten couldn’t tell the difference. The number that had been given was forty million: the number of viewers in primetime, counting livestreams and social. Largely a projection, Tor had told him later, but the networks had confidence. A criminal trial was one of the few happenings capable of anchoring conversation all across the country the way Flux had almost two decades ago. Blue hadn’t yet been asked to explain why he’d agreed to do the exclusive, the only witness still alive and willing to talk on camera, and why now. There was reason to believe he’d had enough of the security during the trial when it had first taken place those years ago, the shuttling between hotels in blackout masks and gloves for the week he spent testifying before court. He took the compensation Tor offered but didn't need it. Was it simply that he had grown accustomed to the attention? He didn't like to think so. In twenty years he had never quite gone so far as to admit that his life had become all the more exciting because of it.

The elevator dinged open into a stark white studio and a single desk out front. Blue was walked inside and showed a stool, which he sat on. Several young people in various levels of business appropriate attire formally introduced themselves like the soldier children in *The Sound of Music* and got to work on him, speaking in loud tones to each other about the sun damage on his cheeks, the wrinkles around his eyes. Something would need to be done about the grey hairs, and the stragglers in his ears and nose. They dispersed, and a young technician wearing a face shield and latex gloves approached him with a chrome-tipped gun in his hands. He looked about eighteen.

"Pleasure to meet you, Mr. Blue, we're going to get your implant in and take you through operating etiquette." He sounded as though reading from a prompter, which he might have been. Blue nodded and, as directed, removed his jacket and scarf. The kid bore down on a spot just to the right of his Adam's apple with an alcohol wipe.

"You'll have to remove your in-ears, please."

Blue dug the white pearls from each ear and placed them in his shirt pocket.

"You're good with needles?"

Blue rolled his shoulders, ambivalent.

The kid didn't say more. After moving a couple dials on the gun, he peered at the chrome tip for another second, lined it up with Blue's neck, and pulled the trigger. A *pop* punctured the air, loud and hollow in the empty space. It didn't hurt any more than a hard pinch, but still, the area on his neck had never quite been handled this way. Blue fought the urge to buck as the gun hummed, and before he had time to close his eyes, a second *POP* hit his ears. He gasped at this one. It felt like somebody had dug a finger straight into his carotid and was rooting around the muscles and sinew for a lost quarter. The gun was removed and sterilized in a lightbox. The kid turned around and dug a cotton wad into the spot, guiding one of Blue's hands up to the spot to keep pressure.

"Easy," was the kid's only assurance. "It'll be sore for a day or two."

He aimed a little black baton at the cotton wad. A whistle sounded from somewhere Blue couldn't hear, then died out. The kid snapped his fingers in rote, hard-angle formations all around Blue's head, instructing his eyes to follow the noise. He was made to open his mouth and move his tongue to each corner of his jaw.

"Okay, Mr. Blue, you lost the ability to speak when you were twenty-nine years old. It says here cerebral hemorrhage, correct?" Blue nodded, weakly, his head still spinning.

"It's a smoother transition with people like you. Your brain is still technically wired for it. Normally I'd lead you through some exercises, but you were late."

He checked his watch. He looked more excited than annoyed, Blue thought.

“Fuck it. We don’t have time. You’re a smart guy, Mr. Blue, you can jump straight to sentence recall, can’t you?”

He held the baton up to Blue’s neck another second, then lowered it. “Repeat after me, please: *I’ve seen things you people wouldn’t believe.*”

He blinked, expectantly, and Blue cleared his throat. He opened his mouth.

/ / I’ve seen things you people wouldn’t believe. / /

The voice that came from him was harsh, a smoker’s rasp that didn’t sound like anything he’d ever heard before. It had the character of a much older man, Blue thought. Though he *was* that much older man now, wasn’t he? The implant in his throat had vibrated with a strength that tickled his ears while he said it, speaking the words for him. The kid’s eyebrows raised a centimeter. He looked around, as though for support, and found only the girl who had offered the Fiji, who was swiping through the air with her in-ears on.

“You’re a natural,” the kid commented. “I’ve never seen this kind of efficacy before.”

He continued. “Attack ships on fire off the shoulder of Orion.”

/ / Attack ships on fire off the shoulder of Orion. / /

“I watched C-beams glitter in the dark near the Tannhäuser Gate.”

/ / I watched C-beams glitter in the dark near the Tannhäuser Gate. / /

The kid slapped his knee, an oddly provincial sort of gesture that didn’t seem to fit the rest of him. He looked at the girl again, who glanced his way with disinterest.

“*Blade Runner*,” he said. “You know? Final monologue? It’s like the most iconic monologue in film history.”

"Is that a sci-fi thing?" she said, placatingly.

/ / I've senescened it / / said Blue. He frowned. The voice had skipped a beat, then doubled back over itself to correct, moving his mouth of its own accord. He tried again. / / I've seen it. / /

"That's going to happen," the kid explained. "The gear isn't perfect. It's an electro-reader that translates brain chemistry and vibrates your larynx at the right frequencies while stimulating Broca's area to form the right shapes with your mouth. Your brain on its own operates at a hundred times the CPU, comparatively. You're going to have to think hard about each word you want to say."

/ / Does it get easier? / /

"Well, you should remember, these are short-term implants, no more than six weeks. You're not going to have much time to get used to it, not if we're filming next week. In a month it'll disengage remotely and pass through your digestive tract. You're pretty lucky to be getting one of these free, you know. They're harder to get your hands on than cow milk. Before I go, finish the line for me. *All those moments will be lost in time, like tears in rain. Time to die.*"

/ / All those moments will be lost in time, like tears in rain. Time to die. Cue dead replicant, flying dove, sad rain, sad, sad Harrison Ford. / /

The kid really liked that one. He packed up the gun and lightbox. He tapped his wrist to Blue's, transmuting their IDs. "Anything out of the ordinary, ping me. You'll see some redness around the injection site for the rest of the day."

He lingered, glancing around him. The makeup techs had

corralled themselves around the lights and had largely forgotten about the two of them.

"So you've like, met her, right? That's why they took you to court."

Blue didn't blame the kid for his curiosity. It was something he was never asked, despite the fact that the privacy agreements had long since expired. Not many had the opportunity to ask him something like that, anyway. And what was one even to say about Io Emsworth? Flux's founder, a billionaire for the span of thirteen months before investors bailed, now tried and living out a sentence of life in prison for the deaths of three employees approximately twenty years ago. A psychopath, a word that most people talking about her were given to throw out in conversation in order to sound knowledgeable. Some Silicon Valley wannabe who got herself tangled up in fraud, extortion, later murder, whose trial mutated under public scrutiny. Whose name, twenty years later, inexplicably had become the number one search trend for the past six months and counting. A genius. The most famous person in the world at one point or another.

And, of course, there was the photo of them. A class photo of sorts, taken in their glass modernism of an office by the piers. Io Emsworth's black, close-cropped hair, shorter than short, like *Cabaret*. Standing next to him. A young man in a blue shirt, twenty years younger, picked up by the feds just a year after the photo had been taken, offered a plea deal in exchange for testimony.

/ / Only once / / Blue said. / / I can hardly remember. No, that's not right. I met her twice. / /

The kid gave a knowing smirk.

"That's what they told you to say, huh. I get it. I guess you couldn't remember very much, anyway."

/ / Do I look that old to you? / /

Tor had hung up his call and joined them, putting his hands on each of Blue's shoulders.

"Magic, isn't it? That little Froot Loop in your neck costs a hundred grand."

/ / I don't need this. You could've hired an interpreter. / /

"Yeah, and have you karate chop the air for an hour on live television, right. Split screens kill engagement, you know that. We're not trying to have half our audience click off in the time it takes them to realize they can't focus on two faces at once. You're missing the point, buddy."

Tor was known to talk like this, cauterizing people around him in a way that Blue imagined he probably got off on. He was young, not older than thirty, but wore suits made of heavy fabrics and barked loudly on calls with his in-ears on in public places to make up for it. Unlike most, he was conspicuously apathetic about the Flux talk. It didn't seem to interest him like it did everybody else. Blue granted, the company had been shuttered for years, the deaths had occurred decades ago, Tor was too young, anyway, to recall the brief year in which Io Emsworth appeared on the covers of every business and newsmagazine in print. There was print, back then. There was talk of humanitarian prizes, the MacArthur grant, among other accolades. Flux was streamlined, optimistic, and dangerously sexy. All the best ideas were. A twenty-five-year-old business school grad had invented the closest mankind had ever come to perpetual energy. Once the media had kicked in around her, it didn't matter exactly how. A single Lifetime Battery could power most appliances and other tools for longer than the tools themselves could survive habitual wear and tear, no charging, no replacements, nothing. Though disclaimers later clarified: the batteries had a "Lifetime" of around twenty-five years. Those were the words, anyway. Words with more power than the things they described.

It collapsed after one of the dead employees' families spoke with the media. Io Emsworth fled to the Turks and Caicos, where it was alleged that she married a local. Investigators spent almost a year extraditing her, during which Flux was ransacked for assets, all of its employees either fired or tried for the cover-up. The cargo yard on which fifty million dollars had been spent building a glass office space that Io Emsworth and Flux's board of directors had dubbed "F1" was cleared of property, taped off, and left to rot. They brought her to trial for negligent manslaughter, wire fraud, convicted her on all counts. As of today, she'd been in prison for seventeen years. In the past year there had been a movie, several movies, a prestige streaming drama. Kids dressed up as her last Halloween. Products, no doubt, of that strange and unknowable storm of interest that led an entire world to start talking about her again, as though her name had been on the tip of every tongue, waiting for an opportunity.

A team had descended around the area where Blue sat, massaging the sore spot on his throat. He persevered through several floodlights shined directly in his eyes. They agreed a matte blush would work best on his cheeks. Several more minutes were spent discussing a scar above his right eye.

"It's distracting," said a tech. "Nonnarrative. If we leave it, they might ask about it."

"Unless you've got some kind of story?" said another, hopefully. Eyes fell on Blue, who had been trying his best not to move his head while his eyes watered from the light.

/ / Scraped it a long time ago. Nothing special. / /

"Cover it," said Tor. "Remember, this has got to be as quick as possible. We'll need this done for the location shoot Monday."

"How remote?"

"You get one van."

"We weren't told that."

"Need to know only," Tor said, loudly. He got a glint in his eyes, squeezing Blue's shoulder. "Site visit. Nobody's been inside F1 since the feds shut Flux down. We're getting a skeleton crew inside and letting Mr. Blue here do a walkthrough, show us the back doors, tell us stories."

Chatter erupted around them. This would no doubt leak within an hour's time, which is what Tor wanted. More cameras.

The makeup team started their work. Voices hammered away around him as the wrinkles around Blue's eyes and mouth slowly vanished. His hair, grey around his ears and neck, had been made uniform again. They'd done something to his eyelashes, suddenly full and longer than they had ever been in his life. He moved his feet around, uncomfortable. When they were done they ordered him to pace around the floor, watching his gait for imperfections, the way his hair and face looked under alternating lights. This was all deemed satisfactory.

He was guided back to the stool where, after the logging was done and at least a hundred pictures were taken of him from every angle, the techs set about taking it all off. He watched in the mirror as it all melted away. He was nearing fifty. Seeing it all at once seemed to make the bags under his eyes even darker in response.

It was all packed away in a matter of minutes. Tor led him back to the elevators, where the doors closed on the noise of the floor and whooshed them back down to the lobby. Some activity had started up again around them, workers in glow vests hauling carts of bottled water, four stacks of trays holding a hundred wrap sandwiches each. Somebody was holding an event upstairs.

"You're gonna love how it looks on camera," Tor whispered into his ear. "I've seen some ladies cry. A segment we did about a bunch of divorcées knitting hats for some kind of relief aid bullshit. We had them all to the studio, and they said it was the best they'd looked in decades."

Blue had nothing to say to this. He was shown out into the street, where the remnants of snow landed delicately around them, vanishing on the sidewalk.

"We'll pick you up, day after Christmas, from your address," Tor said, already turning away. He stopped, glancing back.

"Gonna be a mindfuck to be back there, won't it? After so long?"

Blue had seen a photograph of F1 taken just last year. The glass—bulletproof all around on Io Emsworth's insistence—had fogged all the way over with dust and rain. The lots out front where they'd all parked their cars had started to crack, moss and weeds coming in on all sides, climbing up the empty light poles.

/ / I guess. / /

"You don't guess, Blue, it's what we need," Tor said. "Remember this: you told us you needed to find closure. That's narrative. That's what we're going there to get from you."

Blue straightened his face. / / That's what I meant. I'm sorry. That's what we're going there to get. / /

This was a satisfactory answer for Tor, who left without another word and ducked back inside the lobby. Blue fumbled in his shirt pocket for his in-ears and switched them back on. His face felt tight after the vigorous scrubbing by hands and cotton pads. He checked his wrist, then called his daughter. Her face, a two-year-old photograph from her high school graduation, appeared in the left-hand corner of his eye. It clicked, he heard jumbling and voices on the other side, but otherwise nothing.

After a while she spoke.

"Care to explain the point of calling me?"

/ / Just wanted you to hear me before I come by. / /

Another pause. In the background Blue could make out a voice, male, young. Laughter. His stomach constricted.

"What the fuck? Is that you?"

/ / In the flesh. / /

"How are you—what—holy shit! What the fuck? How are you talking to me right now?"

/ / I was waiting to surprise you but thought . . . I wasn't sure if it'd freak you out. / /

"You got one of those Froot Loop things, didn't you?"

/ / Somebody else called it a Froot Loop today. Is that what they're called? / /

"How the hell did you get one of these? My roommate told

me her grandpa paid a year's salary for his, and that was with insurance."

/ / You're comparing me to a grandpa, that's great. / /

There were a few moments of silence between them. He had lost the ability to discern her jokes from her seriousness, probably when he and her mother had divorced.

"So I'm going to get to hear this weird new voice tonight, am I?"

/ / You don't have to. I'm still getting used to it. It's not as easy as it seems. / /

"You're going to have to try it out for Mom," she said, not listening. "She'll lose her shit. What time are you getting in?"

/ / I'm . . . not sure. Have a couple of things to get done before I leave. Around eight? Am I supposed to bring anything? / /

"Bring your Christmas spirit. And pick up some cognac." She said something just as a laugh erupted in the background "—really likes cognac, don't you?"

A noise of agreement came over the other end of the line. Blue set his lips together hard, waiting.

"Yeah, cognac would be good," she said. "We'll see you soon, okay?"

/ / See you soon. I— / /

She had already hung up. He looked at the space on the sidewalk where her face had been before it vanished. He cleared his throat. He turned around and headed for the subway. He'd told her eight. That gave him four hours. His neck was sore. He was going to be doing quite a bit of talking. Practice was good, he told himself. The kid had asked him to practice, somehow. As he walked, the setting sun turned the streets grey.

3

There were fingers in my mouth when I opened my eyes, two pinched around my tongue and moving in and out of my mouth. I strained, squinting at a bright light shining directly into my eyes. My resurrection caused a wave of chatter around me. I swayed where I sat. Hands held me up. Voices commanded me to blink, to smile, to stick my tongue out, and I complied, trying to speak words at the same time.

"What happened?"

"Tongue out, sir, follow my hand in the air with your eyes can you feel your feet can you feel your fingers—"

We continued on like this, not listening to each other. It felt pretty nice to be propped up like this, not responsible for my own body. Very, very slowly, the glass dome roof of the mall came back into view, steel latticework swam spiderweb-like above us.

I remembered that I had fallen down an elevator shaft, how many floors I didn't know. There was a piece of muslin tied around my head and another around my shoulder, which I could tell looking down at was marked with a bit of my blood, but not much. Hands angled my head one way, then another, making sure each of my joints still worked. Somebody had fished my wallet out of my back pocket and was reading me its contents, asking me to nod at my name, my address, most everything else. In the left field of my sight there was a gurney, an ambulance waiting outside through the windows. I wondered who had called them. I was trying to remember which realty trust's name was listed outside the lobby's entrance, whichever one had installed elevators that decided capriciously to open to unassuming guests even when there was no car inside. Would I sue? Would I win something in return? Maybe an apology. Would I go viral? Would it be worth it?

I pushed somebody's hand away and got to my feet, praying I wouldn't teeter and look foolish. I didn't, and drew myself up to height, blinking my eyes.

"I just fell," I said, "is all. I'm fine."

"Sir, you're exhibiting symptoms of a concussion."

"I feel fine."

"Your eyes weren't following my hand. That's—"

"That's because I wasn't awake," I said, blinking and moving my eyes in each direction around the mall floor. "I'm really okay."

"Sir, I really—"

"There's something I can say to make you go away, right?" I said, "I deny service. Begone. No, wait—I refuse service. Treatment. I refuse treatment."

I didn't know what I was expecting, that there were some magic words that would make the paramedics disappear as though they were ghosts summoned by séance. I certainly sounded that way, hearing it. What I certainly wasn't expecting is that it would work. They stopped their moving, all six of them in their bright yellow jackets and flashlights.

"This really isn't a smart thing to do," the one who had his fingers in my mouth said. "You'd be a lot better off coming to the hospital to get checked out."

He was young, or looked young. Nice arms. Bet he worked on them four days a week. I shook my head.

"I feel dizzy tonight, I'll call you guys up. Sound good?"

He smiled.

"We're just trying to help, sir, no need to be sarcastic."

"I'm not sarcastic. That's just my voice."

He didn't have a response to this. He muttered something passive into his walkie. One of them handed my wallet back to me. They left me there at the foot of the elevators. There was a small crowd around me, some parents staring with their kids in tow. I looked around. I did feel fine, it wasn't a lie. My shoulder hurt, I could feel my lip swelling where I'd probably clipped it with my teeth. Would I live? Yes. That was enough for me. There was a ding from behind and the elevator doors opened, letting a group of tourists out.

"Hey."

I turned around. It sounded like Gil but wasn't. The man holding my new belt bag in his hand was a couple inches shorter than me and decked in all spandex, which bulged—extra padded for comfort—around his dick and balls. The biking jersey was Toyota brand, and he lugged a gym bag on one shoulder. His head was a shock of silver hair that didn't match his eyebrows.

"Hey?" I said back to him.

"This is yours."

I took my new belt bag from him, looping it around my shoulder. I was fascinating to him, judging from the look on his face as he watched me.

"It's a great bag," he said. "Fall/winter collection, right? I was at the show in Milan. It's a Galliano knockoff, but you wouldn't know that."

I blinked at him.

"Are you okay?" he asked me. I glanced around the marble floor as if in answer. The crowd around us had dissipated.

"Doing all right, notwithstanding."

"Notwithstanding," he repeated, smiling, "that's pretty."

I waited for more, but that seemed to encompass enough for him. Warily, I searched my bag, finding my stapler and, crumpled near the bottom, a piece of paper I didn't recognize. His number, for sure. I fought not to roll my eyes directly at him and zipped it back up. I wondered if he might have taken it off my unconscious body while the ambulance arrived.

"Takes a lot of self-possession to just fall down an elevator shaft like that," he said, a joke. "You know, the *confidence* of it. People usually look where they're going, is all I'm saying. I was just coming out of my gym when I saw you fall. Funny thing, I wouldn't have seen it if I'd stayed the rest of my class. High intensity interval training. Shit kicks your ass. I tapped out after ten minutes, sorry to say. The instructor's some new guy, not really with it, you know? He doesn't have the vibe."

"Funny." I turned my head toward the empty boutique. Min was gone. Another girl had taken her place and was sorting through the scarves she'd left near the register. "I'm gonna go now."

"You work around here?" the man called after me.

"Yeah. No. Sort of. Used to."

"Ah. Francis Corp buyout, wasn't it?"

I saw his face again. He'd caught up to me in front of the boutique. Maybe the open space around us made me feel safer. After all, he had not in fact stolen my bag, though he seemed keen on letting me know he definitely could have.

"How did you know about that?"

His lip curled ever so slightly upward.

"I work in markets," he said, shrugging, without bothering to hide the fact that he was completely and unashamedly lying. "Seemed inevitable at this point. What magazine do you know of that's not sold or being sold today? They're dinosaurs. Bet the board's up there on the fortieth floor saying, 'just pay a porn star to hype the brand on her socials, triple the engagement.' There's tons of them out there, I mean, open Twitter for two seconds."

I had no response to this. He continued on, undeterred.

"So you lost your job. Whole team gone?"

I nodded.

"Sorry."

"Thanks for saying that."

"You know . . . " he said, "we're hiring at my firm. If you want, I could put your name in, figure something out."

I frowned at him, unsure of whether to laugh. I could see his entire dick pressed up against his left leg through his shorts. The sheerness—both literal and figurative—of his absolute bad guy vibes was hard to ignore.

"You don't even know what I do."

"Do I need to? It's marketing. Consumer insight. It's why they hire theater majors out of college to do it."

"You wouldn't hire me."

"I would," he said. "You're a young guy, recently unemployed, hard worker. Passion for fine leather goods. Besides, it's Christmas."

"I really don't know," I said.

"Come on now." He said it theatrically, every word enunciated, like they do all the climactic arguments in Hallmark movies. "Give me a reason why I wouldn't."

I stopped short, hearing it for the first time. It was a perfectly normal thing to say. *You* don't even say it most of season one. And it certainly doesn't start to fit you until a couple of episodes in. In the late '90s, when there was talk of a *Raider* movie with all the original cast, it was the tagline they used. "Give me a reason." Fan posters everywhere, people made a ruckus over plot, whether we'd just pick right up after the end of the show. More still, debated a retcon of your sidekick Moto. Late cast additions often killed shows looking for new material as time went on. There was an entire wing of the fandom, surprising to find, that despised him, and argued that the inclusion of his character took too much bite out of the dark edge of the show. Which was true. I'd never deny that. In any case, Maxie Lang, the Vietnamese-Canadian kid they'd hired to play him, was almost eighteen and had dropped out of show business by then, arrested once for cocaine possession, another for drunk driving. He would die in a couple more years, the autopsy leaked to *Star Mag* revealing both trace amounts of heroin and HIV positivity.

And in any case, Moto or not, the movie never progressed beyond fans yammering at each other over message boards. Haubert himself never even mentioned it, refused even to talk about it. The show didn't exist after he'd stopped making it. The guy made *award winners*, now. People gave a shit who he endorsed for president and voted accordingly. A foundation in his name recycled textiles into sustainable utility wear in sweatshops all over Malaysia and Thailand.

I stopped myself going further. This was always what happened, every time I'd hear those words and think about you and end up angry again.

The big-dicked stranger checked the step counter on his wrist.

"Tell you what. I'll be down at that coffee spot"—he pointed above my shoulder at the bakery on the other end of the floor—"8 a.m. tomorrow before my spin class. If you want to meet me there, I could tell you some more about the gig. You can ask any questions you want."

Again he smiled, disarmingly. I could tell it was a thing he did to force people off their guard, and it was working. Like doing it made me forget exactly half the words I knew and forced my neurons to take tedious paths around my brain to form suitable English. I waited for him to admit he was playing an elaborate prank on me. Or maybe just cruising. I was into that, I admitted. He was short but looked like fun. I didn't suggest any of this, in the end. I just pulled my bag tighter over my shoulder and said: "I'm seeing someone."

"You sure?"

He said it without changing a muscle on his face. I looked around, for cameras, for whoever hired him to fuck with passersby on video for likes.

"I'm gonna go," I said again. I turned around and walked back toward the lobby. My phone rang, Gil calling again. I sent him to voicemail a second time that day. I didn't look back around until at least a good jog away and saw the area he'd been standing in was empty. I opened up my bag again, finding the crumpled paper. Unfurled, it contained a phone number, which I was expecting, but on the back, something I wasn't: a name scrawled in the corner. *Min.*

I looked it over a couple more times, then back toward the boutique, where the other, new girl was still folding scarves. I dug my phone out of my pocket and dialed.

She picked up on the first ring.

"Are you okay?"

I let a pause linger far too long, shocked as I still was that her number had been real. To think: I'd misjudged the big-dicked stranger. I wasn't as hot as I thought.

"I'm fine—"

"Are you at the hospital?"

"No—"

"Are you filing a complaint?"

I paused at this.

"Complaint against . . . "

"The elevator company, the people who own the mall, I don't know. Jesus, I'm really sorry. My dog sitter was about to leave and I didn't give her a key to lock my door and they brought you out of the elevator shaft and you were still unconscious so I just—"

She broke off.

"Just left your phone number in my bag," I said.

"Are you sure you're not hurt?" she said.

"I hit my head, but it doesn't feel serious."

"You were gushing blood."

"Not anymore."

Min let out a small breath the moment I realized she had been holding it in the first place.

"Seriously," she said, "what kind of elevator just opens without the . . . the elevator part."

I had stepped outside, unprepared for the cold, and started to make my way home. The ice bit at my ankles, but I decided on walking. It would take some time. Which was okay.

"Do you want to have dinner with me tonight?"

4

Bo sat in the backseat of the car with his brother while their father drove them home. Snow had begun to pile against the glass. Slowly, it blotted away the orange lights streaking by, turning them from comets to glowing balls of gas, passing one by one along the highway.

Bo's brother Kaz was making bubbles with his mouth, uninterested. Their father Hal was driving with one hand, pressing his other fist into his brow. They hadn't spoken to each other for at least half an hour.

"Did Umma make dinner?" Kaz asked. Hal glanced back at them, as though remembering for the first time that evening that they were there. He drove on another few seconds.

"No, Kazzie, I'll make you something when we're home."

He spoke Korean to them, something he only used to do in front of their grandparents, adhering to some code, determined to impress their mother's parents with the sight of a white man grasping the language the way that he could.

"Grilled cheeses," Kaz ordered. To this, Hal said nothing. They turned off the interstate and onto the quiet roads. Banks of snow were piled high on each edge of the road, leaves and dirt mixed in so that they resembled hulking mounds of sludge. Bo let his gaze fall on the space between his feet a couple inches off the floor of the car. He saw his right shoe was missing, and the underside of his white sock had gone black with grime. He looked halfheartedly around the car, hoping to find it, but gave up.

"Is Umma making dinner soon?"

The word, like it had the first time, sent a charge through the air. Bo's stomach knotted upon itself, hearing it the second time. He could not see the bottom of Hal's face through the rearview mirror. The fist he held at the top of the steering wheel was clenched tight.

— CLICK —

Jacket Guy never misses a shot, not once. He is given many opportunities, perps that run, perps that jump into cars, perps that fire their guns over their shoulders or through walls and doors. Jacket Guy always nails them. Always. And while the thought does occur that Jacket Guy may not ever miss because Jacket Guy only takes the shots he knows he can't miss, it is not dwelled upon for very long or for very hard. This is, after all, a great way to live. Jacket Guy may lay claim to an absolutely perfect shooting record—in rain, in wind, in the dark, while running, while hanging from buildings, while fighting through busy and unsuspecting crowds—and it completely works, it's perfect, and nobody can question his authority on the matter; it cannot be disproven and never will.

Jacket Guy has a name but wears the same jacket every episode, so he's Jacket Guy, and it is not a lack of interest in Jacket Guy's real name that has effectively erased it from existence in this viewer's mind but rather an easier route to identification. It has never been particularly important what Jacket Guy's name is, or what Jacket Guy's commanding officer's name is, or what Jacket Guy's Girl of the Week's name is. The allure of Jacket Guy has always been the yarn. It is generally understood that Jacket Guy lives through a great many yarns that do not eventually make it to air because they are not the most interesting, nor the most perfectly portioned for Jacket Guy's 9/8 central time slot. A guess, for sure, but a guess that makes sense in-universe and cannot effectively be disproven, much like Jacket Guy's prodigious skill with the state-issue Smith & Wesson Model 39 tucked into his belt at his hip. It is the first thing onscreen as season 2, episode 2, "The Mighty and the Weak," gets rolling: close camera trained on the handle of the 39, pan out to Jacket Guy—and his jacket—headed inside the precinct gnashing his teeth on a steaming hot dog. A cinematographic move that accentuates Jacket Guy's humanity and hints at a life outside his work that portends itself as lonely and grim, as anyone may easily picture. Jacket Guy's commanding officer scolds him for the hot dog, warning him that the cart on 71st once gave his wife food poisoning for three days.

"Don't joke," says Jacket Guy. "You don't have a wife."

"Funny. I want you to get your ass to the McAuley shipyards. Homicide called in this morning."

"Perp?"

"That's for you to decide."

Their voices are blurred by the sounds of a busy office,

raggedy men in handcuffs being walked to the jail cells in the back by petty officers. Jacket Guy almost rolls his eyes.

"I'm not your guy. I don't know the first thing about Little China," he says, throwing the rest of his hot dog in the trash. Douche Cop pushes past on his way out, earning looks but no words. There was reason enough for Douche Cop—a sad, burly guy who towered over Jacket Guy and the rest of the precinct, designed by production and casting crews to be both pathetic and formidable—to be upset. There had always been a notorious, unhinged intensity behind his face, underneath his plastic bravado. Jacket Guy had solved his two-month sting of the West Antioch gambling ring operating downtown in just a single episode, the season 2 premiere, "Dark Reckoning."

"You're right about one thing," says Jacket Guy's commanding officer. "You are definitely not my guy. But you're all I've got. Ask your questions when you get there."

"What am I looking at?"

They turn around and scrutinize a bulletin board stuffed with shipyard photos and grainy shots of three people, a woman and two men, all Asian.

"They found a six-month-old girl still in her baby carrier by the dumpsters on 115th. Hypothermia. Left out all night."

"Jesus. Parents?"

"Devastated. Windows broken in the baby's bedroom. They're saying botched kidnapping. Dad's some kind of locksmith. New parents. Live in a one-room situation above the store. We haven't gotten through to them so far. They talked to us through the door this morning, pretending the shop's closing. Not much room here for a warrant, yet."

"What makes you think I can get through to them?"

Jacket Guy's commanding officer gives him a look, and the meaning of this look is partially lost, perhaps by evolving customs of social signaling that do not carry over from the 1980s to the early aughts in which this viewer is watching a rerun on tape. But whatever the look is or what it entails, Jacket Guy gives a little nod of his head, takes the file from the top of the desk along with the three photographs, makes it to the doors at the end of the hall. He stops, looking just slightly over his shoulder. It is not only the solemn quiet of the moment, given that a little girl has been found dead; it is almost as if the whole look of the world around them has shifted, sideways, into an entirely new tone. This is, of course, the episode that changed it all.

"How cold was it last night?"

Jacket Guy's commanding officer puts his hands on his hips, formidable and dark. But his shoulders fall. It is apparent that Jacket Guy's commanding officer, himself a tall, imposing man with broad shoulders and greying hair, has, in fact, thought deeply about what he says next. That death, though commonplace in their line of work, has never truly softened its edge on his mind, not in the decades he has been on the force, and never will, no matter how much longer he stays.

"Nine Fahrenheit. Kid that young, dead in an hour, two, tops."

— C L I C K —

They pulled into the driveway, over the rough seam in the asphalt that separated them from the street. Bo undid his seatbelt and stepped outside. His shoeless foot made contact with the ice, which felt like needles digging into his skin. Hal was busy with Kaz's booster chair. Bo made himself think of the tree inside, how he had spent a day placing their ornaments all around it. It was placed in a corner of their living room at an angle visible to the road and greeted them every time they came home. It wasn't lit tonight. They hadn't been home all day, not since morning, in which Bo's mother had seen the boys off to school. And despite his exhaustion, the numbness he felt in his limbs as they drove, it was the only thing he was really thinking about: that the corner of the house was as dark as the rest of it, dark as the street and the trees around. They proceeded to the door, Bo stepping carefully over iced-over tire tracks in the snow. The house was a wall of hot air that hit them when they got inside and shook themselves out of their coats. Hal set himself about the place, turning on every last light in the house as though trying to flush it all white with illumination. "Guys, stay in the living room where I can see you," he said over his shoulder, and they did not answer.

— *C L I C K* —

Jacket Guy enters the rickety lock shop from his car parked outside, shaking snow off his shoes. An old Asian man sits at the counter, counting bills, lifting his eyes up to meet him across the counter when he approaches. Each spends a few moments staring at the other.

"You own this place?"

The old man speaks a few syllables, shy and without moving his lips. Jacket Guy looks around for help, but the shop is empty.

The face is one of the photos he'd received from the precinct. It has been several stops along the way to decipher the lock shop's location from passersby he'd managed to stop on the street. The address he has been given does little to place him accurately among the makeshift shacks and cobbled alleys. Little China was a twisting maze of alleys just outside the McAuley shipyards. Jacket Guy had been silent passing under several strings hung up between apartments with ragged white clothes hanging from each, glancing only briefly up at them. His breaths, even in the store, come away as fog.

"You want," says a voice from behind the beaded doorway. The old man turns, pronouncing urgency in chattering, rapid-fire language, but the young man who emerges waves him off.

"Your father," Jacket Guy guesses.

"What you want," the young man says. "Close."

"I'm not here for locks, I'm trying to find whoever's the owner here. I have some questions about Hui-Ling Tao, I'm looking for her father or her mother."

Jacket Guy opens the right side of his jacket, revealing, pinned to the inside, the gold badge, weathered and pock-marked. It is a quick and subtle display of authority that electrifies the room. The young man's face contorts as though pulled in opposing directions by invisible strings. For the first time since Jacket Guy has walked into the lock shop, the air turns thick and dangerous.

The old man puts a hand on his son's shoulder but is almost beaten away. He retreats behind the beaded curtains and is not heard from again.

"You're Hui-Ling's father?" Jacket Guy asks. The young man

doesn't answer, bustling angrily around the counter. He fumbles with a mess of keys on a chain around his neck and uses one to open up the register.

"Go away."

"I'm not doing that until somebody answers my questions."

There is a deafening smack across the counter as the young man brings his hand down hard on the surface. Jacket Guy doesn't react, though the crack of skin on wood has echoed many times over in their dingy space, making the keys hanging around them tingle against each other on their hooks. It is a sound that suggests making it caused a great deal of pain to the young man's hands, but he is trying not to show it. The young man turns around, facing Jacket Guy with their noses only six inches apart.

"What there talk," he says, quietly. "Hui-Ling dead. No talk. Get out."

"Do you know anybody who might have had a reason to hurt you or her?"

"Don't know nobody. Ten, fifteen people in my store every day. No work. My bàba know nothing, bàba half blind, not see anything."

"What about your wife? Is she upstairs during the day?" Jacket Guy asks several more questions that go unanswered. The young man leaves the counter and begins to tinker on a worktable off by the doors. For a minute, the sounds of his tools are the only noise in the store. Jacket Guy puts a hand through his hair, and his exhaustion, set against the hard overhead lights, is painfully apparent.

"Jiao-Long," he says, finally, and the name, unlike the others, appears to stick so much better, as Jacket Guy does not say many names. He says it with such self-assured clarity that the young man's head dips just a centimeter over his tools, hearing it.

"I know you don't think anybody can help you," Jacket Guy says, "and maybe nobody can. Maybe I won't find out who did this to your little girl. But I'm who you've got on your case. And if I don't find out what happened to her, they're going to put this file in a drawer and leave it open. And you're never going to know why somebody out there wanted her dead. Trust me. You're not gonna want to live with that."

Jiao-Long raises a screwdriver that is held so tightly in his rugged fist that his knuckles are white around his grip. There is a brief moment, unmistakable in the light, in which he appears to entertain lunging for Jacket Guy with it. The urge is clear on his face from where the camera lingers, in high detail, while Jacket Guy looms in a blur behind him, over his shoulder. But seconds pass, and he puts his screwdriver down, and turns his head.

"Get out."

— C L I C K —

"I'm not hungry anymore," said Kaz, whose jacket had turned inside out and clung to his wrist by the cuff. He swatted it back and forth to get it off. Bo sat on the sofa and peeled off his soaked sock. His toes had gone wrinkly and white, going red only for a moment where he poked them hard with his finger. Kaz took a running leap and landed on a cushion, snatching up the remote. The television was still set to the news channel, which their parents had typically kept on in the mornings up until the boys left the house for school. It was airing the nightly show, and they caught a section about a gang robbery at a Domino's across town. Bo felt his back seize, afraid to see an establishing shot of his school, his picture, even. It was late enough that it might have already made the headlines. It was news enough for their town, he was sure. Kaz watched, enraptured for a moment, then changed the channel—click—past a parade of infomercials before settling on *Rudolph*. Hal made cooking noises in the kitchen, opening and shutting the refrigerator, starting up the stove. Between them stood the tree, still dark. Bo raised his head a little and saw that a red ornament had bent the branch it hung from almost to the floor and was dangling less than an inch off the ground. On the screen, the Abominable Snow Monster tore open a space between the trees and opened its mouth to roar. Kaz screamed along with it, and the noise made Bo's ears ring long after he'd stopped. Bo conceded to his brother most days when the television remote lay in contention. But he wanted to watch his show. Perhaps Hal might even be convinced to watch an episode if he went to the cupboard and took out the tapes.

Kaz had always looked so much more like their father. His hair was brown, his eyes big and wide instead of like their mother's. They heard noises, a banging pot, hissing steam, some bad words. Hal appeared briefly in the doorway, framed by light, and it seemed for a moment that his head had blackened to shadow and all that remained was his silhouette.

Winter was long and dark in their part of the state. Bo had fought all month to stay interested in his classes and had mostly succeeded. Second graders were not allowed reign of the playground to wait for the buses and had to be corralled in an area close to the doors at school, which was where Bo and his brother waited each afternoon for the buses. They had been warned all week that the snowfall had caused road blockages all over town, which had forced the buses onto alternate routes. Bo hated these afternoons the most. He didn't particularly enjoy looking after Kaz, especially not at school where Annamarie Watkins and her friends could see him. Kaz always wanted to play pretend, demanding he be the Abominable Snow Monster and chase him around the snowbanks. It was something they did at home while outside. Halfway through they'd tire and start throwing snowballs, after which one would hit Kaz in the face and he would start shrieking until he got something to eat. Kid stuff. Bo couldn't be caught indulging in that sort of thing while the girls watched; it impugned his character.

Annamarie Watkins told him the previous day that her family was taking her to Colorado for winter break to see their aunt, who lived in a wooden house that she said slept eight plus kids, comfortably. There was a hot tub, a barbecue, and a Finnish sauna downstairs that she had never been in because she didn't like to sweat. On Christmas day, they were going to Maui. Bo had never heard of going away for Christmas, especially to someplace that didn't have any Christmas trees, but that was what Annamarie Watkins had said, and without sounding at all like she was lying or exaggerating for dramatic effect, and so he had believed her. The only Christmas he had ever traveled was to their cousins in Miami one year, and the trip, which had required a connecting flight, had been so difficult that his parents had vowed never to fly so near the holidays again. He knew enough to know that they didn't have money for things like a trip to Maui, but he still enjoyed hearing Annamarie Watkins talk about it, describing it all to him so that he might picture it for himself.

And so he'd woken up today, the last day of school for two whole weeks, thinking singularly of the Watkins' vacation. He dared not ask if they could travel for the holidays, knowing what his mother and father would say, but didn't police himself so harshly as to avoid imagining the possibility.

They sat now at the table, in front of three bowls of corn flakes with whole milk. Hal had thrown the remnants of the cheese still burned onto the pan into the trash. It seemed silly. It had only been a number of hours. It was strange how much could be bent around time to look so different on the other side. Hal ate wordlessly. Kaz dripped milk all over his side of the table as he ate; it ran in rivulets down his chin. Bo hadn't touched his food, stirring the flakes into soggy meal while taking small glances his father's way. The three of them stared into different spaces somewhere beyond the walls of their kitchen. It had been so loud and bright in the hospital. By comparison, the soft yellow light from the lamps around them made their surroundings old, near rotten.

"Guys," Hal said, finally, and both boys looked his way. He turned words over in his mouth, trying to choose.

"I'm going to call your grandparents after dinner, figure some things out. We're going to talk about some things I don't want you to hear, so after you clean up, I want you both upstairs and get ready for bed."

"Umma always reads me a book before bed," Kaz said. A dark

line crossed Hal's face. He placed his hands flat on the table.

"I can't read you something tonight, Kazzie, I'll be busy. Why don't you ask Bo?"

"I don't like Bo reading," Kaz said, sticking his lip out like a shelf. "Umma always reads me a book."

Hal looked at him for a long time, at the pouty face he made with milk all over the front of his shirt. He let out his breath, and the air seemed to come from his shoulders; they sagged as though deflating. Their father was hugely, inhumanly tall, so much taller than their mother. When he put them on his shoulders they felt as though they could touch stars, bend the curve of the world back around to them. On his left ring finger was the gold band. Bo wondered if he would take it off tonight. Wait until the morning, maybe.

"I'll read you whatever you want tomorrow, Kazzie."

"No—" Kaz pounded his palm onto the table, causing vibrations that unsettled their plates. "No, No, No—"

He pounded again and again, until he'd tired himself out. Bo realized his hands had fallen to his sides and were clenched into fists. He blinked, finding wetness in the corner of one eye.

— *C L I C K* —

Jacket Guy has found the crowbar used to dismantle the window into the apartment in a dumpster four blocks from the lock shop. He spends a great portion of the episode pacing the long alley that leads from the lock shop to the dumpster. He is on a third trek across when he notices a young woman enter from the street. They lock eyes. It is clear from the look on her face that she is

Hui-Ling's mother, whom Jacket Guy has not been able to find for several days now. He has been back to the McAuley shipyards each day for the past week, walking the neighborhoods, and has never found her or anybody willing enough to tell him where he could find her. The young woman ducks her head, walking faster as he chases, shouting her name. She has come to the set of steel stairs leading up to their second-floor apartment, locking herself inside the gate before Jacket Guy can reach her.

"Please!" he shouts after her retreating back. "Please, talk to me."

The young woman has nearly reached the door at the top of the stairs, past the garbage bags taped over the broken window to the right when he puts his hands down, calming himself.

"Your daughter deserves justice."

The young woman glances at him, and it is the lines carved on her face that fill the screen, they are all Jacket Guy—this viewer—can see.

"Not care," she says, quietly. "Police come last week, not care, either. You care justice? You want? Somebody come and break windows, somebody take Hui-Ling and leave her in the street, trash. You all same, you laugh, us animal to you."

"That's not true."

"Lie." The young woman does not cry, gathering herself up, taking several steps down to Jacket Guy. Her eyes are dry, but her face is deathly red. "You cannot help us. We go police, they deport. Husband and I, husband bàba, all of us. Done. Nothing back home. Home, we die."

The young woman leaves him pressed up against the gate and slams the door behind her. Jacket Guy keeps his eyes on the door for a while, curling his fingers around the wrought iron. The staircase is a caged area that climbs up to the roof, chain link on all sides. It is evident to this viewer that he has lost control of his witnesses, that they revile him, that he will never locate their daughter's killer and it will haunt him for the rest of his life. Jacket Guy is young, a little too young to be in this line of work, and it has never seemed to bother him until now. It is perhaps the first time Jacket Guy has been confronted with a situation to which he perceives no immediate solution. The camera lingers on his face through the bars, he would scream, were it allowed, but he is too much of a man for that. He presses his palm to the keyhole lock.

— C L I C K —

Kaz pounded his fists a few more times against the table, petering out his strength, giggling to himself, having already forgotten his anger. At last Hal noticed Bo's full bowl.

"Bo? Not hungry?"

Bo shook his head, forcing his lips shut. He felt along the outside of his pocket the little lump of paper, the crumpled visitor's pass he'd unstuck from the front of his shirt as they found their car in the hospital parking lot and come home. He curled his fingers around it, felt Hal's hand on his chin.

"You wanna watch an episode with me tonight?"

Though the idea had crossed his mind favorably just minutes earlier, Bo shook his head, confronted with the look on Hal's face. He did not want it anymore, not like this. He remembered the day Hal had set the tapes in front of him, just a few years earlier. "The greatest TV show on the face of the planet," he called it. "I loved these when I was a kid. I've been waiting to show them to you until you were old enough."

They fell in love with the darkness, the grit and fog. Bo's mother protested, but only lightly. She saw how happy it made them, the words and energy it seemed to bring out of him. Bo sat there, shaking his head, and felt his eyes grow hot. Hal grew pale.

"Bo—"

"Appa, can I watch *Rudolph*?" Kaz said loudly, swinging his legs back and forth from his chair. "I'm done eating, can I go watch—"

Bo raised his eyes just an inch to see Hal's looking back at him over the noise. In that moment Bo pictured the bus that arrived that morning, the way he had raised his arms and accepted a hug and kiss from his mother before pulling Kaz's hand out the door toward the street. Hal had already gone to work like most mornings but had promised to come home before dinner. He worked in a plant that printed copies of local newspapers and had taken the boys there on a weekend. They'd wandered through the machines, huge hulking ones that spun sheets of paper high over their heads and drew them like threads from big rolls of it as large as bales of hay. Hal had taken them to a stool on the right side of a conveyer that ran the length of the floor, almost too big to be seen all at once, curled together in angled variations like an imposing and guarded creature.

On the bus that morning, Bo had spied from the seat he shared with his brother near the back the vague form of his mother in the window, arranging the pillows on the sofa, her shoulder just barely touching the tree, already lit.

It happened just twenty minutes after they had arrived at school.

Kaz had been herded to his class by one of the teachers, and Bo had settled his backpack in his proper cubby. He had never heard the voice that came on before and had only enough time to recognize they were saying something to the effect of "stay inside your classrooms" when Jordan Hinson shrieked from the open window that there were police cars outside. They clambered for the windows and saw it over the shouts of Mrs. Aronson and a room mom from the hall, a yellow bus parked haphazardly on the curb and a small crowd around the drop-off zone. He didn't recall what was said, or even much of the view himself, as he had been near the back of the crowd and had only gotten a glimpse before Mrs. Aronson had closed the blinds shut and ordered them back to their desks. They protested, especially the boys, and were shouted down. They had never heard Mrs. Aronson's voice get that way before, loud and high. They heard the sound of an ambulance right outside as it pulled around the corner, and several imitated its siren, earning more barks from the front of the room. Another five minutes later, their school principal, a bald man who wore polo shirts tucked into khakis every day, appeared at the door.

"Bo," he heard. "Bo, honey, you come with me."

Had it been Hal who had driven him and Kaz to the hospital? Had he come to the school and found them? Had a parent volunteered? Bo didn't remember, he tried again, and again, in that little split second, something kept misfiring.

— C L I C K —

"Jiao-Long and Fan Fan are going to be deported in two weeks," says Jacket Guy, back at the precinct. "I got it out of her. She told me if they went to the police and we kept snooping around they'd be sent back to China, but it's not true. I found the transcripts in the courthouse records, Jiao-Long's been appealing their case for months now. No dice."

"This doesn't fly. Why wouldn't Fan Fan know about this?" his C.O. asks.

"He must not have told her. He's been to court alone every time. I have the visitor logs."

"Still. Why keep it a secret?" he asks.

Jacket Guy turns away from the bulletin board, facing the window. It is dark, from where he stands he can see tendrils of steam coming off the buildings, in the distance the steelwork that marks Little China. He'd never paid it much attention before. All of the city had long become alien to him, no longer a place where people lived quiet lives but a maze of interlocking pathways, hideaways, dark corners where shadowy figures lurked. But Little China, more alien, still. He is thinking it when something in his face changes, amid a swell of music that cuts to silence.

"The lock." The lock on the stairway cage. It had been worn, slightly, but not forced. He recalled the path up the stairs to the window, shattered and taped over. There was no other way inside the fire escape. Whoever had taken Hui-Ling had used a key. One of a number of keys. Perhaps in a mess of keys, hanging off the end of a chain necklace.

"Holy . . . "

He is already running for the door past his commanding officer's repeated yells, sprinting to his car.

"Please, Appa, please can I watch *Rudolph* now? Watch it with me, come on, Appa—"

And it was true, in the end, that it didn't matter much whether he had been driven to the hospital or ridden along in the ambulance. As many times as he wracked his brain it didn't come, and Bo couldn't help but think it was for the best, or at least what he deserved. Because it had been his fault. His mother wouldn't have come to school to drop off their bagged lunches if he hadn't forgotten them in the first place. Isn't that what he saw in Hal's eyes? What he already knew to be true? He gritted his teeth. Kaz continued his noisemaking. "Umma always let me watch *Rudolph* after dinner. Why can't—"

"SHUT UP." Bo brought his fists down, bracing his shoulders, and rocked the whole table with his weight. "SHUT UP KAZZIE SHUT UP—"

It was over. Hal's hand on Bo's wrist was so tight that it hurt. He felt his pulse throb, shockwaves over his body. He had stopped shouting and he couldn't have gone on even if he'd tried. It was as though the heat had all come out of him and had dissipated, instantly, into the air. He went limp. Kaz had fallen silent, the color had drained from his face. In their silence hung the ends of Bo's words, consonants that pierced them like shards of glass. Kaz began to cry, and it was not his shrieks that they had heard before and grown accustomed to but darker, deeper noises from his belly. They shook his entire being. What seemed like a minute passed. All they could hear were Kaz's screams. Bo's hands were open in front of him. He didn't dare look at his father. His cereal was a yellow soup of oatmeal. The hand around his wrist loosened. There was movement as Hal stood up and scooped Kaz into his arms, let him sob shuddering breaths into the shoulder of his shirt.

"Kazzie, stop crying, show me *Rudolph.* Show me your favorite part, huh? Can you do that?"

Bo sat alone at the table, in front of their bowls. Hal's: empty. Kaz's: half of it spilled over the table. His. He dug his spoon into the sludge, ravenously hungry, ate until his stomach hurt.

— *CLICK* —

Jacket Guy finds him on the edge of the docks, shivering in the cold. The back of his head is visible as he climbs out of his car and sprints to the water, the camera following, jagged and jumpy, above it the ice-cold outline of the city and the vault of the stars.

— *CLICK* —

Hal stayed downstairs for what seemed like hours after that. Long after Kaz had fallen asleep on his side of the room Bo lay there on his back, staring at the ceiling. Certain words he could hear floating up from downstairs were twisting themselves into shapes he thought he could see in the darkness.

They had gone up to bed as they'd been told, stood side by side at the sink as they brushed their teeth. Kaz didn't brush if he wasn't made to. They didn't usually say goodnight, each of them lying there, content to talk in whispers until one of them fell asleep and the other followed soon after. Kaz had calmed down after about a half hour but still hadn't said anything to Bo. They went to their beds this same way, and Kaz, after much tossing and turning, had finally dozed off and was breathing loudly with his mouth open. Bo didn't know what he was waiting for. Maybe for Hal to turn off the lights downstairs. He could see out his window the flood of yellow from the living room on the snowy yard that meant the lights were still on. As soon as he looked, they shut off, throwing the snowscape outside into darkness.

— C L I C K —

"Jiao-Long." Jacket Guy comes to a stop twenty feet from him. Jiao-Long turns his head, and his face is streaked with tears, though they are half-dried, leftover tears. The certainty in his eyes is chilling.

Jacket Guy takes another step forward, and Jiao-Long dangles a foot off the dock.

"Don't do this."

Jiao-Long gives a short little laugh. The tips of his fingers are blue. "Good man, so far. Lock shop, apartment. Bàba comfortable, enough eat. I do my work."

"You left her out in the cold. You killed her, Jiao-Long."

Jiao-Long opens his mouth and gives an anguished roar that pierces the dark. His face is sickly white, a mask of hate.

"Two week, we go back to China. We no home, we no family. We starve. We die, months and months, keep dying, Fan Fan no more milk for baby. She watch Hui-Ling, dry up, every day lose weight. What I do, strong. Nobody could. What I do."

"There was a way out of this, you didn't have to—"

Jiao-Long turns fully to show Jacket Guy the screwdriver still in his hand.

"Think, Jiao-Long. You still have a wife, a father. You need to think about them."

"I save," Jiao-Long whispers. His lungs are scarred by the cold; he can barely get the words out.

"I save. Daughter dead," Jiao-Long says, and it is quick enough for the cadence to match, the way he has picked up Jacket Guy's words, how it echoes around his head. "Hui-Ling dead, either way."

"We can help you appeal your case. We can get you a lawyer."

"Daughter dead," Jiao-Long says again, "either way."

He is standing at the very end of the dock where the frozen water froths below them. He turns the screwdriver in his hand, every muscle in his chest bulged and tense.

"Stop me?" he asks, gritting his teeth.

"I'm trying to help you."

Jiao-Long steps forward, making a sudden arc of his arm toward the sky with his makeshift weapon. Within a half second Jacket Guy has already pulled his Model 39, aiming it silently at Jiao-Long's chest. A man faces death or death, and the choice is both impossible and inevitable.

"We're not going there."

Jiao-Long is not breathing so hard anymore. He raises the screwdriver like a baton, pointing it at Jacket Guy's face.

"You stop me?"

Even in the whispering cold he looks rather comfortable.

Several seconds of silence play out over a low, brooding simmer of background music. This viewer can see it coming, can already hear it playing on Jacket Guy's lips.

"Give me a reason, man. Just one."

— C L I C K —

Below, he heard the stairs creaking, Hal making his way to the second-floor landing, then to the first door on the left. Bo closed his eyes as the bedroom door opened an inch, slowly. For a few seconds, he heard nothing.

"I know you're awake."

Bo kept his eyes closed, turning his head just a little farther into his pillow.

"I'm sorry."

Hal slipped fully into the room, rounding the corner of Bo's bed. He sat. Bo felt the warm weight of his hand on his leg.

"I know you are. I'm sorry, too."

Bo allowed himself another moment in the spot he'd warmed against the sheets with his body heat, then sat up. In the dark, they could really only make out little silhouettes of each other. Some moonlight dancing off the top of Hal's hair when he turned his head.

"I know today was hard," Hal said. "You have so many reasons to be scared, and angry."

It had been in the hallway just outside the second-grade classroom, hadn't it? The moment in which Bo was told that his mother had gotten into an accident on the street? Or had it been in the lobby of the hospital? Where Hal had sat them both on each knee and told them Umma was very hurt and wasn't awake right now, that they were going to have to wait here for the doctors to tell them what was going on. It was not the moment itself, this much seemed clear to Bo, but the change in the world around them, the way it grew so large and fearsome. Two realities, one in which their mother had remembered the two brown bags sitting on the counter and passed them to Bo as they left for the bus, or perhaps just one in which Bo hadn't forgotten in the first place. And another, a new one they lived in now, in which an old man in a white coat had met them in the lobby, with families and other doctors and nurses milling around, and let them know that their mother had died fifteen minutes ago, without ever waking up after the moment in which she had lost consciousness on the side of the parking lot, fifty feet from Bo's classroom.

Hal's hand moved in little circles on Bo's leg. They paused when Kaz made an impatient groan, turning over in his bed.

"You're gonna have to be brave, Bo. Okay? I need that from you. Your brother needs time to figure this out, same as us. We're all going to—going to process this in different ways. You know what process means?"

"Yes."

"Yeah—" Hal rubbed his eyes. He must have been exhausted. Bo hadn't even asked what had happened at his work, if he'd gotten in trouble for leaving the floor. Would they go back to school? Bo remembered he had homework. He'd asked Jordan Hinson to fax him a worksheet he'd forgotten once already. He didn't like to ask favors. He was going to be in trouble.

And yet there was a moment in the hospital, and it was all Bo could picture when he looked at his father, that seconds-long slice of time in which nobody else existed, when their eyes met, and the doctor had explained how sorry he was, and that she had gone very peacefully, and without pain. He saw all of time stretched out in that moment, could see it the way Hal saw it, all their lives stretching out beyond now, all without her. Allowed himself to see it for just a moment before Kaz pulled on his hand and asked what was going on. None of them had cried. That had been the strangest thing about it, that in all their time left in the lobby, after they went downstairs and were given a little baggie with a watch and a golden wedding band inside, not a single one of them cried and still hadn't, not about her.

It was that which he looked for, trying to reach out with his vision to make sense of the black blot in front of him, his father's face in the darkness. Something, permission, maybe. An allowance to feel what he was trying not to feel. He had no mother. On Christmas Day they'd steam fresh white rice and make spicy curry from the little packet of dry powder in the pantry, they'd open the little pile of presents under the tree, they'd sit and watch the snow fall, all without her.

— C L I C K —

"Jiao-Long," says Jacket Guy, taking more furtive steps. "Jiao-Long, listen to me—"

It comes very quickly after that. Jiao-Long steps backward off the platform, his body falling out of sight over the side of the dock. Jacket Guy roars and lunges for him but is too late. Jiao-Long hits the water, disappearing under. The punch to his chest by the freezing cold is assumed to be quick and subtle.

Jacket Guy watches the inky black surface, hoping against hope. But nobody surfaces. Like a stone, he has already sunk below, succumbed. Lights appear over Jacket Guy's shoulder. Cars pull in beside his unmarked sedan, blaring their sirens. Jacket Guy gets to his feet. The camera lingers on his back as he shakes the cold from his limbs, casts one last glance over the icy water, and heads for the headlights. Credits roll against his back. And it is not just the heavy shadows and swelling music just before cut to black that always fill this viewer's eyes with tears, but a darkness that takes on new meaning, and will continue to do so for the rest of his life upon watching this episode. Because it is the last episode this viewer watched before his mother was killed and his family had broken. For years he cannot bear to see it again, will not picture the fiery whiteness of Jiao-Long's face flecked with snow and slush on the docks without thinking of the day it happened. And it will be observed in the months afterward, in the years to follow, that Jacket Guy is not only ionized pixels on a glass screen but an extension of this viewer's courage, or rather, the courage he wishes he had, courage to speak, to keep living, to ask his father for a hug, for permission to cry that night in his bed while his brother sleeps, unaware his mother lies cold in a fridge downtown, for one last night in which they might pretend none of it has happened at all, that they could take their dinners to the couch, slide the right tape into the player just under the television, take up the remote, press play, with a click—

But Hal only leaned close and kissed Bo on the forehead, gone a second later. "Goodnight. I love you" was all he said. Bo felt the mattress under them shift again as his father lifted himself off it and made his way to the bedroom door, shutting it behind him. Bo lay back down against his pillow, straining to hear more, and gave up.

He didn't want to sleep. Inside, his chest buzzed, vibrations that reached the tips of his fingers and toes. It was so dark that it made no difference if he closed his eyes. He thought maybe he could exist like this forever. He thought of the snow, the way it gathered in clumps on the car windows as they drove home without her. Then his ears pricked when he heard the floor creak in the hallway. He sat up again, wondering, but the door didn't open again. The house made its noises, small whispers as wind passed around the walls and the heater clattered to life in the crawlspace. But nothing more. He sat up, waiting, and found he couldn't distinguish the howl of the wind from his little breaths.

5

Blue didn't find himself around this part of the city for any other reason. He wasn't even sure if Lev was allowed a phone anymore. The rules were stringent, he knew, and had changed many times without notice over the years. Lev wasn't allowed outside the building without an escort. His food was brought in at the beginning of each week. As of yet, they hadn't barred visitors, or so Blue thought. He was hoping to be lucky this time. It had been a few weeks since they had last connected, though the visits, Blue thought, had now continued for at least a decade. Blue entertained for a quiet moment as the train teetered around a bend in the tracks the possibility that they had finally decided to just cart Lev off to a proper prison. Even if there had never truly been enough to criminalize him in the first place. It was an affordance granted by the media saturation around Io Emsworth that her lieutenants had by and large escaped blame. He was afraid, briefly, that he'd forgotten the address, but off the subway and farther into the city a couple blocks, he saw the building fairly quickly, all glass and spiraling up into the sky at least forty stories. Snow fell around him in halfhearted wisps. In the lobby, a girl at a desk took his name and, hearing Lev's, brought a separate tablet out from a drawer. His palmprints were taken, his in-ears removed, turned off, and placed in a lead box along with his wallet. A discreet monitor had already scanned his body for metals as he'd walked through the revolving door to the desk. He was ushered to the near walkway by a guard and escorted up to the penthouse. After a minute, while his ears popped, he was deposited in front of the double doors at the end of the hallway.

"You have ninety minutes."

The guard stepped aside, folding his hands in front of his waist. Blue caught the black grip of a pistol on the inside of his jacket as he opened the door and stepped inside. The door was not locked.

He found Lev in the kitchen, like he had done most other times he visited. He made espressos at all hours of the day, stirring it together with a few tablespoons of sweetener and a thimble of cream.

"Make you a double, shall I?" Lev called over his shoulder.

/ / Nothing for me today. / /

He watched Lev's head rise a couple centimeters, turning around. Lev wore a spindly velveteen robe off his bony shoulders. His hair was nearly gone. He'd started to look this way in the last few years, Blue suspecting a cancer that Lev wasn't telling him about. Lev chewed the inside of his lip, trying to make up his mind.

"You didn't. You couldn't possibly."

/ / It's for the news special. Not permanent. / /

Lev set down his espresso, hobbling over. Already, his hands skirted the bandage around Blue's neck, as though feeling for the implant with his fingertips.

"Unbelievable. And they gave you this little thing for free, did they?"

/ / Again, temporary. / /

Lev put his hands on each shoulder. With a look, he appeared both animated and exhausted, as though a manic-only energy was keeping him from collapsing altogether. He leaned in and kissed each side of Blue's mouth. "I do enjoy you. Take me to the parlor."

Blue led them into the adjoining room overlooking the city, wide windows that extended the length of the wall. Lev hung onto his hand, creaking his way across the floor. He was in worse shape than Blue remembered. The place was impeccably neat, as always. On a visit a month ago, the ornate credenza that once held a collection of antique china was replaced with a wholly modern glass and onyx television that blared faces twice real-life size. A news bulletin was on mute; Blue wondered again how much of the trial and its subsequent talking-head coverage Lev had seen, was allowed to see. He had never been given a clear answer.

"Shut that ugly thing off," Lev told him. He sat, winded. Blue fumbled for the remote as he sat down with his drink.

"I swear it's the only exercise I do these days, opening and shutting my eyes, reading closed captions," he said. "I can't tell the sitcoms apart from the dramas. Such beautiful people. It hurts my head."

/ / Why aren't you taking your walks anymore? / /

Lev gave him a look.

"Have you ever thought that the concept of taking a walk around a predestined course, day in, day out, down to the exact number of steps, calories burned, joules of work produced, is perhaps the most fascist thing any of us could ever do?"

/ / Just a question. / /

Lev gazed at him a second longer. He had lost so much weight.

I really can't stand this voice of yours, he signed, impatiently. Speak to me with your own words.

This is not just an excuse for you to remind me how fluent you've become?

"I take offense," Lev said, "I didn't learn it for you."

He had, in fact, learned it entirely for Blue. He had said so many times before. And American Sign Language, though complex, had barely taken him more than two weeks. Lev was older, beaten, falling apart, but not any duller, and it made Blue happy. At least he thought it did.

/ / I'm supposed to practice this voice so that it can appear more natural on camera. / / said Blue. / / You'll be helping me out. / /

"You sound very natural already, you don't need any help from me," sighed Lev. He downed his espresso and wiped his mouth with his sleeve. "Lay it all out for me. I want to hear everything."

/ / That's not really why I came by. / /

"Oh, come on now, you're the only interesting news I get anymore." Lev crossed his legs in front of him. They paused a moment to catch the last glimpses of the sun dipping out over the city. It wouldn't have surprised Blue to know some legal clause afforded him the penthouse apartment gratis to serve out his house arrest. Lev had always commanded presence like that. It made sense that he'd demanded a penthouse and they had obliged, no matter what the cost had been. Blue had seen Lev make a great many things happen in the time they had known each other, this much was true.

/ / They're picking me up a couple days after Christmas. It'll be me and a camera crew, they say. / /

"Fascinating." Lev observed him. "Just fascinating. How do you feel?"

/ / I don't feel anything. They've paid me a lot of money to do the news special. / /

"You have never struck me as somebody who cared for those sorts of things," Lev said, "the future, I mean. It's always escaped you. Don't tell me I'm wrong."

/ / How do you know? / /

A smile crossed Lev's face. He smiled like this often; Blue was used to the comfort it generated in him. It was comfort he had never quite learned to distrust the way he should have.

"You've come almost every month for the past ten years. You've wanted to know everything I could bother to tell you about it all—Flux, Io—and I've told you. I've left nothing unsaid, no stone unturned. I don't mean to flatter myself, but I didn't have to. You made that call for us when you tattled."

/ / Hardly tattling when under oath. / /

"Oh? Is that what you call it?" Lev turned his head at the sound, sharp shoes hitting the floor. A young woman had emerged from behind a door, carrying a mess of shopping bags. She stopped, gazing at the two of them with an empty look on her face. Lev waved in the direction of the left-hand wing off the great room where he and Blue had taken their seats.

"Find something to do," he told her, briskly.

"This was supposed to be our night," the girl pouted, but Lev had already turned away, ignoring her. The guard who had showed Blue up to the penthouse closed the door behind her. Within another moment she had taken her bags and clicked down the hall, away from them. Lev raised his hands, extending his fingers wide.

"What were we talking about?"

/ / Under oath. / /

"Under *oath*," Lev repeated. "That's it. Incrimination. I surrender all my receipts to a judge. I need court approval to buy a ficus for my informal lounge. The police academy dunce listening outside my front door is, undoubtedly, going to be the last face I see before I die. Did you hear what L'Aspirant said about Io? It was this week, wasn't it? Quite the uproar."

Blue screwed up his eyes. He had heard enough about L'Aspirant for a lifetime. It was pitiful, the value people claimed in the words of those running for president. An election loomed, Blue thought. He didn't know more.

"He might be the highest profile to call for a pardon."

/ / I think the government has better things to do than debate the merits of one woman in or out of the jail time that she deserves. / /

They had called him L'Aspirant—in the French military, the word for an officer candidate—for the first time a month ago, when he announced his run, and the name had stuck. It was unknown what the man genuinely thought of the moniker. It wasn't particularly flattering. Blue didn't watch much television anymore but recalled the video clip of the previous month in which L'Aspirant paid a visit to a children's hospital in the wake of a bus accident. He had taken a makeshift podium, with almost comical solemnity, and vowed greater protection for the country's children. Many believed the stunt to be pure performance. It was only a bus accident, after all. The worst of the injuries had been a broken wrist, some concussions. But Americans respected his stoicism and vast wealth, his handsome face. Empathy often won elections. An election more than a year away, in which L'Aspirant had become the single, most logical, most enrapturing choice, of course, but all the same, Blue thought.

Lev raised his right wrist, showing Blue the scar where the tracking implant had been installed.

"You couldn't have made it at least a little interesting, could you? I mean, house arrest. Wire fraud. You sell away the company that bought you your house, paid your little daughter's child support, for an oath you don't even understand. Because we are to believe the great myth, that you, all this time, were that Good Samaritan who saw something, said something. I must sound so bitter to you, darling. Believe me, I'm not."

/ / In any case, Io is in jail because of me. You were served much better, because of me. Why are we talking about such old news? / /

Lev turned his cup over in his hands. "Really, the only things I envy you are the airs they've put on your shoulders. Out of all of us, you're the only one they call a hero. The way things are going, L'Aspirant may make you attorney general. He *will* win."

/ / I don't care. / /

Lev snorted.

Blue wasn't in the mood to be called a hero. It didn't matter to him anymore, little had in the intervening years. So Io would be pardoned once L'Aspirant took office; who was this show of moral generosity even for? The young ones on the internet who'd obsessed over the movies made about her in the last year, acting as though they'd uncovered some secret tantalizing history twenty years obscured? Blue was no hero. Nobody even knew his name. Lev cocked his head to the side.

"Why don't you ever humor me anymore? You used to. Call it whatever you want, but admit, we've shared a great deal of fun together."

/ / Do you know that you're the one always talking about the past, not me? / /

"I've earned that allowance, haven't I?" Lev asked him. "It's my past, and yours, that made a billion dollars from nothing."

/ / I've already heard this story. / /

"Companies like the one Io built are made of nothing." Lev ignored him. He was in one of his moods and could never wait for an audience once he got started. "It's hot air, bending light around it to fool everybody looking at it into seeing something worth seeing. After which—"

/ / After which three people died. / /

"Everybody dies," Lev said. "I'm watching the dumbest old show about some cranky little cunt doctor who treats his patients like dirt. He says that all the time. 'Everybody dies.'"

He laughed, when Blue said nothing.

"I'm not smart enough for you anymore. You're bored of me."

A thought appeared to cross his mind, smooth so as not to appear manufactured. "Yet you keep coming."

/ / Can't I visit an old friend? / /

Lev's hand grew white around the cup in his lap. For a moment he looked ready to throw it. But the seconds passed, and neither moved, and Lev's knuckles faded back to pink as he loosened his grip. The girl was making some noise in a nearby bedroom. They jumped as the timed lights, calibrated to the setting sun, sprung on all around them.

"We are not friends," Lev said. "You despise me. You always have."

He stood, gathering up his robe around himself and hobbling past Blue's chair to look out the window. He was a small man.

"You'll have to tell me now what you want. You are different, today. I can tell. There's something you've done, something you've decided, and it's changed everything about you: the way you look at me."

Blue was quiet for a long time. He had not forgotten the request his daughter had made of him. He didn't know where to find cognac nearby and didn't want to show up with something cheap.

/ / You're always right, Lev. / /

This made Lev happy.

"I am sorry," he said, "for the dead ones. It shouldn't have happened that way. And I know you didn't mean for it to happen, either. Nobody blames you."

/ / It's very late for that kind of thing. / /

Lev shook his head. "This voice of yours. It's insane. I can't stand it."

Blue stood, joining him by the window. The light was dull and orange and would be gone soon. He was already exhausted. He had much left to do.

/ / I need some reassurances / / he said, finally. They were an arm's length apart, standing together. / / In a few days, they're going to take me back inside F1, and I need to know some things before I go. And it's very important that you tell me the truth. / /

"What will you do if I don't?"

/ / I'll break your skull open. / /

Lev smirked, Blue could see out of his periphery. At least a minute passed before either of them spoke again.

"That caveman standing outside my door will take great care of you if you do."

/ / Doesn't matter. I'm very quick. I'll get it done if you make me. / /

"You mean to say: right now." Lev looked at him, for the first time surprised. "Right here?"

/ / I'm through wasting my time. And fifteen of your ninety minutes are already up. / /

It seemed as though Lev wasn't going to give him what he wanted. Which would make sense, Blue thought. There wasn't much sane about the way he lived anymore; it was something they had in common. But at last, Lev nodded. As if they'd thought of the same exact thing, they retreated to the couch and seat where they'd positioned themselves previously. The moment between them passed as though through water, slowly and silently. Then Lev crossed one leg over the other, leaned forward.

"Go on, then. Ask your questions."

6

Min said she liked Korean food, commercial and authentic, she didn't have a preference. There was a fine line growing finer between the two in the city. I was talking about the places in the lobbies of luxury condominiums that sold galbi tacos with kimchi pico de gallo. Compare that against the basement holes deep in the heart of K-town where one grandma cooked all twenty-five broths and cut the noodles herself. I used to be able to tell them apart. They grew closer and closer together until it could hardly be said which had adopted the other. Who was to say this was not the ultimate goal of immigration itself? Synthesis. It was more than simple cohesion. I'll give you an example. It was all Mandarin on *Raider* so I'm not sure you'd know this, but they don't eat beef in Korea, not like we do here. The piles and piles of barbecue grilled on charcoal at the table is as rare and spendy as prix-fixe caviar over there. The notion of it did not exist before the techniques were developed in the States. Leading us, the sickly hybrid generations that came after, to wonder what exactly we had done to our culture.

She'd told me to meet her at a noodle shop where she said she'd only ever been for lunch. I was early. My hands were blue from the cold; I had been walking down every street that presented itself, turn after turn, for most of the day, taking shelter from the snow wherever I could find it. My head still hurt, but I'd stopped bleeding, so I left the bandage around my head in a garbage can outside the Jewish museum, where I'd spent an hour inside a display of paper cutting by an artist from the twentieth century. Giza Frankel was her name. She had emigrated from Poland to Israel in the '50s, and I'd memorized her life story by the time my hands had gotten their feeling back.

It had been a long time since I'd eaten Korean food, but now, plied with vapors from the kitchen, my memories were fresh. The place was modest and lit with too-bright overhead fluorescents. On two television screens on each opposite wall blared a glossy drama. An old rich type was meeting a young man for dinner at a restaurant that looked exactly like this one. She was crying, while his eyes were bulging, frog-like. There was a fight coming. Somebody was in a coma and there was money left to be paid out of the young guy's inheritance; I caught the gist over cooking sounds coming in from the kitchen. I lingered by the door, looking around for her, and seeing the place nearly empty took a seat under the window and neon signage. My belt bag took the empty seat beside me. There was activity from the farther tables where the grills were, but I didn't feel very hungry for meat. A teenager brought over some hot water and disposable wipes, and I took them silently.

"Just you tonight?" he asked me, in English.

"I'm waiting for someone."

The kid set down another cup and a spoon, its head wrapped in paper for cleanliness, and saw himself back to the kitchen.

Over the course of the show, I saw you eat about fifty hot dogs and not much else, the exception being season 2, episode 17, "Checkmate," in which a young witness to a bank shootout makes noodle soup for you and Moto in her kitchen. There were plenty of ways in which the show could have denigrated ethnic food, like it was always done on TV at the time. Her, lifting up a pot cover to reveal a pile of squirming bugs, duck tongues, monkey brains—played to death over sounds of plucked guzhengs and imperial cymbal crashes. But the camera, and your eyes, are respectful. You watch her chop, peel, and ladle. Moto licks his lips and speaks in chatters, and you have to hush him for his rudeness, though it is cute the way you do it. When the meal is ready you lift the hearty bowl to your lips with both hands because you saw her do the same, slurp the noodles in quantities too large for your mouth, and she smiles at your choking noises. She would be dead in a hit-and-run just fifteen minutes later, after a commercial break, but there in that kitchen there is safety. You understood that. The soup looked hardly tasty, given the spare couple of minutes she was shown boiling the beef bones, but I didn't have it in my heart to be choosy, I never did. And besides, I didn't have anything else.

Sometimes I forgot the ways I did things just because I saw you do them. Walked with my head down and feet falling squarely in front of each other, like I always had places to be, though I almost never did. Stood with my hands in my pockets, balled into fists, looked and stared without changing a single muscle in my face with my jaw set just a bit farther out than was comfortable. I wanted to smoke so badly, like you did, but my dad would've killed me. It was the one thing I never tried, not even in secret.

I looked up as she passed me in the window, appearing not to notice I was sitting right there, and shouldered the door open, stamping her boots free of snow on the mat. She was dressed in the same dark colors but was buried under a thick scarf and woolen hat. I saw her eyes scan the place, coming to rest on me. She stamped her boots a couple more times and made her way across the tables. She looked different, out of her work habit, like she had put on a shiny film when at work that had now been taken off. Her cheeks were rosy from the cold.

"I was afraid you wouldn't come," she said, sitting down.

"Wasn't I the one that asked you out?"

"I don't expect much from men." She took a long drink from the steaming cup and tried to shake herself warm. We wiped our hands clean with the disposables and crunched them up together at the corner of the table. She smiled at the belt bag I'd slung over the empty chair.

"Are you okay?"

"My head hurts." I shrugged. "I guess I'm not that worried about it. Otherwise I'd be in the hospital."

"That sounds like something you should be worried about."

We sipped, and took turns watching the K-drama onscreen. The teenager returned, dipping his head slightly to Min. She ordered, surprising me. The kid took another glance at me.

"He eats spicy food, yeah?" he said in Korean. "Doesn't look like it."

"He'll be fine," said Min.

We were left alone after that. Somebody switched the television closest to us to the news, which was still running coverage of the blackout. A portion of the ConEd plant just by the river was still dark.

"Crazy," we both said about the television, nothing more. I remembered the office that morning and turned around, trying to find the clock. There it was, analog, white face, probably a little battery-operated ticker hidden inside it, moving the hands, chugging away. It made me happy.

"Do you get that a lot?" Min asked me. "People assuming you don't speak Korean?"

I nodded.

"Does it bother you?"

"Well, I don't, really," I said. "I stopped when I was a kid. I was bilingual once. Not so much anymore."

"Want to practice with me?"

I put my hands together and bowed so low my nose touched the tabletop. She laughed.

"You don't look Korean."

"I don't think I do, either. Probably why people assume. What's up with your dog sitter?"

"She's giving me the impression that she's overworked. I don't know how much longer I'm going to keep her. Honestly, causes more stress than just leaving him at home."

"What kind?"

"He's a rescue. I think some poodle, somebody told me English Pointer. Don't know what you'd call that."

"Pointy-poo."

Min made a big, flourishing wave in the air, as if to congratulate me. Banchan arrived, in a dozen lacquer bowls the size of my palm. We broke our chopsticks and picked at the good ones, candied sardines, fish cake, there was potato and mackerel in soybean paste that made the back of my throat burn.

"I'm sorry I turned you down the first time," she said with her mouth half full.

"You don't have to be."

She gave me a look. "Yes, I do. I wasn't being very honest. And it wasn't because I didn't want to. You just caught me off guard, and I took the easy way out. That tends to happen with me."

"You're here now, aren't you?"

"I am." She rose a little higher on her seat, straightening her back. "Tell me about that job you lost."

I told her, trying not to think about Gil, who had called several more times while I walked through the city, the big-dicked stranger in Lycra who was expecting to meet me tomorrow. I left him out of my retelling but left Gil in. Min ate the last of the fish cake.

"I used to get *Metropol* delivered," she said. "I thought they always had great spreads. And the interviews. Are you keeping up with that Antonin Haubert stuff?"

"Yes," I answered slowly. "Fucked up."

"The most fucked up," Min agreed. "As if anybody needed reasons why nepotism is poisonous. Just waves and waves of generational wealth propping these people up until they don't even understand what they're doing is wrong. I honestly doubt the old guy really knows that. Sad for the kid, though. He's literally everywhere. Did you meet him when he came in for the cover shoot?"

"We don't meet them, usually. Not the marketing people."

"I heard he's tall," she said. "I also heard he doesn't use shampoo."

"I'm sure," I said.

We picked at our food for the next minute or so. I asked her about the store.

"It's a job," she shrugged. "I wanted to be in fashion, but I couldn't get over the subjectivity. Something I thought was beautiful doesn't even get in the door because somewhere high up a senior buyer doesn't think green is it this year. Infuriating. I'd already broken my parents' hearts getting the fine arts degree. And I'm a terrible sketcher."

"They let you do it, though. Your parents."

"I don't know if they really had a choice," Min said. "I wasn't very kind to them about it. Anyway, I'm okay with it. The pay's good."

"Don't forget the discount."

"Yes, can't forget that," she said. "I'll be in this job, selling bags to people like you until I die."

"I don't think I want to know what you mean by people like me."

"You're right," she smiled. "You don't."

Her phone buzzed, I could feel it through the table, but she ignored it.

"I really can't imagine what that Haubert kid is thinking right now. He hasn't said anything, has he?"

I shook my head.

"I mean, I read the profile. They're obviously not close. But they've got basically the same name."

"He'll probably get by," I said. "They always do."

I could tell my answer had almost irritated her, but, in my defense, I was only trying to steer us away from you. I wasn't ready. A pot of ddeok-bokki arrived on a portable stove, and Min dug a spoon straight into the boiling sauce to eat. We juggled the steaming hot rice cakes in our mouths and chewed like raptors. I was into the way we could eat like this. I hadn't had any food all day and was glad she wasn't somebody all that interested in talk when there was a meal to be had. It was the kind of date I would have guessed I wouldn't enjoy.

"Do you know what they're going to do with the magazine now?"

"They told me they'll sell. It's pretty prestigious, so I wouldn't be surprised if some rich guy picked it up as a passion project."

"Are you sad?"

"About my job?"

"About the magazine," Min said. "It's one thing to be fired. But getting let go while they just junk the whole thing seems . . . different."

It *was* different. I'd been getting *Metropol* and a couple other titles delivered monthly ever since I'd worked for the conglomerate. It was a casual presence on my table back home, even if I rarely had time to read it. My name had appeared on the second page under the sales department for a single issue before they nixed the masthead page to make room for advertisers. I'd kept my first issue in a folder under my bed, and in the years since, the paper had yellowed to the point of eroding the ink. We printed on the kind of paper that stayed ripe only for a year or so before stacks and stacks of them were ostensibly thrown in a landfill. I still had the page. I imagined showing it to her someday.

"It might not be over yet," I told her. "We don't know who's going to buy it. Gil—"

I stopped myself. Min stayed put, looking at me. A sizzling plate of short ribs had come to the table.

"Is Gil somebody you can talk to about this?" she asked. "Maybe he can help you find a new job."

"He could," I said. Min selected a steaming slice of beef off the hot plate and held it in the air.

"You're really cool."

"How do you mean?"

"That's the impression you're trying to make on me, isn't it?" she said. "With your fake brooding? Not telling me anything about your life?"

"Who says it's fake?"

She looked at me, smiling. "Me."

I left her most of the barbecue and settled for the soup that came afterward. We packed it away. My fingers were swollen from the salt by the end of it. She didn't like green melon, she told me, when the teenager brought it over sliced and skewered with toothpicks, so I had that as well. We split the check and walked outside together. There persisted a few seconds in which I was looking for her to show me where she was headed, and she waited before speaking.

"This was nice."

More silence. Snow had started to fall around us. Somewhere on a balcony, or maybe out a window, somebody was blasting Christmas music, an old Bing Crosby, and it was pissing everybody else off. We heard shouts from the apartments above. Frost coated the street, a single track of tires running through it from a recent car. My phone buzzed again, and I, knowing Gil, pressed on its side through my pants to send it to voicemail.

There were two feet of space between us. Big crystalline flakes had dusted our hair by now. My stomach was still hot from the soup.

And it's that thing I've imagined happens upon realizing somebody has seen you for who you really are despite your best efforts. The feeling of being given just a split second to make the choice—in or out—before any of it becomes real. I remembered the first time I watched all of *Raider* through and realized there would be no more episodes. I think I actually cried. I was much too young to be watching it in the first place. I'd practically ruined my mother's life badgering her to let me, and she blamed my father wholly for introducing me to it. Whatever meaningful bond made between us obsessing over the same show was not worth the violence it preached, to her. It had been the moment I realized that I had seen all of you, every moment now uncovered. You were as available to me as my own thoughts, and it made me afraid, because first and foremost I loved the questions you posed. I loved knowing that I didn't know, that there would be more, next episode, next episode. I wouldn't be able to watch you quite the same way. I'd never wonder about you again. I'd never be surprised. There you were: Raider, for all you are, and there would be no more.

I stopped looking at her.

"I have no idea what I'm doing."

Min seemed about to say something about that. I wasn't expecting her to but braced myself anyway. Then her phone buzzed, I heard it through her coat. She kept her eyes on me but dug it out of her pocket. She rolled her eyes.

"Jesus, do you know how to turn these off?" She showed me the screen, a Twitter news alert. "It's the dumbest shit they bother me about and I can't figure out how to turn them—"

I had taken her wrist, holding the screen steady because I had, in the split second she waved it in front of me, recognized a name. *Hadrien Haubert.* I read: *Actor Hadrien Haubert releases statement on abuse allegations against father Antonin Haubert.*

"What?"

"Can you—" I made a gesture with my hand. "Would you—"

I looked away while she unlocked her screen and handed it to me. Ten thousand tweets already on the topic. With our heads together, it took a while, scrolling, to find the original. Hadrien hadn't tweeted in two weeks, not since the *Times* article. Just twenty minutes ago, he had posted a screenshot of a white Word document with no caption.

> Like many of you, I am shocked and appalled by the allegations that have surfaced concerning my father, Antonin Haubert. The alleged assaults of

coworkers, spouses, and others have shaken my core. I am disgusted, and ashamed. It is difficult to find the right words.

I am not a close contact of my father's. As he raised me, I often felt oppressed by his domineering and perfectionist attitude. This callousness has more than once led to disagreements between us, after which I saw it best to limit our contact. I understand this news is difficult and upsetting for many who have supported and admired him over the years. Many of you grew up watching him on the screen, just as I did. But violence is inexcusable. My father cannot be forgiven for the sake of his stature and influence. In an era in which the bravery of victims has at last resulted in deserved repercussions for their powerful abusers, I am adamant that we cannot allow my father's victims to languish in silence any further. He must face consequences for his actions.

As of tonight, I have filed paperwork to legally emancipate myself from Antonin Haubert's estate. I am named in his living will as next of kin along with my step-siblings. These connections, with him and with them, will be severed.

I am also exploring the legal adoption of my mother's surname. I am reminded, in taking

> these steps, of her strength and bravery. Last year, I celebrated the founding of her women's health initiative, which seeks to provide support for victims of abuse. Please donate at the link in my bio. Peace and love.
>
> —H

We read it through, pulling apart afterward. The snow had picked up speed around us and collected in larger clumps around our feet. Min stamped her boots again, and the sound echoed across the street. Hardly anybody left in the city so close to Christmas Eve. We could tell from the empty air.

"What does that really mean, legal emancipation?" she said, finally. "He's over eighteen, isn't he?"

I shrugged. I'd gone over the words enough times in my mind. It was easy to see Hadrien's way out of the mess. He was banking on culture's overwhelmingly liberal lean and his own independent success, success I didn't know he truly had without his name attached. It was a gutsy move, but things worked out his way, always. He was one of those people.

"It sounds pretty bluffy to me," Min said. "Changing his name? What good would that do? If he really—"

She stopped, seeing the look on my face. I tried to stop myself, to bring myself back down to zero, but it had escaped me and she had noticed and there was nothing I could do.

"You okay?"

I nodded, shakily. I was okay, I thought. There was no reason I shouldn't be. Min looked over my shoulder, then behind her.

"Let's walk." She took my hand and steered me to the direction of the sidewalk. I went. It was some of the most beautiful snow I had seen in a long time. With the lamps overhead it seemed to just appear out of the dark, floating silently down to the ground in front of us. All the dirty light down here was reflected in the clouds, turning them brown. We didn't talk to each other for four blocks, tiptoeing around slush puddles at each of the intersections. We found ourselves in a place where the cars were loud, kicking half-frozen water up onto the pavement where we were as they sped past.

"Why aren't you with your family for the holidays?"

She'd asked the question, finally, as we found a larger, more spacious sidewalk and continued on. Her hand was warm in mine. I'd expected this question much earlier and had forgotten the answer I'd rehearsed in response.

"They're not very accessible," I decided to tell her. "It's hard to make it happen most years."

"I think you took those words out of my mouth," she said. It seemed like it was all she would say about it for a moment, but she continued. "It's actually my first Christmas alone. Plus the bonus wages for staying over the holidays, it's not so bad."

We stopped for a moment, looking up at the sky.

"Were you outside, when the lights went off?" she asked me. I shook my head.

"I was a few blocks away from here," she said, "coming home from dinner. Seeing's one thing. I've never heard anything like that in my life."

"What did it sound like?"

"Just, nothing," she said. "Total darkness, no beeps or whistles, everything gone. And afterward, the five or ten seconds we all spent, just waiting for the lights to come back on again. My mother was doing laundry in her basement. She said she almost had a heart attack."

She sighed.

"What can I tell you, the world's a strange place. Being our age in the world is a strange place, too. Our age and single . . . that's—"

She looked sideways at me.

"We are—our age—aren't we?"

"Twenty-eight."

"Which month?"

"February."

Min tugged a little on my hand. "May."

Where the Christmas carols blasting out of the neighboring apartment balcony had since died out, new ones replaced it, this time from the open doors of a souvenir shop, bright as a diamond. We passed it, listening to the music, and were both a little sad when it, too, faded away. We were headed west, generally, but I didn't know where exactly. Min didn't seem to be leading me anywhere, but I couldn't tell for sure.

"Do you think he's going to go through with it?"

I knew what she was talking about. I hadn't quite shaken the words yet, either.

"He could. It'd probably be good for his PR. His *Metropol* cover might even sell better because of it." In fact, I was sure of it.

"That's what I think," she agreed. Then: "You care a lot about him."

I laughed, half-assed, so that it came out as one big, exasperated breath, which I supposed was how I felt. We were walking slower, stepping around large paths of ice that hadn't yet been salted.

"I used to watch an old tv show his dad used to do. It's—one of my favorites, actually."

"Oh—" She frowned, and seemed to mean it, "That's terrible. I'm sure it meant a lot to you."

"It's just the character," I said quickly. "Because it's not even really Haubert, I mean, not anymore. And the idea that we should just dissociate from something that big, like a show, with so many moving parts and other actors and writers and producers who are probably really proud of what they did there and what it means to so many people, doesn't sit right with me. It's not fair to everybody else. The people who made it or the people who watched it. It means so much more than the one actor, even if it's his face on the poster. A lot of work went into the craft all around him and it's—it's—"

Min listened to this quietly, still holding onto my hand. There were a precious few people in the world who could listen like that, Raider. You know it when you see it. The way somebody can make you feel like you make sense even if you might not even think you do. She didn't speak for a while.

"Nice hill to die on," she said, finally smiling. "You know, a lot of people still watch Woody Allen's movies. Not the new ones, of course, but the classics. They're still on every list of the best out there, still, and nobody really wants to explain why."

"—and he's not the same as somebody like Woody Allen. He put his wife in the hospital for—"

"I know, but still," Min said, "like you're saying. Antonin Haubert is a different guy than the fictional. You're talking about that show, right? The Chinatown detective one?"

I felt my breath flood slowly from me. We were almost stopped on the pavement now.

"Yeah."

"I've read a lot of good stuff about that show," Min said. "Asian representation, and all that. And maybe people say they're still just one-off, supporting characters and whatever, and yeah, by modern standards a lot of it is still pretty insensitive. But somebody had to take the first step, and it was them, and I'm proud of that. Look at me, not even Chinese, and proud."

I'm pretty sure Antonin Haubert didn't ever think about the show anymore. There was so much else on his resume. Which shouldn't hurt your feelings. You still made a killing in syndication. There were entire subreddits dedicated to analysis of key episodes that still buzz with active members—I've both checked and participated. To this day, Haubert has never made an appearance at any live fan event, any convention that has ever been organized, despite his face on all the merchandise.

Min stopped me in front of a building on the north corner of the block. I realized I'd walked her home. Under the canopy, we dusted off our coats and the tops of our heads. Min still hadn't let go of my hand.

"I really did have a good time," she said.

There wasn't much else to say. Still my hand in hers while she led me into the little lobby and into the keyhole elevator. She made a big show of checking that the elevator car had in fact arrived in its proper spot before stepping inside with me, which made me laugh. She lived in a single bedroom on the third floor, overrun with plants on the ground and in the windows that were silhouetted like many-armed creatures when she showed me inside. We took off our shoes, she hung our coats up in her closet. The dog sauntered up to us, sniffing at my knuckles. I put my palm on his head and felt him push against me.

"You've passed his test," Min commented. "Tea?"

I shook my head.

"Toast. I can make you toast. Or coffee. I've got an apple I can peel." Again, I declined.

We were a foot apart. I had to bend my head down to look at her properly. Somewhere below, a siren was going off. I looked at her then, probably the first good look I'd gotten of her since we'd left dinner, and saw her cheeks had gone red again like they had been when she'd met me.

"Have you figured it out?" I asked her.

"Have I figured what out?"

"Why an elevator would open when the car isn't there?"

She said she hadn't, and I kissed her.

The ceiling was popcorn. Min's apartment was low enough in the building that passing cars' headlights threw shadows all over the walls, including on the little kernels in the paint, so that the ceiling moved with the lights like the hide of a spotted animal stalking in the grass. I was in her bed, waiting for her to finish in the shower. I didn't know what time it was. I made a move to get up, maybe peel that apple she had mentioned for us to eat when she came back. I picked up my wrist and clicked it a couple times, contented.

There was barely enough room for Min's bed here, but off at the other end by the window was a little desk and a closed laptop. On top of her dresser were several folded scarves, and the black woven wallet she had showed me that morning in the store. I looked for my underwear, finding it balled up and still wrapped around one of my ankles, and hiked it back up to my waist. I wanted to look up whether any of the outlets had picked up Hadrien's letter, but doing so would involve finding my phone and having to count all the missed calls Gil had left me, which I hadn't checked since early in the afternoon, and I was far too guilty to do anything like that. I sat up and turned on Min's bedside lamp. The walls were mint green, I realized. I wondered if she'd done that herself or hadn't had the heart to repaint it when she'd moved in. Out in the hall, I could still hear the water hitting the tub. I got to my feet.

The scarves were elegantly placed, each folded in a round with their adjoining tassels tucked in for neatness. I fingered open a drawer, seeing the assorted waistbands of lacy underwear, and shut it quickly. The rest of her drawers included pants and shirts, a few dark-colored dresses that were soft on my fingers. I thought about looking for the expensive boots she'd told me she bought but couldn't find them in the little closet off to the right. My eyes fell on the desk. I pulled out the chair and sat, still warm enough from the blankets not to feel the cold. She had a great view out onto the street from here, through the sheer curtains. It made perfect sense to put a desk here. Nice coffee, watch the morning, something like that.

On the right of the desktop was a little drawer. My fingers

curled around the knob, then pulled it open. Inside was a paperback copy of *Tess of the d'Urbervilles*, some pens, and a discarded phone case scratched to hell. I picked up the paperback. It looked new, never opened. I wondered how best to ask her about it. I made to replace the book and saw the letter, folded and pushed to the corner of the little drawer. This, I knew, was wrong, you don't have to tell me. I'd been in the wrong ever since getting out of bed. There was nothing I knew about her, really. Nobody deserved intrusion like this.

The note was handwritten, and in Korean. I glanced over my shoulder again, ensuring the shower was still running. I was a better speaker than a reader. Min's slanting handwriting was already making it difficult. But slowly, with my lips moving trying to sound each syllable in my head, I read it.

> Appa, you have hurt me more than you could ever know. I am so ~~angry~~ heartbroken by the way you've treated me. I have given and given as much of my time and energy as you've asked, but I cannot go on any ~~more~~ longer and live with your disappointment. Nothing I do is good enough. I hate going home. I hate seeing you and Umma because every time I do, I expect to be hurt. This

I turned the note over, expecting something, but the rest was blank. In the drawer I saw the pen she had used to write it. My chest hurt. What had been the point? I was breathing hard, holding my head, which had started to throb, when the shower shut off alongside a slick noise of the opening curtain. I folded the paper again, placed it under the book, and pushed the whole thing closed. I stood, just as the bathroom door opened and she stepped back into the room wearing her pajamas, squeezing a damp towel around her hair. She saw me standing, smiled.

"I can turn the heat up," she said.

"It's okay," I told her. "I—"

I looked around for my pants, somewhere under the bed.

"I should go."

She didn't say anything as I got on all fours and fished my clothes out from under the mattress. I dressed, hastily. I kept my back turned on her. When I saw her face next, she had dried her hair and was looking at me with something like hurt.

"You can shower," she offered.

"What? No, why—" I was stammering. She could tell I was sweating. I didn't dare glance over at the desk again. "I mean, I should get going. It's pretty late."

"Yeah," Min trailed off, confused. "You're being weird."

"I'm not being weird."

"Whoever says 'I'm not being weird,'" Min said, "is usually being weird. What's up with you?"

"Nothing."

"Did I say something to you?"

"Of course not."

Shut the fuck up, I told myself. Stop talking. None of it was working. I saw it dawn on her moment by moment, before I could even tell what was happening. Her eyes fell on the desk behind me.

"What did you do?"

"Nothing—"

She stepped forward. "Tell me the truth. What were you doing in here?"

I couldn't look at her. In my mind all I could think was Jesus Christ are you a pussy, you're a fucking pussy, just say something, say anything. It was a moment in which all I was made of crumbled away to chalk dust and I was alone, all alone with her. I shook my head. Min's face hadn't changed. If it weren't for her fist on me I could have convinced myself we were just talking.

"I wasn't doing anything."

Something in her relaxed, just as I said it, coming to the thought, arriving at it.

"Did you fucking go through my desk?"

"I didn't—"

I didn't get a chance to say anymore, because she had shoved me back toward the wall with enough strength that I would've bowled over on my ass if I hadn't grabbed her wrist on reflex. Which was a bad idea, the badness of which occurred to me when she ripped it free and, with her other hand, punched me clean in the face. I went down. I'd never been hit so hard. It was not dissimilar to the cold after a couple hours outside, the dead weight of it, only this time it was seized locally on the right corner of my skull. I saw her feet, keeping a wide distance, used the bed frame for support, and got up. Min was looking at the desk in question as I pulled my shirt back on and hobbled around her. There was no more talk. I left her in the room and found my coat and shoes by the door. The dog had risen from its spot by Min's couch and was staring at me, his orb eyes caught the hallway light like flares. I stumbled out into the hallway. I had the sense of mind to pick my belt bag off the floor near her shoes before the door shut. A few seconds later, the lock clicked shut behind me. I'd done all this still without the use of my center of gravity, and fell on my knees by the stairs, hard. I put my head between my arms for a bit, which felt nice, and when the swelling had stopped I opened my eyes. One was still blurry. Her knuckle had almost juiced it like a common grape, I was sure of it. I got myself down the stairs and back out through the lobby.

I deserved this. You'd agree, and you'd tell me something like "rats get what they deserve," or "you're past the point of asking why, you should be asking how," or something, I didn't even know if those made sense. The whole left side of my face throbbed hard through my fingers when I touched it. I didn't want to find my phone, afraid of what I'd see.

I turned around and just started walking, back down the street we'd come from. Over my shoulder I looked up at all the windows and tried to visualize, spatially, where hers was, without really understanding why I was even looking. I put my head down and got to the end of the block. My fingers were already numb. I needed a car. There was no way around it. They'd find me all ravaged and frozen behind some dumpster if I tried to walk home the way I was now. I dug my hand into my coat pocket and found my phone, lighting the screen. It was near midnight. There were two little pop-ups simmering urgently on the screen. One was a group of four missed calls from Gil, who had given up around three in the afternoon. I frowned. The second was another chain of hang-ups, this time from my father. I put my phone away, walked another few yards, then pulled it out again. I dialed, bringing it to my ear. He picked up, in the middle of a sentence.

"—son's calling. Hello there? Can you hear me?"

"Yeah, Dad, I'm here."

"Hello?"

"Dad, I'm here."

"Aw, honey, how are you? What are you calling for?"

"You called me four times tonight."

My father made a whistling noise through his teeth.

"Not sure I did. Are you okay?"

"Yeah, I'm okay—"

"Do you know what kind of batteries I need for my remote? I've got the double As but I can't seem to get them to work."

A great crunching noise sounded over the phone, and I winced.

"Dad, you called me four times. Are you okay?"

"Yeah, I'm okay, what are you talking about? What are you calling for?"

"You called me—"

He didn't say anything for a while. It was getting worse. I tried not to listen to it, but it was harder and harder to ignore.

"You okay?"

"Dad," I closed my eyes. I took my breath in, expanding my chest. "Just hang up. I'm fine."

"You know, I can't seem to get in touch with your brother. I was wondering—"

"I don't know where he is, Dad. Just keep calling him. He'll pick up."

"You don't pick up." His voice had gone flat, saying it.

"I'm—talking to you right now, what do you mean I don't pick up?"

"You don't pick up. Kazzie, he always picks up. That's why I'm a little concerned."

"You should ask him that."

"Honey? What are you calling for? You there? You th—"

I'd set my phone down and hung up. I waited, a minute, two minutes. He didn't call back. I tried to imagine him in his chair, still talking without noticing. I stared at the blank screen, beginning now to shiver. After another minute, I found the right number in my contacts and dialed. As simply as I could, I told the voice on the line that my father was sounding a little more confused than usual and asked if it was possible that somebody could come by the house and get him to bed. The voice assured me somebody was on their way and was in the middle of wishing me a happy holiday when I hung up on him, too. I walked up the street, away from Min's building, and within a few blocks had soaked through my shoes in the new slush. My face still hurt. I couldn't make out much in the darkened windows and so carried on my way, past the big department store. It was the only one that hadn't closed in the past decade, the only one whose handlers hadn't made the foolhardy decision to try and open an offshoot in every strip mall in the country. They were known for these windows. There had been several documentaries made about the people who put these windows together, all the prep work, the visualizing, the buying and draping, the custom-made mannequins and their props. Only a few stragglers dawdled around the window displays, big, elegant squares draped over with fabric and impossibly decadent crystal chandeliers. I passed each one, raising my head just a little to look before continuing on. I had never gone a year without seeing them.

Maybe it's getting old, hearing this. Maybe you have important things to do and don't have time for people like me, for fans, for whatever it is that I am. I know. I know it was you. I know that there's a little piece of the past that I keep holding on to, years ago, on a snowy night just like this. When I was eight years old, holding my wrist the night that I broke it while you carried me home. It's funny, the way that sparks create flames create wildfires, bringing it all down, changing landscapes, altering the ecology from a single step, a single motive and action that, at first, don't appear to mean shit. There's a word for that, I forget what it is.

I woke with breaths feathering gently into my left armpit. The falling snow had blasted Gil's windows white again, heavier than the day before so that I couldn't even see the street from them. I sat up, gently, without waking him, and rounded the side of the bed to Gil's closet mirror. My right eye closed and opened normally but had gone purply-blue. It was so seamless that it looked like a birthmark. I flinched, touching it: still tender. My phone was near dead when I picked it up off Gil's dresser. I saw that my father had called one last time around two in the morning. There was no telling when the next would come. If he had gotten through to Kaz, I didn't know.

Gil made a noise and lifted his head off the pillows. He squinted at my face, trying to find it in focus.

"You're not swollen anymore," he commented in his gravelly morning voice. "That's a good sign."

I read off my phone that it was near eight. Gil watched me look at it for a while, making my choices. Then I started to dress.

"Going somewhere?" he asked.

"Home," I lied. "Job search starts today, remember? Can't waste any time."

He was silent as I found my pants, my socks and belt, the leather bag that I'd hung off one of his bedposts and looped once more around my chest.

"You could stay."

I didn't answer this. Gil would keep bothering me until I did what he wanted, and I didn't know if I had the courage for that anymore. Things were different now. Maybe they always had been and I hadn't noticed, but whatever it was, I wasn't going to stay here. I could see out of my periphery the look Gil gave me as I patted myself down, locating my wallet and keys, and made for the door.

"Brandon."

He was doing this to get to me, I knew he was, and it would have been funny if it weren't always so successful. You wouldn't understand the way people look at me. Nobody looks at you like this, like somebody who needs protection, who needs help, who is one step from total chaos and teeters so precariously on its edge that it's almost sickening to witness. This is how you looked at perps, I'd seen it many times before and imagined as a boy: what did it feel like, to be looked at this way? In the light, Gil's shoulders looked even slimmer than they were, his top sheet bunched around his lap. He spoke.

“Are you always going to be such a fucking asshole?”

I tilted my head one way, then the other, with nothing to say, and closed his bedroom door behind me.

The bakery had just put out a second tray of blueberry muffins when I stepped inside. My stomach ached, looking at them. The spicy food we’d had for dinner had upset my chemistry in a way that I usually dealt with by downing something carb-y for breakfast. I had made half a mind to buy something with caffeine but he was already there, sitting at the farmost table in a new set of duds, all white this time, cycling shoes perched neatly on the table near his coffee. He waved me over and I sat. As though preempting me, he poured me a coffee, clapping me on the back.

“You look like you’ve been through hell to make it to this breakfast,” he commented. “Neighborhood scuffle? Big kids took your lunch money?”

“Can I eat that?” I pointed to the other half of his muffin. He smirked and slid it toward me. I wolfed it, still a little bit warm. He watched me with a strange, clinical curiosity. Everything I did seemed to fascinate him.

“Crazy news out there last night, about that Haubert kid,” he said finally, as I licked crumbs. “I saw Antonin was dropped by his agency this morning. They’re saying he might even be arrested later tonight, unless he turns himself in. Seems like the honorable thing to do. Getting pretty serious.”

“I think people need to find more important things to do with their lives than read celebrity news.”

He snapped his fingers, pointing at me. "You are absolutely right. Isn't that in vogue now? Try the one percent, eat the rich, blah blah. These people aren't people, they're not *real* people. What the fuck do we think we're doing, eating it all up. It's imprisonment. You know, that's something about you that I noticed straightaway. You're honest. And you're not just honest. You cut through. You're not afraid of it. It's what you are. We're looking for talent like this. There is so much goddamn corporate obfuscation around buzzwords and meaningless lingo. You know what that is? It's noise. Entropy. It's never produced a single good for anybody. Us at the firm, we're not concerned with language, conversation."

I wiped my mouth, looking for my coffee, and downed it.

"What is your concern, then?"

The stranger smiled, again that arresting, unreal smile that I couldn't ever define if I tried.

"Something better worth our time. Our planet is dying. We no longer have the resources to sustain our growth. And don't say I'm just shitting you. You want to call me pessimistic? Fuck you. I'm the most optimistic person in the world. I know exactly what we can accomplish if we have the money, and the time, to do it."

The coffee had stirred some life back into me, and I fought the urge to laugh. It was the kind of thing somebody might say at the end of a pivotal scene in a movie, cut to black, main titles, yadda yadda.

"That is some heavy stuff for so early in the morning."

"You've seen the blackouts. You've seen the way this entire

country panics when they happen, you tell me what needs to be on our minds," he said. "And the most ridiculous part: most of us seem contented to live with it. Not me. Not my boss."

"You're doing quite a dance to get me to fuck you," I said.

"I'm not trying to do anything you're thinking about," he said. "I'll give you the pitch, yeah? And if you buy it, you're in. I've seen enough of you to be sure you're a fit. I'm putting my money behind you."

He blinked several times, for dramatic effect, and smiled. It was difficult to place this look, as it was right here in this moment, and as it would be almost every time I saw him in the months thereafter. A kind of knowingness in him that suggested all the things that lay unavailable to me about him and would remain so forever, like he held a shiny treasure behind his back at all times. I promised to give you the reason, to tell you how it all happened, how I came to be here just four months after that stupid meeting over coffee. Lying in a clean bed smelling of bleach, hearing only muted bass sounds, IV drips, vibrations through my fingertips, and blackness. I promised you a reason, Raider, and we are, more or less, halfway there. But it really is funny, how much I'm learning alongside you. This look on his face, I'd forgotten the way it scared me, then and now.

"I'm not here to fuck you," he said, finally. "I'm here to offer you a job."

He dug into the little zip pocket on his spandex shirt and pulled a business card from it, sliding it across the table to me.

"My name is Lev. And I want you, first, to ask yourself what it is you know about the state of our world's energy. Competing industries, overpopulation, blackouts that—we all agree—

will just keep coming. Then I want you to comb through all the things you can name about the way people of our world consume energy, conserve energy, waste energy, how we are primed to accept the system for what it is and do nothing about it under a complex of fear. And when you're done with all of that, I want you to forget it, all of it. I want you to listen to me and learn a new word: Flux."

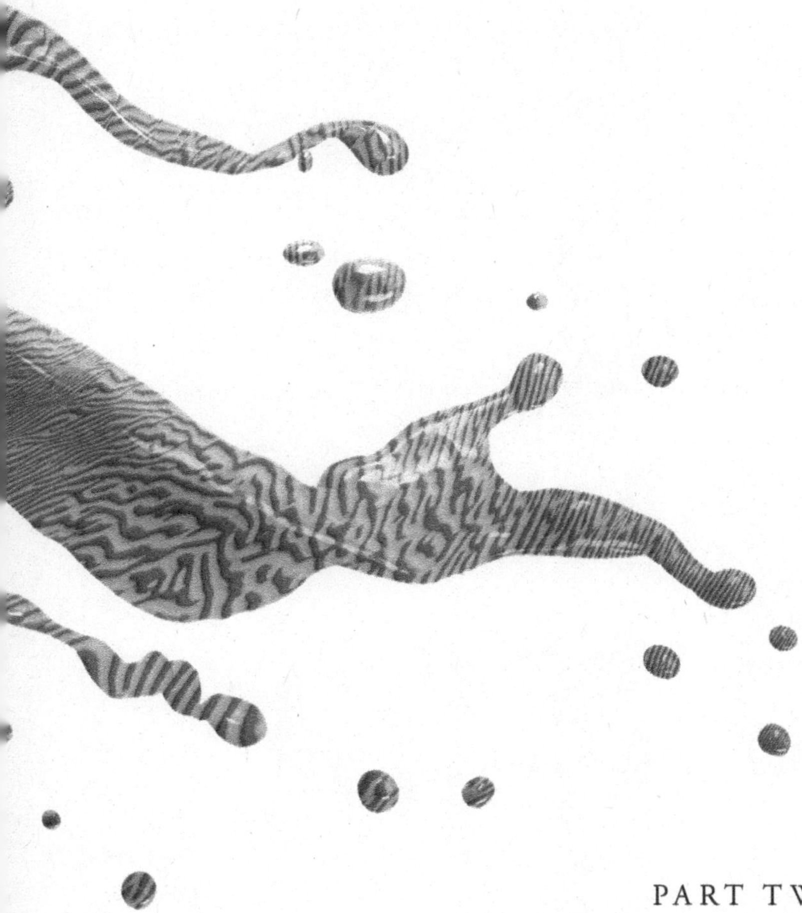

PART TWO

Signing

7

IO EMSWORTH WILL CHANGE EVERYTHING.

That was her cover headline, her very first. I can't remember if it was *Forbes* or *Fortune*. But I remembered the photograph. The image was oversaturated, pop-artish nonsense; only somebody famous could have gotten away with submitting a photograph like that. She was sitting on a barstool in a stark white box with her elbows resting on her knees, black blazer, wide-legged Balenciaga trousers ripped all the way up the sides and secured together at strange angles with duct tape, pink stilettos. On top of it all was that expression on her face—so calm and assured for her age—one that I supposed the photographer wasn't really responsible for because it was, generally, the face she made at all times, though nobody, and I do mean nobody, noticed her face on account of the uproar over the way her legs were spread. "Are we surprised that YET ANOTHER female entrepreneur is being bullseyed by the male gaze?????" tweeted a feminist digi-magazine called *BIT(c)H*, which wasn't wrong. It was the pink heels, in my mind; the cover was noticeably trendier than anything *Forbes/Fortune* had ever done for a hundred years and nobody could really explain why Io Emsworth was to be the poster child for a completely right-angle turn away from their more conventional covers to something better suited for a fashion spread, something a lot edgier than glossy finance. Maybe she'd insisted. She styled herself a sexy dictator, marched out of obnoxious LA boutiques with truckloads of garment bags, sky-high heels, always-slick bowl-cut hair, and thick, caterpillar eyebrows. It was apparent she might have made it as a model in another life, perhaps even in this life, if she wanted. She was certainly tall enough.

Apart from her legs, the thing they noticed was in her hand, held loose between two fingers like a cigarette in a noir movie: the Gen. 1 Lifetime Battery. Slim, chrome-plated, tipped on both ends with cyan lacquer the color of Flux's logo and, coincidentally, the same color of the sparks that appeared on the DeLorean whenever it jumped through time in the *Back to the Future* movies. This was no secret. Io Emsworth loved those movies and the era they represented, she told *Forb-tune*. She had named her company after that little piece of mechanical fuckery that the films claimed made time travel possible: the flux capacitor. She was a self-professed fanatic despite being only two when the movie had premiered and had told several outlets that she had watched the first one at least fifty times, though by now she'd lost count. "It was on when I slept. It was my night light. I wore out so many VHS tapes that I'd get one new each Christmas." It was a detail of the profile that won her points across Twitter. The woman was a geek! A *normal* girl who was also one of the boys and therefore anything they could make her out to be. There was talk, around the time the profile first appeared about a year earlier, that she played in a rock band at Stanford before dropping out, and that somewhere on the internet were a series of topless photos she'd taken for a student art show. I'd since seen the fakes. I was pretty sure they were fakes. It was hard to tell, so many different versions had been drawn up by internet pervs around the globe that the real one was undoubtedly lost somewhere among them, never to be found, perhaps by design. How many JPEGs were out there, in the cloud, copied to servers and hard drives and labeled *IO EMSWORTH HOT PIXX TITS ASS VULVA*. The intimacy of hyperfame. Did Io Emsworth wish to comment on her forced sexualization by the male-dominated intersection of media and tech? "Thank you for blurring out my crow's feet," she said, only.

The company had begun for her, she said, in her grandmother's house in Miami, when she was a little girl. A tropical storm had downed power lines in the area and left them huddled in the dark as the wind howled outside. Io Emsworth recounted in detail the twenty-four hours that followed in which she learned how to kickstart the gas generator kept in the basement and switch out the plugs to power in succession the fan, the kettle, and the freezer in shifts. "I thought to myself: this is really what people do every time the power goes out. Lives get upended. And it would be okay, if we had stronger systems in place. But outages, especially in rural areas, are unavoidable. They cost labor, they cost gas." The first idea, she said, always had to be simple, or it wouldn't work. The needs of people were simple, and thus it only followed that their solutions were simple as well. She was an only child, daughter of a Canadian diplomat and a patent lawyer, high marks in school, Model UN, debate. She talked fast, the profile mentioned several times, and flitted her eyes around the room as though she were thinking ten steps ahead in the conversation, like a chess player. Two years into her bachelor's at Stanford, she dropped out, incorporated Flux just six months later. A Lifetime Battery was built to power anything with a AA or AAA slot; a second, more sizable model, Gen. 2, could take an electrical plug. Each contained a core not of lithium but of an aqueous ferrochromium alloy that replenished its raw materials from the inside of the battery itself in a continuous reaction that decayed five times slower than in regular batteries. In the profile, she mentioned the team she recruited from CalTech, MIT, who had invented the technology. A former Secretary of Defense and two former National Security Advisors, friends of her father's, joined her board of directors. Best Buy nearly bankrupted itself flushing them with a cash order of 800 million, betting billions on a robust and ambitious production timeline. The unthinkable happened: the first blackout, the entire West Coast went dark for nine hours. Plans were drawn for a household generator using the same technology, a device that could power a house for days on end without replacement cores. Soon after, the government expressed interest in retrofitting high-profile buildings and facilities with generators. Sixty days and four more blackouts later, Flux went public at ninety-nine dollars a share, making Io Emsworth the twelfth wealthiest woman in the world. Not a single battery sold, yet. A representative of Best Buy insisted the venture involved innovating an entirely new line of production. A year's wait was expected, maybe two.

"I was taught: look forward. It is the only direction you can look while moving at the same time," she said. She was speaking with *Forb-tune* at her home in Seattle, behind a glass desk the size of a two-man skiff with absolutely nothing on it. Behind her on the white wall was a single sheet of paper stapled to the drywall, two words in felt marker: *Perpetual Motion*. The profile made numerous depictions of the sign over the course of the article, explaining in detail the various ways those two words, Flux and Io Emsworth's informal motto, seemed to characterize both the company's product and workflow. "Perpetuity is not a myth. The only reason infinitely renewable energy is a concept we cannot yet understand is because the technology isn't there." Scientists scoffed at this, but she had said it, staking her fortune on the peoples' trust of her, and who really knew anything about science, anyway? "Oh, and yes," she said with a smile, she was single.

The cover image had been blown up to the size of a canvas and framed on the wall when Lev showed me inside his office exactly a week after I'd met him for coffee. We had ridden together in a chauffeured car to a warehouse park by the river docks, where the company had bought up several million square feet of office and manufacturing space that an outside design consultancy had named F1 in an obvious effort to be as sexy and at the same time as disgusting as possible. The lot and the surrounding dockyards had been textile factories in the early twentieth century and had fallen mostly into marshy desolation in the past few decades as foundations sunk slowly into the river, reclaimed by nature. The company had carted a hundred tons of sand into the area and kept only the bare wirework of some of the larger warehouses, retrofitting the entire interior at a cost of almost an eighth of the funding Best Buy had provided. The car, Lev had explained on the way there, was going to pick me up every morning.

We were driven past a gate flanked by armed guards off the highway and continued underground, into the foundation floor of a car park Lev said could one day hold twenty-thousand cars. There, at the bottom, we were let out onto a paved circle, flanked with glass, a deceivingly nondescript lobby and reception that led, behind a hundred-foot wall of frosted glass, to a stack of twenty escalators. I had stepped aboard, following Lev, and had been lifted, foot by foot, into the single biggest building I'd ever seen. The warehouse stretched so far that the back seemed to converge and darken like a horizon. The air was open, breezy. The building had its own atmosphere. Trees poked from convenient holes in the plaster tiling. Greenery and water spilled from eddying man-made rivers. Above, skybridges spanned, suspended by cables thin as hair. F1's ceiling was entirely glass, bathing me, us, with sunlight. I was led to an elevator and keyed inside, then, up on the tenth floor, closest to the ceiling, we walked across open air and saw ourselves inside Lev's office. The space was newly laid with bleached white wood and glass paneling, one in a suite of workspaces looking back out over the city through the glass. It was at least five times the size of my apartment. A desk sat in the corner with a single laptop on its corner. He showed me to the chairs on a white shag carpet around a retro iron fireplace suspended from the ceiling.

"Custom," he told me, gesturing around the space, immensely proud. I told him it was very nice. Lev took his seat across from me, spreading his arms wide. He was clearly intensely focused on showing me how big and alpha his office was, and I arranged my face into something of admiration. My new boss, after all. I had impressions to make, regardless of whether I wanted to or not.

"We did the interiors with Porsche Design," Lev told me, "soon as we signed the lease on the building. Place was a dump when we got in. You know that kind of dirty cement look everybody's horny for these days? It was all over. Gave me hives. I saw this carpet in a music video."

I jumped as the entire back wall started to sink into the ground, revealing a stark wood-paneled space outfitted with a bike, three yoga mats, and a television the size of a chalkboard streaming an on-demand class.

"You really couldn't be without"—I waved my hand in the direction of the gym—"one of those. It completes you."

"It's my nirvana," Lev said, entirely serious. "I'm spinning in twenty minutes, so I'll make this quick."

"It's a big place."

"We're expanding, too," Lev said, pointing over my shoulder at the windows, through which we could see an empty lot of grass and gravel the size of a football field. "Own production, you know? Get our own plant in here, our own labor. Io's impatient. She told us Q4 next year, have it done. I told her to eat my ass. Here we are."

He laughed at his joke. He was dressed again in compression shorts and a windbreaker but appeared to be the only one in the entire office booking it with his balls out. I decided to let him be.

"Lev," I started, "I'm excited to be here—"

"You are," Lev said. "I can see it in your energy. Perfect stuff."

I looked around the office, as if for clues. In a week we'd been out to drinks, then dinner. I'd come by an office building somewhere downtown that I thought was Flux's headquarters, only to fill out my paperwork. The car (and Lev) had come for me the next morning.

"I really need you to tell me what you hired me for."

Lev snapped his fingers at me, far too quickly to be responding to something I'd said.

"You hungry?"

"No."

"You look hungry. Breakfast?" Lev stood, making his way to the white-paneled cabinets on the far end of the office. One, pulled out, revealed itself to be a pantry, from which he fetched a bowl and a box of cereal. From another, a fridge, he hovered his hands over glass bottles of whole, one percent, almond milk, a jug filled up with something green. Matcha? He looked over his shoulder, expectantly.

"Whole."

Lev obliged, pouring me a generous bowl. He laid it on the coffee table, emphatically, then reclaimed his seat. I reached for the bowl, took it. Cinnamon specks floated in the milk like ants. I ate.

"You've been very patient with me," said Lev, leaning forward, putting his elbows on his knees in an almost exact replication of Io Emsworth's slutty head-of-state pose on the wall behind him. "I'm grateful. The thing about this job, this company, is that we often don't have space for patience like yours. It's why we wanted you in the first place. You're injecting something valuable into our work."

"That's kind."

"By next year, we'll be at two hundred percent. I'm talking workforce, revenue, influence. I've told you about the Best Buy deal. The Lifetime generators are going to take us into an entirely different market. Not just electronics. Energy itself. We're about to become our own industry. It starts there, with the generator tech."

He gave me a moment. "You know how the Lifetime batteries work?"

"Ferrochromium."

He was watching me eat with an absolutely manic look on his face, as though I were turning him on. "The tech is there, but it's old. Three years old. With the cash infusions we've been able to pour our resources into something of an R&D wing. We've been teaching ourselves new things, diving into the science behind it all. Call it what you want. Genius, luck. We have unlocked something nobody has ever heard of."

His eyes darted to the door for a split second, closed behind us when we walked in.

"Are you ready for this, big boy?"

I didn't like the name, but didn't say anything. I told him I was ready, because it was what he wanted to hear.

"Are you?" he asked.

"I'm going to do whatever you tell me," I said.

"You've been so patient," Lev said, "all this time, wondering. Exciting, right? Makes you fucking horny, doesn't it?"

"I just . . . " I shook my head, "don't even know what to say to that."

"What do you know about brain activity?"

"Very little."

"It's electrochemistry. Neurotransmitters within the brain: devices that are biologically wired circuits made of neurons and the spaces in between them. Processes that we are able to measure using electroencephalography. Brain scans. The sticky little fucks attached to wires that we can put on your head. Do you get me?"

I was halfway through my cereal. He looked impatient, and for a moment I was afraid of disappointing him. Lev stood, abruptly, crossed the coffee table over to me and put his hands on either side of my ears. His fingers, cold and smooth, encircled each half of my skull.

"Brain tissue emits electrical fields outside of the skull. Add up as many neurons that fire simultaneously inside you all at once and you begin to weaken the inhibitor chemicals built into your system. What do you have? Endless, repeated wire systems. A hydrogen bomb that keeps performing fission, keeps replenishing its source. In a word: renewable. In two: perpetual motion."

I felt him angle my head upward to look at him. My chin was level with his waistband.

"So somewhere," I said, "in a back room, you've got a bunch of brains in liquid goo like Frankenstein. Is this a hit job? Am I your next import?"

Lev's hands remained firm around my head. Held there, for just a second. Then, without warning, he burst, coughing huge, ugly laughs that didn't sound at all like they came from him. How the sound didn't carry through the glass to our neighbors, I had no idea. He flopped himself on the couch opposite me, laughing, laughing for way too long. Little by little he calmed himself back down with tears in his eyes before considering me there, opposite him.

And he said it, quietly, as though whispering a secret.

"Do we look like killers to you?"

I had nothing to say. I finished my cereal.

"What does this have to do with me?"

"What I'm going to tell you," Lev said, looking again at the door, "should not leave this room."

"I signed enough papers to assure you of that, didn't I?"

Lev smiled.

"You know, we've done a lot of growing here, at a pace you wouldn't believe. But we're still a collective of like-minded people, interested in the advancement of the science, solutions to the problems of life and the world. I have—we all have—given up a lot of our lives for this to become reality. All this, the company, F1 . . . "

He sat forward on his chair, staring intently into my face.

"While you're here you'll run point for me, make appearances, give media access, be a full, invigorant partner in this business. But to retro-engineer the circuitry, we need access to brains. Healthy brains. So every now and then, you'll come down to R&D and you'll lend yours to us. The generators are very, very new. We need all the help we can get systemizing the tech before we can draw up the prototypes. We've got volunteers from all over the company coming in. They did it on me for an entire year."

Lev took the bowl from me, washed it at the wet bar, and replaced it in his pantry. He talked over his shoulder. "Ask your questions."

And there *were* questions, in the span between the moment I'd met him and the moment at which we'd now arrived, that I should have probably asked. Was I here to pencil push or to participate in something jarringly scientific, something I didn't quite understand? What were Lev's expectations here? Brain-powered cars? Dildos? Nuclear bunkers? Maybe he meant all of it. There were questions about the way that I could tell he had already guessed everything I would do and everything I would say. The way the job was both real and fake and utterly, diabolically fucked. The way I'd fallen through the elevator shaft a week ago and come out the other side . . . someone else.

That was the hard truth of it, wasn't it? Isn't that what I was afraid of admitting?

I hadn't slept well the past few days. My apartment, far uptown, was ice cold when I'd come back there the first time in a couple weeks, and I'd laid curled on my couch for an hour or so, like a reptile, until I felt warm enough to move. I had to buy my own groceries and toiletries for the first time in months; Gil hadn't reached out again. After a week, my punched eye was still sore, but no longer black. It still felt just a little bit like my eyeball had grown about a size too big for the socket and ached when I blinked.

"This doesn't make any sense," I said. He didn't seem to hear me. "What did you hire me for, Lev?"

"If I give you what you want," said Lev, "does it matter?"

He gestured around the office.

"Do you like it?"

"I've told you many times I do."

"I hoped you would," Lev said. "Because it's yours. The car, too. You'd prefer to drive yourself, I can arrange that. I'll give you benefits, retirement plans. Keep to yourself, you'll go VP in two, three years. I'll give you stock. I'll give you a large enough budget to relocate yourself anywhere you want. I wasn't lying, then. I see something in you. But I'm too smart to know that sparks like yours can be crushed to death under the right circumstances, under the wrong ones. You need guidance and information. The rest will come naturally. I'm giving you what you need to become who you've always wanted to be."

Above us, the clock had just about hit 9 a.m., sixty seconds away.

I didn't know exactly when I stopped calling my father Appa, the way I had as a kid. It was not recent enough that I could pin it to a single moment. Yet the memory was not old enough for me to ascribe it somewhere in my nebulous childhood, something I couldn't exactly explain, as I wasn't that little kid anymore. It was probably around the time I stopped trying to learn Korean, and started allowing what shaggy knowledge I had to break off, piece by piece. It was a shame. When I looked at my face, I saw his. And yours. And Haubert's. The thing is, when they found Antonin Haubert hanging in his closet two days ago, there hadn't even been a formal investigation, state or federal. His assault charges, just a handful over thirty years, had all been settled out of court. There were incidents of menacing, intimidation, threats of violence. But more threats than action. What I mean to say is: he could have lived, Raider. They rushed to explain why, when the world found out he was dead. Surely something stranger was at work, something that hadn't been found out. What kind of man kills himself over bad press? It was a delightfully Eastern thing to do. In Seoul, the last Samsung VP implicated in the bribing scheme that brought down the president several years ago was found dead in his apartment in almost the exact same way. People spoke of something like antiquated honor, around that case. The kind of thing that would never happen in America. The men here were too brave. They were born under protection. People like Antonin Haubert never *really* went down because of these things. And yet there he was, blue and cold, and we would never know why.

I was told there was to be a funeral, that a social war had started among Hollywood's elite over who would show their face, as Antonin's will had made arrangements for a public service. Hadrien hadn't say a word. We knew he was in London, with his mother, and that production on his latest film had stopped just to lend him the personal time.

So no, I didn't know why I called my father "Dad," now. He didn't seem to remember the difference anymore. My head hurt. Thirty seconds to nine. I found that I'd been watching the big hand cross the clockface in an arc all this time.

"The exams," I said. "What happens in them?"

"They're very simple," Lev told me. "You sit down, we examine you, run some tests, hold a magnet to your forehead, and look at the way your activity varies. Stuff I don't understand. It's not our job to understand. If we knew more about it, we'd corrupt the sample pool. The only thing that you need to know is that in our research lingo, we call them commutes, the sessions."

"I miss him," I said. "I'm sorry for what I've done."

"I know you are."

Ten seconds.

"When are you going to put me in my first commute, Lev?"

Lev cracked a smile, and it pierced, like stonework suddenly coming to life. Meanwhile the room had begun to spin and my neck, my hands, all my joints had come free, adrift in deaf space. So much so that I could barely hear him when he spoke and said to me: "Haven't you noticed? You're already in one."

— C L I C K —

My phone was ringing. I could hear it somewhere to the right of my head and moved myself around my blankets, swimming, trying to escape. Finally I got to my hands and knees, crawled across to the other side of the mattress, and found my phone, yanking it from the charger. The room was dark; through the sheer curtains I could see my view of the city, the park below. The tallest buildings rose like dark spires lit from the inside, glowing ominous against the night sky. I'd never get tired of that view. The windows were floor-to-ceiling, framed in white lacquer, dressed with sheer curtains so soft that when I ran my fingers along them it was like touching air, the ghost of fabric. Lev was calling. I picked it up.

"Big boy! You awake?"

"Hardly."

"Come down in ten. I'll be outside with the car."

"Why?"

There were laughs on the other end. I realized Lev was shouting at me through the pounding of music. "He says 'why,' little fucker. We're coming to you, okay? Get dressed."

He hung up. I sat up, feeling my head, which felt heavy but at peace. Slowly, I reached over and flicked on the lights, and the strips built into the crown molding slowly raised the ambience to sunlight, late afternoon. I stood, leaving my phone where

I'd found it, stripped, and took a shower. I held my head still against the hot water, scrubbed with soap. The drain in the floor was a long grate that ran the length of the marble and—despite its pretension—did not drain very well. After I shut the water off, I dragged my foot across the floor, herding the water into it, satisfied with the gurgling sound it made as it emptied. I didn't know where Lev was taking me, and the past few places had been more formal than I'd been comfortable with, so I wore a jacket. Shoes, discarded in the corner of my closet but new and starched, I put on, tossing aside the tissue paper stuffed inside the toes. In the mirror at the end of the room, I thought I looked all right. My eyes were bloodshot, but it was evening. Nobody would notice. In the kitchen, I passed a basket wrapped in plastic that had come the other day from which I'd torn the chocolate almonds and the beef jerky. As I rounded the corner of the island toward the fridge I saw that the basket had also included several pears, slightly bruised but still good, which I picked like from a tree and left to finish rotting at a slower pace in my refrigerator's crisper drawer. I leaned against the countertop, looking at the sky from my windows. The string ties on the furniture cushions out on the balcony swayed in a shy breeze. It was starting, finally, to warm up. The last of the snow, ice the color of shit caked against the sidewalks and gutters, was hanging on but would be gone soon. I drank a glass of water, thinking I'd need it.

I keyed my door closed with the smart card in my wallet and crossed the hallway to the elevators. This building was clean and largely empty, from the looks of it. I didn't recall seeing many people in the lobby, though by now I'd come and gone at most times of the day. The lobby was pulsing with some lo-fi club music, a weird choice. A young woman behind the desk and in front of the pink salt tableau hanging on the wall nodded at me as I passed through. She was wearing earrings that dangled past her shoulders, little strings of chain that I couldn't imagine *didn't* drive her absolutely insane every time she moved her head.

Outside, the SUV was waiting on the curb, swinging its door up and open for me as I approached. Several shouts from inside. It was too dark to make out any faces but his. I was clapped several times on the back and around the waist as people wished me a happy birthday, and I thanked them. Some discussion was made about my shoes. "They don't like sneakers. They're gonna kick us out."

"Nobody's kicking us out," Lev said, pouring me champagne. We pulled away from the curb and were headed uptown. "You know these guys, don't you?"

There were girls engaged in their own conversation in the back seats who didn't seem to pay us any attention. Two men sat on either side of Lev. One had his knees out, poking through gargantuan holes in his jeans. The other was wearing mesh. A jeweled bar had been shoved through two points on his left ear.

"Twenty-nine," Lev commented. "Big fucking year. You've got a lot to be proud of. This is Ry, you know Ry."

He nearly hit the last girl directly behind me with his glass. "Ry's on the engineering team."

"Happy birthday," Ry said. The dress she wore reflected a hundred speckled lights up at the ceiling of the car as we jolted and shifted down the street. "Why is it you never come out with us?"

"I'm a busy person."

They all laughed. The twink with the bar in his ear was closest to me and hadn't said anything as our driver turned the music up higher.

"Lev, you are not taking us to Dream, are you?"

"Lev, I had my ass eaten in the bathroom at Dream."

"Everybody shut the fuck up." Lev raised his glass, already empty. Ry accepted a bump off her girlfriend's knuckle. "We are going to Dream because it's our big boy's favorite fucking place on earth. And if only we'd be so lucky to all get our asses eaten in the bathroom. I say keep an open mind. It's only eight."

There were shouts and groans. We took a hard left, which crushed the twink wearing mesh against my arm. It was motive enough for him, finally, to talk to me.

"My name's Kodi," he said, spelling it out for me. "With a K, and an I."

"No, it's not," I said.

He laughed and didn't dispute it. Lev was telling a story about something I'd done the last weekend. Kodi shifted himself closer, so that our shoulders touched.

"So is it really your birthday or do you just tell people a random day?"

I stared at him.

"Who do you know that just makes up their birthday?"

"No one."

"Then why are you asking?"

Kodi shrugged.

"Making conversation."

We were deposited on the corner of the street outside a line circling down the block. We were swept inside over catcalls from the crowd and shoved into immediate darkness. A fog-wave of sweat and oil had hit me straight in the face as a girl showed us to our table on the second floor past a few boys on poles. One of them leaned off his pole and screamed over the sound of the music to identify the birthday boy among us. Lev pushed me to the front of the crowd. What felt like the entire place howled as one when the go-go-boy bartender pushed his tongue into my mouth, then fed me a shot. I was deposited back on the ground. I was already dizzy. We settled into our seats, laid out with bottle service and sparklers, one of which Lev lit with a lighter and passed to me. My ears rang; I was still adjusting to the sound barrier shift inside these walls. Dream was a two-level situation with some of the hottest guys I'd ever seen tending bar and milling around the floor. It was not in any way my favorite fucking place on earth, but I decided to let Lev have that one. In any case, he was paying and couldn't be talked out of it. Ry was on her phone next to me while the rest of them dropped their things and splintered out onto the Day-Glo floor. In seconds we were left alone at the table. She smiled, awkwardly, looking around for the girls.

"Having fun?"

I shrugged.

"You know, it's really hard to get a table here, it's not just expensive. I was here last week and saw that guy from *Justified* at the next table over."

"Yeah," I said, "crazy. I haven't met your friends before."

"They work with me," she leaned forward. "I'm glad you came out with us. We don't ever see you in the office. How long have you been here? Three months? Lev says you get up to the wildest things."

I almost frowned, hearing her. I'd been here a week, almost two.

"I'm sure he'd say that."

"Big office," Ry agreed, half-listening to me, "I was hired last year. I practically broke my lease and signed for a condo the next day when I saw how much they were going to pay me. Shit's like a Ponzi scheme. I hear Lev's taking us out to the beach after this."

"What do you think about him?" I asked her. "Lev, I mean."

"He's great, he's so much fun," said Ry. "I've been out with him more than I've been out with my friends."

She moved closer.

"Why? What do you know?"

"Nothing."

"He as close with Io Emsworth as he says he is?"

"I don't actually—"

"Because that's bullshit. Google her top to bottom and you can't find a single thing about him. And the titles. Director of Outside Ventures. Executive Vice President of Communications, Chief Innovation Officer. I can't even keep track anymore. Guy's had like four promotions this past year."

"Wouldn't that mean something good instead of something bad?"

"In tech, sure." Ry shrugged. "Or, you know, it just means he's fucking her."

"Lev?" I turned around, scanning the area, and saw nobody. "No, that's—that's not possible. Lev's—"

"Actually," Ry said, "that's a pretty good point. I wouldn't know. I mean he hired that guy to suck you off tonight, more if you wanted. That's what he told me."

"Who? Kodi?"

Ry smirked at me. "Is that what he told you his name was?" She glanced downward at my feet. "I love those shoes, by the way. They've been killing it the past few years."

I didn't know who "they" were. Somewhere inside me recoiled at a concussive wave of loneliness as Ry returned her attentions to her phone, as though I wanted to stay here with her and talk about nothing. Which didn't make much sense because I could barely hear anymore. It would be hours before I'd be allowed back to my apartment. I tried to think, moving sluggishly, and realized I didn't know what day it was. With any luck it was a Saturday night and I'd have some time to myself the next morning to puke up the tequila and eat something starchy.

"Big boy—" Lev shouted, cutting me off. He had appeared at the foot of the table and held out his hand. I took it. "Come up here, we're waiting for you."

Ry was gone from the table when I turned around. Lights threw beams all around us, hitting smoke and dust in the air, like solid arrays of matter floating around me. Lev led me to the center of the floor, where, shunted side to side by sweaty shoulders and stomachs, I tried to stay afloat, seeing double. I didn't know how long it had been since I'd left the table, since we'd come in. I felt along the lining of my pocket for my phone. There was a bathroom somewhere on this second floor. The music had stopped for a brief moment as the hoarse-voiced DJ at the front asked all the Jersey whores to raise their hands, to which several around us did, snapping their fingers and screeching. I made for an exit. I felt Lev's arm on my wrist as I turned to go and shouted "bathroom" in his direction, shaking him off. I was losing air. There was an absence where the light didn't reach around the corner of the floor, the halls leading to the bathrooms, which I followed, snaking along the corners of bodies and hands until I reached a lull in the fever, and let myself inside the stuffy, black-tiled men's room. Somebody was getting a blowjob in the farthest stall, so I picked its neighbor and shut myself in. My phone was reading out several emails, company newsletters from Io, a text from a shoe brand I didn't recognize begging me to capitalize on their thirty percent–off deal ending at midnight. I deleted the text and blocked the number.

There was a chance I could stay here the rest of the night, at least just a half hour more, until such time that they might leave and I could slip away, quietly. I didn't know if that was what I wanted. It was shitty of me, there wasn't any doubt about it. Lev would be disappointed, if he remembered the next morning. There was a chance he wouldn't.

The week had passed at a pace that I couldn't confess myself happy with, which was to say so fast I could barely keep up. I recalled being home early each afternoon, languishing on my couch, watching the sunset off the balcony. Despite this, I wasn't sleeping well, I knew that for sure. There were bags under my eyes that I didn't know I had. In the stall I turned on my phone's camera and trained it on my face, examining myself. Somebody, maybe the go-go boy who had frenched me at the bar, had smeared glitter all over the side of my head and into my hair. I tried with my fingers to comb most of it out but the deed had been done, as there was no un-glittering to be had, at least not here in the Blowjob Bathroom. My neighbors were almost finished. The one being serviced was making some high-pitched noises that signaled he was close. Slowly, they became still. Through the muffled music, I heard the sound of muscles relaxing, breaths returning to normal.

"I love you," one said to the other, and I could've cried, hearing it. It felt real and true, no matter what it really was, and I could appreciate that in any case.

I'd read on the news several days earlier that the Cheez Wiz billionaire had bought *Metropol* from Francis Corp for nineteen million, which didn't make much sense to me. In ad revenue alone the title pulled more than half that. Relatively speaking, among the world of dying mags, that kind of shit was *Seinfeld* money. Surely the entire business was worth something more. I felt angry, at whoever owned Francis undoubtedly taking the lowest-ball offer just to get the whole thing off their hands. It was dirty. There was no other way to put it. Thirty-five-year legacy gets little more than a toot of a dying breath. Who knew what Chairman Cheez Wiz was going to do with it. All this, despite the fact that it was stupid of me to get sentimental over it. Nobody else was, clearly, or a title like that might have been treated with a little more respect. Some of the more famous covers had trended on Twitter for a couple days before the whole thing was swept aside. The *Metropol* archives had officially been offloaded, its freelancers and editors fired. People had moved on.

I supposed it was time for me, too. I exited my stall. An older guy had taken up post at the leftmost sink and was scrubbing his hands hard. He settled down as I washed up. Out of the corner of my eye I could feel him leaning my way, and edged slightly out of reach. I didn't try to look at him, to ward him off. I didn't have the energy tonight. The stall door behind us slammed open and the couple stumbled out, laughing to themselves. There was movement, shoes squeaking on the wet ground. At last, I saw their faces. They looked me up and down and nodded, shamefully, both young, both sweaty. They didn't know a single thing. They had so much time left. I wanted to tell them not to have anything to be ashamed over, that their love was beautiful, because it was. But—without me saying a word—they both washed their hands, one gargled water from the tap, and left me in there, opening the portal into the wall of sound for a brief moment before closing it back up again.

I didn't think much about my old job anymore. Because perhaps that had been the greatest lie, that for everything I'd hated about the ingratitude our team received, the hopeless helplessness of beating back an onslaught of bankruptcy with little slips of renewal notice cardstock, I'd had a good job. I'd had a good boy at that job. I took my phone out and called Gil and it went to voicemail. I took in a breath to say something when the beep sounded, but changed my mind at the last minute and hung up. I realized I'd forgotten entirely to piss in the stall and aligned myself with one of the urinals. Bass reverbed dangerously around me.

Outside, the table was full of strangers. Lev, spotting me, gestured me back toward the crowd, slamming his hands onto my shoulders.

"If you'd left, I would've fucking killed you," he said. "Group of us are going out to Long Island. A friend of mine owns a house on the beach. We'll fly up there, sleep over, come back in the morning? You okay taking tomorrow off?"

“It’s not Saturday, is it?”

I didn’t hear Lev’s answer to that question, only that afterward he said something loud and unfunny that I didn’t hear over the music, announced that we were leaving, then pulled me away, and I let him.

I could hear the ocean soundly, through the open windows where a few of us sat with our shoes off. Kodi and two of the go-go boys we’d picked up at Dream were naked and doing shots in the pool. I was feeling hungry but there didn’t seem to be much of substance in the fridge when I’d checked. There was, as I was told, a service kitchen downstairs where the good stuff was, but I was dizzy. The drop-away feeling in my stomach that had occurred as the helicopter carrying seven of us lifted off the docks had not completely gone away, nor had the rocking in the cabin as we hit high winds over the Atlantic. I remembered looking down, trying to focus on the spot between my legs, and seeing my knuckles white over my knees. They’d laughed at me for that. I wasn’t drunk, though nobody would’ve noticed. Lev was busy cutting lines on the table from which I was sure I’d probably have a heart attack if I indulged, at this point in the night and in my stomach. The boys came in from the pool with their hands cupped over their dicks, earning catcalls.

“I need to ask a question,” Lev slurred, wobbling dangerously on the spot with a ratty-looking handle of Jack. “Who here works for me?”

“Birthday boy,” said Ry, who had followed us to the house and was on the lap of the meatiest guy I’d ever seen.

"You do, too, Ry."

"Absolutely not."

"Never mind," Lev said, shushing her. "Notwithstanding. You know our big boy taught me that word? First time we met, swear to God. Whichever one of you works for me, I'm here to tell you all, I love you."

He lifted his glass, which was empty, and almost fell over doing it.

"A toast to Io Emsworth. And the money."

Groans.

"Regardless of what you might think, Lev, we're not at work right now."

"I told you all, she's coming back from Sri Lanka next week. Doing a couple TV spots in the office. Big media presence. It'll be killer. Again: To Io Emsworth. And the mother*fucking* money."

The conscious ones repeated half or less of Lev's words back to him. Kodi, wrapped in a towel, collapsed next to me. Whoever had connected their phone to the Bluetooth had passed out because the past twenty minutes had been the same song on repeat and nobody but me seemed to have noticed. Kodi giggled to himself, soaking the cushions with his back and soaked hair. Up close, I saw that his ear bar had a little pewter skull on the end of it.

"You've got some crazy friends," he said, quietly, surprisingly clear for the level of wasted he appeared at present to be.

"Can't really be sure if they're my friends," I told him. "I know . . . three of them. You included."

Kodi shrugged.

"You can make new friends, can't you?"

“No.”

He laughed.

“You’re funny.”

He was cute. There wasn’t much to come from denying something like that, when it was staring me in the face. I missed Gil. It had been a mistake to call him. I’d been thinking about it for the past two hours.

“I’m funny,” I repeated. Kodi nodded, sliding farther down the couch and exposing his balls, which I threw the end of his towel over to hide.

“Are you gay?” he asked me.

“Yes. Maybe. I don’t know.”

“How couldn’t you not—not know?” Kodi said, struggling with the logic of his sentence composition. “You’re thirty.”

“I’m twenty-nine. And I don’t know. I’m both.”

“Boys and girls,” Kodi supplied for me.

“I have better luck with boys than girls.”

“Who’s the last girl you slept with?”

I smiled, saying nothing, until he nodded, shaking his finger at me. I would tell him, probably, given enough time. He had that way about him. Min hadn’t called me since the night she’d punched me in the face, which I didn’t blame her for. It was thematically sound, to never speak to me again. It was a story we could both tell when we were older that felt complete and fulfilling.

“You’re good,” he said. He stared at me, hard and disarmingly, for a second or two, then threw up in my lap.

In his defense, it was mostly sugar water, maybe champagne. There was a brief scuffle as the soberest of us, the meaty guy

Ry was sitting on, used a towel to sop it up from the cushions and off my pants. I looked around, fearful. Lev was going to call the police, or toss Kodi out of the house, something that I wouldn't be able to live with. But Lev was already gone, upstairs somewhere, or outside. Things had become so loud around me that I couldn't look around fast enough. Kodi mumbled his apologies, holding onto my arm while the rest of them laughed. His towel had come loose and was pooled around his feet.

"Dude," the meaty guy said to me, "I'd take him upstairs, dude. He looks done for tonight, dude."

I did what I was told, securing Kodi's towel around his waist and leading him to what I thought were the guest rooms. In the first one I could find, I walked him to the shower and told him to get inside.

"I'm sorry," he said. "I trashed your sofa."

"It wasn't my sofa."

"Come in here with me," Kodi said, fumbling with the water tap. A hiss of steam came up around us.

"I don't think that's a good idea."

"If you don't come in here with me I'll fall and break my head," he pleaded. "I know it."

He asked a few more times, and eventually I told him I would. It was a tiled shower, not like the marble death trap I had back home, and we maneuvered around it easily. I took care not to touch him, watching for signs the heat and steam would knock him out. Evidently, purging his stomach and the hot water sobered him up; he eventually got around to balancing on each foot to scrub his soles with the loofa we found in there.

He passed me everything he used, and I replaced them in their spots along the rack built into the wall. When he signaled he was ready I shut off the water and got us towels. The one he'd been wearing most of the night lay soiled on the floor. I led him to the bed and pushed him under the covers.

"I'll get you some water."

"You think Lev's going to pay me even if I don't let you plow me?"

"Jesus."

Kodi propped himself on an elbow, looking up at me.

"He told me to make you comfortable."

"You've already done that, Kodi. I'll tell him."

Kodi looked pleased with himself. After a moment, he scooted himself sideways, making room for me. I shook my head.

"What? Aren't we friends?"

I came up with no good responses, looked around for my underwear, and slid them on. He rolled his eyes as I joined him. We were close, just a few inches between our faces.

"Your job's really weird," he said after a while.

"I could say the same thing about you."

"It's not a job," Kodi said. "I'm trying to act. I've almost got my MFA. I got cut from a scene in *CSI* last month."

"Impressive."

Kodi's eyes were the color of clear sky, and probably the reason apart from his dick that people hired him to do things like fuck guys whose birthday it was. I'd never seen anybody with the same color eyes.

"I know I have a weird job," I said. "I'm trying to decide whether it's worth staying."

"Having a lot of money gets old, for sure," Kodi said. "You're lucky you can think that way. My grandma lost her Medicaid a year after she had her stroke. My mom had to sell our car."

"I'm an asshole."

"Yeah, but you've got a cute little chin, and eyebrows. Are you Asian?"

"Half."

"My best friend's from the Philippines."

"They should give you a medal for lifting marginalized voices."

"Can you tell me something about yourself?" he asked me.

I shrugged.

"Something personal," he clarified, "something you don't tell people."

"Why?"

"Because something you *do* tell people wouldn't really be all that special," Kodi said, "and we have something pretty special."

"No, we don't."

"You don't see it," he said. He reached forward and ran his fingers once through my hair, which felt good, but I didn't want to admit it. There was still glitter in it, probably.

I let myself follow the lines in his face, smooth and contoured. He was—perfect. I hadn't noticed his perfection until then, and afterward, it was clear. The blanket between us was heavy and had begun to warm our legs. He didn't move when I reached out and held his face in my hand, just closed his eyes with my thumb as though I were lulling him to sleep. His chin and jaw were hard and angled. My fingers came to rest in the divot at his neck. He nudged my hand, delicately with his cheek.

“I know what you can tell me,” he said. “You can tell me how you got this scar on your wrist.”

I followed his eyes to the point he was looking at. I raised it up in front of us, angled it in my special way, and sounded the little click between the joints. He winced.

“That sounds like it hurts.”

“It did, when I broke it. I was eight.”

“What happened?”

I tried not to. Tell him, I mean. There was no use in doing so, nothing he could give me for it. I didn’t want to know anything about him in return. He was a lot of things, but he would never hurt me.

“Just fell. You know, kids fall all the time. I was out in the snow one Christmas and it happened. Somebody had to carry me back home.”

He waited, patiently, thumbing the little divot scar on the inside of my wrist.

“Who carried you home?”

“Somebody, I don’t know. I don’t remember,” I lied.

“You owe me a good story,” Kodi said. “I told you about my grandma.”

“How often do people pay you to pretend to like them?”

“I’m not pretending,” he said. “I’ve been in love for a night, two nights, maybe a weekend at a time. Feeling like somebody loves you back, even if they don’t. Taking care of them, drawing a bath for them, washing them with soap, cooking them food, feeling them fall asleep next to you. It’s the greatest feeling in the world.”

“You’re twenty-two. You don’t know anything.”

“You don’t need to know anything to be in love.” He poked my forehead with a straight finger. “Idiot.”

He was still rubbing my wrist when I started talking, and once I’d started it was hard to stop, not with him looking at me like that, listening.

“I’ve been dreaming about my mom recently. She died just a bit before I hurt my wrist. There was an accident outside my school. It was . . . hard on us. It still is. But in so many years, I’ve never really dreamed about her, not in ways that I remember. Which makes these past few times—I don’t know. In the dreams, I’m standing on the street, watching her. It’s my old school, the parking lot. And I can tell, she’s about to go inside. And I know it’s the day she died, because I remember what she wore that day, green pants, this white shirt with string ties on the sleeves. And I know, when I look at her like this, I’m about to see her die, because it’s right there, outside in the parking lot, where she got hit by a bus while crossing the street and died in the hospital a couple hours later. And in the dream, I’m thinking say something, tell her what’s coming, please, just think of something to say, and it’s like my mind can’t work fast enough. I never see the car coming, maybe it never comes. And each time, I get so sad, thinking there’s nothing I’ll be able to do to save her. So I find myself reaching out my hand, trying to reach her fingers, where she’s waiting on the curb. And every time, right before I wake up, when I get my hand around hers, she kind of—jumps—looks around, turns her head toward me. And . . . that’s it. I wake up. I’ve had it so many times it’s just—it’s always the same.”

Kodi hadn’t said a word through all of this but, as I finished, opened his mouth several times, taking breaths. I shook my head. I felt drained. More than anything I wanted to sleep and a small part of me was glad that he was here. He pulled himself closer.

“I’m sorry about your mom.”

“Thank you.”

“You want me to spoon you?”

This made me laugh for the first time all night. Without saying much more, he turned me around, bringing his body up against mine. He put his nose right on the back of my neck but didn’t kiss me. I lay there for a few minutes, waiting for him to fall asleep. I hoped he would soon; I was banking on whatever bubbly was still left in his stomach knocking him out for the night, and had just started entertaining the possibility that he might throw up on my back sometime during the night when I flinched; my phone had made an angry noise on the nightstand. There was a single blaring buzzer on the screen and in my blind hope I thought of him for the first time in a long time, Gil, thought that I might even be happy if he’d told me never to call him again, because it would’ve been a text and not silence. But it wasn’t a text. It was an alarm, set to midnight. I shut it up, squinting at the screen’s brightness, and made out the reminder, just one line: *TRY THE ONE PERCENT. —JEM.*

8

"Haven't you noticed? You're already in one."

— C L I C K —

I woke. I could spot the edge of my phone halfway under my pillow and dug for it, checking the time. I'd become used to waking just a minute or two before my alarm and today had been no exception. Sunlight poured through the shielded windows.

I showered. I found new pressed pants hanging up in my closet, choosing a blue polo from the stack of starchy shirts piled on one of the shelves. I saw myself in the mirror, nice blue shirt tucked into my pants, black belt and shoes. I looked like I meant no harm, like I could take any offense, any insult, and just keep on living my life. I looked like someone I wanted to be. I had no bags but the belt bag I'd left on the doorknob, which I took to work each morning. I reminded myself that a backpack might be more useful but overall unnecessary considering I didn't even bring a laptop home. I decided to let the matter be, the way I had been doing every morning recently, and locked my front door behind me. Downstairs, the girl with the long earrings waved, making noise around her face as the jewels whipped around her neck.

"Long night?"

I began to shrug, attempting some kind of conversation. It hadn't been particularly long, no. The smile she was giving me wasn't *non*judgmental. I mumbled something to the effect of "totally, you know, just one of those days, can't complain, ha ha, how are you," and headed out to the curb where the car was waiting. My driver was a short man with dark sunglasses, always with a suit that rode up the back of his neck, always with a can of mints in his cup holder that, as far as I could tell, was switched out for a different flavor every morning, suggesting either he ran a regular rotation or just plain went through a can a day. Given the frozen wintergreen fumes inside the car at all times, I assumed it might be the latter.

"Long night," he said, pronouncing it like a truth instead of asking the question, eyeing me through the rearview.

"Sure."

We drove in silence the rest of the way, through the car park and down a ramp to F1's underground lobby. The visitor's entrance was a big glass contraption on the other end of the building, where Io Emsworth held press conferences and other public events. I'd read somewhere that she owned one of the original DeLoreans from the movies and planned to display it somewhere there. It was a logical enough rumor to be taken as true. The car swiveled to a stop in front of the doors and let me out. I passed through, swept by the revolving doors into the cool air, equally spaced trees and benches coming up out of the concrete. Glass offices rose up all around, connected along some pathways by skybridges, though never too many to obstruct the view of the ceiling. All bulletproof. Io Emsworth had insisted, citing security reasons I didn't understand. A young blond kid was checking bags at the front and nodded at me as I swiped myself in with the badge around my neck.

"You look like you've had a—"

"Yeah, I know. So funny."

I went up the escalators to the concourse. Lev had mentioned there were to be expansions as hiring continued to boom and the manufacturing campus neared completion at the other end of the lot. I was early, only a few stragglers around getting breakfast, though the cook staff kept the buffets stocked at all times. I continued on, toward the elevators, and rode up to the tenth floor, where, after a moment looking out over the skybridge to the atrium below, I reached my office and shut myself in. It was almost nine.

I poured myself a bowl of cereal and placed it, along with the jug of whole milk from the fridge, neatly on my desk. There was a laundry list of housekeeping to do before Io Emsworth came to headquarters the next Monday, Lev had told me. She glared out at me from her pinup on the wall. I didn't want her there but didn't know how to ask to have it removed. I'd been watching emails crawl over my phone since early the previous evening and wasn't looking forward to attending to them. I ate my cereal while scrolling Twitter. Somebody stocked my pantry each week with the cinnamon kind that I liked but the box was running low. I made a note to send down for some more. I drained the last of the milk. The clock above my head struck nine.

— C L I C K —

She arrived by helicopter. Which I'm sure most of us have seen in movies and on TV but is still a spectacle to witness in person, maybe because of the noise, the sheer howl of the rotors that dig claws into our ears. Especially while watching them fly out of the sunset and pass over the river, buffeting the water below. Especially while it hovered and threw bits of dirt and grass where Lev had assembled a greeting party, including myself and four suits I didn't know. Around us, media crews fixed their camera lenses on the field. The helicopter wobbled, precariously, then came slowly to the ground. The whine began to die down. The cabin doors opened. She climbed down the little black steps, tottering for the briefest minute on the grass—just brief enough to humanize her—and continuing on toward us, toward the cameras.

Io Emsworth was wearing a suit, leather pants, one of those weird jackets with cape sleeves and slits for her arms. Her hair, evidently secured with liquid concrete, didn't move in the rotor wind. She was flanked on each end by pro wrestler types with earpieces. Lev stepped out of our group, opening his arms wide. Io Emsworth, at least a foot taller than him, nearly picked him off his feet. Her sunglasses sat askew on her face, big black lenses that shielded almost everything from her nose up. She was insanely hot. She had that way, no matter where she was or who was looking at her. All of this I knew beforehand. What nobody had told me was just how tall she was, how brightly and solidly she seemed to tower over Lev, over me. The two of them turned, briefly, toward the cameras, waving, then proceeded straight past the rest of us and into the building. The media crews hurried quickly past them, shouting over the engines.

"Big boy!"

Lev had called back to me. I turned around, my eyes meeting hers for the first time over Lev's head. I jogged up to meet them.

"Lunch? My office?" Lev asked. I blinked. Did he want me to bring them lunch?

"What are you wearing?"

I looked down at my shirt, a blue polo I'd taken off the first hanger in my closet. I liked the way it had looked on me in the mirror, nice blue shirt tucked into my pants, black belt and shoes. I looked like a good guy; however one could quantify goodness, it was performed a dozen times over by this starchy blue shirt.

"What about it?"

"Unimportant," Lev said, stepping aside. Io Emsworth and her security detail had stopped in front of me. She extended her hand.

"I know you."

It was a supremely bizarre first thing to say to somebody, especially considering: she didn't. But I smiled, shook her hand, and buckled in its titan death grip. Io Emsworth's teeth were whiter than the sun.

"What do you think?" Lev said. "Nobu? Salads? The cook staff has got something going on today, I heard, but they might—"

"I can't hardly decide," Io Emsworth said. "I ate something raw on the plane."

"You and me, then," Lev said, winking in my direction. "You should see this guy eat cereal. Just packs it away, every morning. I've never seen anything like it."

Io Emsworth laughed far too loudly at this.

"A photo," she said, gesturing to the press behind her. "Quick one, you don't mind, do you?"

An aide had already arranged the group of us into a line, Io Emsworth between Lev and I, the glass box rising up behind us.

"They'll thank us for this one," Io Emsworth said.

"Blue shirt," Lev whispered. "That's really how it goes, isn't it?

"What's wrong with my shirt?"

Cameras snapped. We turned around and reached the atrium, where several engineers who had been gathered in small conversation dispersed, making room. Io Emsworth removed her sunglasses, revealing the biggest eyes I'd ever seen, and passed them to one of the pro wrestlers.

"You're a remarkable thing," she said to me. "I've heard Lev sing your praises for months."

Months, I thought over in my mind. She meant weeks. I'd started in January, now it was—

"He's a killer," Lev said. "For sure. I've been on my toes ever since he's come onboard. A goddamn killer."

Io Emsworth laughed again, a noise that appeared to freeze the air all around us now in the quiet space inside. Several up by the dining concourse looked over. This was a mythical sound, no doubt, that only the luckiest in the right place at the right time had the privilege to hear. Io Emsworth did not venture this far east very often. Others in the glass offices lining the warehouse looked down at us through the sunlight glare. All eyes trained on her for that brief moment in which nothing else mattered. Then sound returned, as though she had given the breeze permission again to blow.

— *C L I C K* —

I woke. Spotted the edge of my phone halfway under my pillow and dug for it, checking the time. Nearly eight. I'd become accustomed to waking just a minute or two before my alarm, and today had been no exception. Harsh rays of sunlight bore through the shielded windows over my face.

I showered and dressed. I wore a nice pressed blue shirt I'd found on top of a stack of them in my closet. I liked the way it looked, like I had nothing to prove. Like I had all the time in the world for people and their problems. I passed my refrigerator door without notice. I had found no use for it with so much food stocked in the office. I took my belt bag off the doorknob where I kept it and looped it around my shoulder. Did I need a backpack? Something more substantial? I didn't. I didn't even bring a laptop home. Down the elevator, through the lobby. The girl with the long earrings, stationed as she always was at the desk behind the salt sculpture, waved at me.

"Long night?"

I shrugged.

"You could say that."

"You have a lot of those, don't you?" she said. "Big job, somewhere?"

Again, I shrugged. The smile she gave me was pointed and arresting, but I guessed this was just the way she treated everybody. I wondered if she treated her own mother like this. It came so naturally to her. My car was waiting at its usual place on the curb. My driver, a short man with dark sunglasses and an ill-fitting suit, waved his hello as I climbed inside, wafted with minty smells from the jar he kept in his cup holder. I smelled wintergreen.

"Long night, huh," he said.

I had nothing to say to that. We crossed a bridge and bypassed traffic along the river until we reached the garage underneath F1 by ramp, the building and its trees, manicured and artfully arranged, sprouting out of the concrete at optimal intervals under the vault of the glass ceiling and the blue sky beyond it. I passed the entryway, swept up by the naturally circulating breeze, coming in under my armpits, around my head. The space inside was gargantuan; I wondered every time I went inside just what kind of an industry needed space as big and tall as this. F1 was large enough to hold stacked shipping containers, that was for sure, and this wasn't even all of it. Lev had shared plans to expand farther into the neighboring lots, schematics for in-house production and manufacturing. I saw that many had come in already and were hunched over their monitors in the scores of glass boxes rising up around the walls, some walkways connected across the air by skybridges criss-crossing the bright white look of the skylight, nearly as wide as a football field. A young blond kid checking guest bags at the front gave me a wave with the back of his hand.

"You've been up late," he said. I paused in front of him while he took my ID and swiped it across his desk, granting my entry.

"Married to the game."

"Funny," he said. "Why's everybody talking about security next week? What's happening?"

"Io's coming."

"Du-u-ude," the blond kid said. "I've never seen her here. You think she'll pass through this way?"

I shrugged.

I went up the escalators to the concourse, past the buffets and communal tables, birch wood, sprouting seamlessly from patches of soil in the concrete floor. I rode the elevator up to my floor, walked across the air to the other side of the warehouse, and reached my office with five minutes to spare.

The cereal box was half empty, an even half, when I poured a serving for my breakfast and supplemented with whole milk from the fridge. At the top of my email was a note from Lev: *find me post 11 today, need to discuss Io visit nonurgent but asap*. I ate, scrolling Twitter, finished, drank the last dregs of the bowl. I looked at the clock above my head. Nine.

— *C L I C K* —

Lev showed us into his office on the other side, a corner of the glass that overlooked the dining concourse and an ample view of the park below. Several on our way up had gawked out their windows at us; it was hard not to spot her, harder still not to spot her bodyguards. We sat opposite each other on the white chairs. Lev ordered lunch as though reciting poetry. Io Emsworth stared hard at me.

"What do you think of F1?" she asked. I accepted a glass of water from the girl who had followed the three of us inside.

"Beautiful. Hardly anything like it."

"We hired a Czech firm to design it," said Io Emsworth. "Clean lines, but above all: purpose. On the macro scale it makes the best sense out of what we have. The glass is—"

"Bulletproof," I said. "I read that in the *Times*. You've got everybody talking about it."

She snapped her fingers. Just like Lev. She seemed to be considering the image of herself, the *Forb-tune* cover that Lev had blown up on the wall that was identical to the one in mine.

"That's the greatest thing I've heard today," she said. "It's a matter of security, naturally, but think of the way that sounds. I tell whatever outlet I choose our headquarters is covered with bulletproof glass, what are we inclined to believe about a decision like that? Importance. Integrity. Perception. Do you understand? It's everything. Do you really think I named this company after that ditsy little movie because I'm a *time-displaced child of the '80s* or whatever else that incel wrote about me in *Fortune*? This is about perceptions. Always has been. I polled five points higher among men thirty-five and up after that interview. Probably helped that my legs were spread so wide. Now the nudes everybody says are on the internet. Those are real, you know."

She talked exactly like Lev, which shouldn't have surprised me, but it did. Her face was smoother than marble.

"I know you know that perception is really the only thing worth talking about when you talk about what we're doing here, what we're accomplishing." she said. "We are not a startup, not anymore, but the principles remain. Something from nothing. Lev says you understand that."

"I said that," Lev said.

"He did," I said.

"It's important work," said Io Emsworth, crossing her legs. "We wouldn't be where we are without people who understand that at the top of the pyramid. Do you know how many hours of sleep I get?"

She waited. I guessed.

"Six?"

"There was a time, shortly after the IPO, that I decided to give that a try. I hadn't slept more than three since I left college. There was something those billionaires were getting at with their demented schedules. These guys had all the time in the world, and I was watching them use so much of it to do fucking nothing. I started sleeping eight hours and almost killed myself because of it. It's a fallacy, that hard work and busy schedules disrupt a person's natural balance, their chemistry. What's truer is that some people are better built for it than others. We just happen to live in such a difficult, egalitarian-obsessed world that speech like that is nearly hateful. It makes no sense. Children are taught that differences mount to some of the greatest strengths of any modern society yet the moment we try to impose tiered structure, skill hierarchy, organized tabulations of opportunities and values based on aptitude, background, economic fitness, we're suddenly fascists. Or worse, conservatives."

"That is so right," Lev said.

"You are so perfect for this job," Io Emsworth said. "I can see it already. I've been impressed. Do you like the firm? Are we doing what you want us to do?"

I glanced Lev's way, but he was on his phone. Within the soundproofed glass, I could hear my own thoughts turning.

"It's very impressive."

"And the apartment."

"Yes, I—" I paused. They were both looking at me. I glanced down at my lap. "Sorry, I—"

"He's emotional," Lev said, "Our boy lost his job last year. That's how we met, actually. I saw him outside my spin class."

"I've been told the story," said Io Emsworth. "*Metropol*, gorgeous magazine. My father got it at home when I was a girl. Do you miss it?"

She was expecting a diplomatic answer, I supposed. The door behind us had opened and several paper boxes had been opened in front of us. There was enough food there for at least six, and I expected at least half of it would be dumped afterward. Lev started eating, but I had suddenly lost my appetite.

"It was a good job," I said. "Good brand, like you said. Some great investigative pieces the past few years. It was just a magazine. There wasn't anything special about it."

"I knew an editor there for a time. We met at Stanford. Always great things to say about the work being done there. You can tell. Prestige mag like that, there isn't much better, for a writer."

She trained her spotlight eyes on me, and I felt the back of my throat begin, slightly, to close up. Pinup Io glared out from her cover photo over Real Io's shoulder.

"I'll let you in on a secret. Francis Corp approached me about buying. I said no. Wasn't looking into building a personal portfolio like that. Besides, the new owner, he's a friend of my father's. Much better fit. To think, we may have met in another life, another universe. Wouldn't that have been fun?"

— *C L I C K* —

I woke. I dug under my pillow, having spotted the edge of my phone and checked the time. Nearly eight. I had become used to waking just a handful of minutes before my alarm and—just my luck—today had been no different. I put on a blue shirt from the stack on the shelf, straightening it out, getting a good look at myself in the mirror. I looked like somebody with something to prove. Like somebody with places to be and no free time in the day. Sunlight blinded me through the windows.

Downstairs, the girl with the long earrings shook her head importantly as I passed.

"You've had a very long night," she commented flatly.

"Not so long," I told her. "It's Monday, anyway. Isn't everybody slow on Mondays?"

"You're so right. You're so right."

She smiled wide, showing me rows of brilliant teeth.

— *C L I C K* —

"I want you to know that you're doing some highly impressive work," Io Emsworth said, "to me, to the board, certainly to Lev. I can't tell you how much we appreciate what you've put into your time here. Flux is nothing without dedicated people supporting it. I am absolutely nothing, without the people who lift me up. It's an interesting realization I've had the past few years, building all of this around us. The idea that individual work amounts to very little in the eyes of the collective."

I thanked her. Lev was holding a saucer of soy sauce daintily in one hand, his knees touching as though trying to protect his white carpets. We had evidently arrived at a lull in the conversation that didn't seem to unnerve either of them. Had they been expecting me to come with questions? I had to have known I'd be having lunch with Io; it wasn't something that could've slipped my mind. I tried to think of something to ask, my brain riffling through a bag of *neuroelasticity*, *commutes*, *lifetime* but came up empty, unable to connect.

"Do you know why I don't have an office here?" Io Emsworth asked me, suddenly.

I frowned. "You don't?"

"Absolutely not," she said. "I don't have an office anywhere. I prefer to work off my phone, always have. Took quite a bit of time for our dev team to build out enough security on my handhelds for the top-confidential work to be possible. But it's the way I've chosen. It lets me walk around, wherever I want, and bring everything I do with me, at all times. I feel unmoored, in a way that liberates me. You know, our words are not a joke. Perpetual motion is not fantasy. It's entirely possible given the right constraints, regardless of what the science may have you believe. Look at me, disputing the *science*. But I mean it. They would have us believe that so much is impossible. Would you live, willingly, in a world like that? I wouldn't."

— C L I C K —

My driver was a short man with dark sunglasses, always with a suit that rode up the back of his neck. In his cup holder, faithfully each morning, was a can of mints that appeared to change its flavoring based on the day, wintergreen on Mondays, Peppermint on Thursdays. I hadn't figured out the rest of the pattern. Did he drive me home?

"Long night?" he asked, quietly, as we pulled away from the curb.

"I guess."

"I can adjust your air conditioning if you like. Too cold?"

"It's perfect, thanks."

"Perfect," he commented, looking over the tops of his black frames to squint at me. "I've never heard perfect before. You're a lucky man if you find something perfect, anything in the world."

We arrived at F1 with ten minutes to spare. I stepped out of the car and passed into the entryway, the solid glass enveloping me once I was inside, blocking the sounds of the car park outside, and the wind. All bulletproof, I'd read in the *Times.* Io Emsworth had insisted, citing security reasons that were not elaborated upon.

— C L I C K —

"Do you want to hear something interesting?" Io Emsworth asked. "I didn't grow up religious. My father had outlawed religious texts of any kind in the house. He said they were poison. He used to tell me things like that from the moment I could talk. It was important to him that I be able to make my decisions unaided, uninfluenced. He himself was devout. I've never met anybody more devout. But his love for me was greater than his love for God. And so he raised me his own way and gave me the most valuable perspective you can give a child. I read something very recent in a book. I take to reading every night after the workday. It's something called the Parable of the Friend at Night. Do you know what this is?"

"I'm not religious, no."

Io Emsworth made a noise.

"Korean?"

I blinked at her.

"My mother was."

"I could tell," she said. "Anyway, the Parable of the Friend at Night. The story goes, a man is woken from sleep very late at night by a friend, knocking at the door. The friend, with no business to attend to, beseeches the man to lend him three loaves of bread, no questions asked. The man is tired, he has work in the morning, his children are bound to be up early with their questions and their chaos, and his wife is nowhere to be found. He says to his friend: go away, it's late, I have work in the morning, and every other reason, in turn. And in turn, the friend just keeps asking. Keeps asking, and asking, and asking. And at last, the man relents. He lends his friend what he has asked for, not because they are friends. No, the man is quite irritated at this point. He does not perceive much value to their friendship at this moment in time. No, he acquiesces, he lends the loaves because of one critical factor that supersedes logic, emotion, everything. Persistence. The friend doesn't shut the fuck up and now he's got all the bread he could want. Now, there are genuine religious applications for this story. It's thought to be instructive to the action of prayer. Ask and ask, and ask again, and it will be given to you. But more than that, it's an escape valve in an action. It has no other meaning. It's transactional."

I looked at her, at the way her hands were folded in her lap. Io Emsworth seemed deep in thought, as though she had only just heard the same words spoken by someone else and was, along with me, absorbing for the first time just the same.

"That's pretty sad," I said.

"If you want," she shrugged. "I think it's educational. It teaches us ways in which our connections are more of a numbers game than we think them to be. Even ones between those of us that we love. It's sad but true, which—in my mind—makes it less sad. Doesn't it?"

"It does," said Lev.

They turned, at the same time, to face me.

"It does."

— C L I C K —

A young blond kid leaned over his desk at the front of the lobby and swiped my ID over the scanner, buzzing me inside.

"You don't look so good," he said.

"Thank you."

"No, really. Tired, more like it. Up late?"

I didn't have anything else to say. I took my badge back from him.

— C L I C K —

Io Emsworth leaned backward, settling against the couch cushions in a way she hadn't done before, signaling to us that the conversation was over. Most of our food lay untouched in front of us.

"Lev," she said, "I've got an eleven o'clock."

Lev stood, downing a canned green tea. Io Emsworth stood, extending a hand. Again I shook it. I could feel the pressure in her grip even after she'd let go, in the beat of my blood through my wrist. She stood, and I followed.

"Is there anything you want to know?" she asked me. "Anything at all that I can answer for you? This isn't a test, by the way, I don't test people. I want to make sure I'm available to you. I like to leave people with a sense of fulfillment in the best way that I can."

She waited, patiently. I didn't have anything to ask, I thought. It would have been rude to say so. It was evident that this was a gift that Io Emsworth gave to people who she liked, and to refuse it was to refuse her altogether. I cleared my throat.

"Why did you come here today?"

She considered me a moment longer, folding her fingers together in front of her. When she spoke, she said it quietly, as though she didn't want Lev to hear, which was stupid, given that he was standing just off-center, hanging on her every word. But whatever it was, maybe the way she said it, or the way she seemed to look at things with such intensity that they appeared to burn the rest of the world away, I knew then that we had bonded in some way, that she had let me in somehow and was letting me make myself comfortable, that I was important to her and would continue to be, and—for now—it was enough: "Darling, I came here for you."

— C L I C K —

Lev had mentioned the expansions planned in the manufacturing campus at the other end of the lot. I was early to the office, only a few drifters around getting their breakfast. I reached the elevators, continued up to my office, shutting myself inside. Nearly nine.

The cereal was cinnamon, nearly empty when I took the whole milk out of the fridge and poured it over. I chewed carefully, scrolling Twitter. I made a note to send down for another box. I finished, drank the last of the milk from the bowl. One minute left. I did a strange thing then, just watched the face of the clock as the second hand made its sweep around with nothing else to do. Watching, still, when it ticked away, past seven, eight, nine, ten, and met up with the minute hand back at twelve.

— *C L I C K* —

It was early afternoon. I circled the takeaway bar, thinking if I found something of substance to eat here I wouldn't have to order when I was home. I couldn't remember the last time I'd gone out for dinner. My mind looped around the sensation of spice, bitter, winter melon, then came back to the bar.

I picked up a serving spoon at a tub of beef and broccoli, ladling a helping into a paper box. Steam rose over the glass shields into my eyes. I looked up and saw her. Ry was standing by the other end of the concourse, in line with an armful of laptop computers next to two engineers, coworkers. She was gazing silently out the windows to the docks, the top of the car park, the sun dipping low over the river. F1 was transcendent this time of the day, the white walls and glass turned gold by the light. I packed my dinner and made my way toward her. They didn't notice me until I was only feet away.

"Hey."

She looked at me, oddly. I realized then that she didn't recognize me and was trying not to be rude about it.

"You went to my birthday party," I supplied.

She opened her mouth, then closed it. Raised a finger, pointed at me. "Right. How are you?"

It was an odd move. We'd been in a car, nightclub, car, helicopter, car, and then a living room separated by a coke table for the better part of twelve hours just a week ago.

"You're new here, aren't you?" she asked. I nodded.

"Tenth floor."

"Did you say tenth floor?" one of Ry's friends looked strangely at me. "You're C-Level? You look eighteen."

"I'm not."

"Not C-Level or not eighteen?"

"Neither, both."

One of them laughed, pitying me.

"Do you remember?" I asked her. "We went to Dream together? With Lev?"

"No, no, I remember you," Ry said, nodding. "That was months ago. Fun. Lev is . . . insane."

"What do you mean, months ago?"

Ry's friends had left her behind, and I could feel the glare she gave the backs of their heads as they retreated. She sighed, finally, bringing her shoulders down.

"Dude," she said, "why are you talking to me? We've never talked."

She closed her mouth, I could see she was grinding her teeth. I thought of a number of different follow-ups to this but wasn't thinking fast enough. Each came to me like half thoughts, nothing I could really work with. I probably looked like I was stuttering, trying and failing. I could tell I was making her uncomfortable but didn't know how to stop.

"I'm gonna go," she said, finally, sidestepping me. I could hear her catching up to her friends. I turned, looking after them, but they'd already passed down the escalators to the doors. I turned on the spot, finding the setting sun, and made my way to a chair. I sat, numbly. After a moment, I dug my phone from my pocket to check the date. Two hands clamped down, onto my shoulders, before I could read it properly.

"Big boy," Lev whispered into my ear. "Come up to my office, huh? I want to show you something."

I found his face above me, smiling. I stood. I followed him back up to the tenth floor and saw myself inside. I craned my head out over the window one last time, hoping to see Ry somewhere down below, but couldn't make out the black specks from this far up. Lev paced the length of the couch once, and I saw that he was giddy about something.

"I want to give you something," he said. "It's been a great few weeks, I know you're still getting the hang of things, parsing our systems, whatnot. But I want you to know you've been a great help. I couldn't do half the things I do around here without you. I mean, the level of dedication here, it's . . . it's exactly what we needed from you, and you've delivered. Far and away, you've exceeded every expectation."

He went to a door set into the wall, and opened it.

Rummaging inside, he pulled a black garment bag out from between several hanging coats and brought it to me, laying it on my lap.

"From me to you."

He stepped aside. I pulled at the zipper, drawing it down and slipping from the bag a jacket, a black leather jacket with a loose, torn epaulet on the right side. The leather was worn, flecked with rain and sun damage. My hands went instinctively to the right side of the chest, knowing already. In the inside was a badge, the same make, same color, same orientation, I'd know it anywhere. You know what it was, don't you? Same one you wore every episode, both seasons. The garment bag fell away as I stood, lifting it into the light.

"Authentic, bona fide, Academy-certified. That's the real deal. Worn by Antonin Haubert himself."

I turned, looking at him.

"How did—"

"Don't ask me," Lev said. "Think of it as a signing bonus. I knew I'd get you something. I just didn't come across the idea until recently. I know you've been torn up since the old guy killed himself."

He took it from me, holding it open. I eased my arms into it, lifted it onto my shoulders. The leather, though it looked worn, was stiff and unforgiving. I moved stiffly in it, coming to the window, where, reflected in the glass, I saw my head on top of your body. We looked the same, now, same hair, same shoulders, waist, legs, wrists. It was a moment in which I realized how much more I had become like you, like my father. Did anybody see my mother in there anymore? I peered back into that face, looking for her. Was she always just going to disappear like this, in bits and pieces until I could look at myself and see nothing left? It wasn't supposed to be this way.

I knew you didn't care. That was worse than saying you didn't know, which was also true. And why would you care? This had nothing to do with you, in reality, no matter how much I wanted it to. Maybe that was why I kept trying. There was something to be said about the way that damaged people sought more pain, if only because it was familiar. Comforting, in a way? Maybe.

"Do you like it?"

I was shaking. My eyes were wet. I screwed my fists into them, quickly.

Lev appeared behind me, his face a reflection just beyond mine.

"I've never told you about *Raider*," I said.

"Are you kidding?" he said. "You don't ever shut up about fucking *Raider*. You might have tuned it out, but none of us have."

I was still looking at my reflection when I felt him draw closer, put his mouth right up to my ear. The way he did it, I could hear the way he took in his breath, the lungs expanding, the way his lips parted. I'd experienced this feeling before, though I couldn't remember where. It was a nice feeling, understanding that I was safe, that somebody—him—was looking out for me. You may forget what that feels like, after so long, but it doesn't take much to ease back into it. It's a mode we are built to exist in, naturally, aren't we? It's what we want, isn't it?

"Remember this," Lev said. "Anything you want, you can have. I can give it to you. All you have to do is ask."

He was too close to me, our faces just a foot apart.

"That's nice of you," I said.

"There really aren't many like you," Lev said. "I would know. I've been thousands of places. I've met thousands of people."

He'd come closer.

"If I gave you the chance," he said, glancing down at the space between us. "If I let you."

He didn't say more, asking the question with his eyes. He smelled like sugar. I swallowed, constricting my dry throat in a wave down to my stomach.

"I'd like to ask you to do something," he said.

"What is it?"

Lev's eyes darted downward, for a brief moment. He traced his two index fingers around the shape of my jacket lapels.

"Don't ever talk to Ry again."

— C L I C K —

I woke. I could spot the edge of my phone halfway under my pillow and dug for it, checking the time. I'd become used to waking just a minute or two before my alarm and today had been no exception. Sunlight poured through the shielded windows. I showered, took the jacket off its hanger and weighed it in my hands. The leather had become soft and supple, acclimated to my measurements, the cut was exactly what I remembered. I put my arms through it and saw myself in the mirror as I passed my fridge. I wasn't finding much use for it with the food so stocked in the office.

I passed the sink, stretching my arms above my head. The office had been in high gear for the past week as Io Emsworth's visit drew closer. There were emails from Lev that I knew needed to be attended to first thing in the morning. I took my belt bag off the doorknob and had been about to throw open my door when I heard it, froze, recognizing the sound, my phone blaring in my pocket. I fished it out of my pants, turning it over, read the name of the caller in white letters across the screen. *Kaz.*

9

Jacket Guy steps into frame among the strewn debris of splintered wood and broken glass, a shot tight on the floor interrupted by the dark-wash legs of his pants. Beads of pearls roll around the floor; it is evident that the scene, an antiques storefront on the edge of Little China, has been only recently ransacked, as the paper lanterns strung over the cash register, ripped from the counter, are still rotating weakly over the heads of the officers that canvas the perimeter. Jacket Guy's eyes linger on the desolation. Furniture lies smashed, beaten with hammers, perhaps the discarded pipes on the ground that rollick and roll as personnel step around them. There is not a single inch of the store that has not been ravaged, in a way that might convince this viewer of simple vandalism—that is, if this were a different show, and its hero anybody but the inimitable Jacket Guy. The camera moves nimbly over his shoulder, focusing on the figure of a lion carved from wood whose head is missing an ear and jaw, smashed off by sledgehammer. It is a scene, falling within the first ten minutes of (season 2, episode 6, "Mercy for the

Damned") that lays out in succinct and unmistakable terms the ruthlessness with which Jacket Guy's recurring antagonist, the loan shark and shipping magnate Chien Xi (otherwise known among the shadowy circles as the Demonhead) is known to act. His name is one that instills fear among the organized criminals of Little China, synonymous with unspeakable brutality. Jacket Guy has encountered the name only once before, after questioning a witness to a gang-related killing in a previous episode. Nevertheless, there is little that explains why the store, thought to be the honest business of the family living in the apartment just above, has been destroyed, and the family themselves vanished into thin air.

A cry pierces the room. Jacket Guy whirls around, holding up a hand for the attending officers to freeze, and, regaining his bearings, aims his flashlight beam under a piece of particle board fallen from the ceiling. It becomes gradually clear that the board is moving, slightly. The sounds of little, ragged breaths become apparent. Jacket Guy reaches out a hand, curling his fingers under the board, and lifts it. Behind it is a little boy, cowering, covered in dust, with a fat cut on his lip seeping a branch of blood down into his shirt collar. He does not look to be more than five years old. His eyes are wild, turning nervously.

He attempts to squirm deeper into the debris, away from Jacket Guy's hand. Jacket Guy retreats, slightly.

"It's okay, son," he says, calmly.

It is rare to witness even an ounce of tenderness escaping Jacket Guy's grizzled face and exterior, but the voice that leaves him in this moment is not only level, but warm, even. The ring of the word "son" through the air, through the static, is not without significance, as Jacket Guy, unmarried, childless, barely thirty years old, is in many ways the furthest fit from a parental figure, as has been established over thirty-one episodes thus far. And yet it is clear he has taken to the role as naturally as a fish to water. The officers around him approach but he turns his head, glaring, and appears to force them back with the strength of his gaze.

Jacket Guy puts forth his hand once more, then, sensing the child's hesitance, puts his palm to his chest.

"My name's Tommy," he says.

It does not escape this viewer that this is the first moment, the only moment, in which Jacket Guy introduces himself by his first name, Thomas, miniaturized perhaps for the child's comfort. Or was it that, in identifying himself as such, Jacket Guy has provided a brief look into a childhood he has sworn through successive episodes and intimate trysts with prying women never to elaborate upon? The question arrives to this viewer: did Jacket Guy's own parents call him Tommy when he was a child? It is never confirmed, not for the rest of the show's run, but the clue here, just one clue, is enough. The child offers up his hand, and Jacket Guy takes it, giving it a firm but little shake.

"Will you tell me your name?" he asks, carefully. The child cocks his head, suspicious. It is not altogether clear whether he has understood. Then he coughs, setting loose a layer of dust from his hair and shoulders.

"Moto."

Jacket Guy nods, clears his throat. After a movement—it is not clear whose—Moto is lifted from the debris and loops his arms around Jacket Guy's neck. It arrives to all who witness, from the striking silhouette of the man with the boy in his arms, that something new has been unearthed. With his entrance in "Mercy for the Damned," Moto is the first and only child character to be given lines. With his introduction comes the acknowledgement of new ground, a new atmosphere through which Jacket Guy must navigate, and, more importantly, a new and laborious facet of his personality that is given in part to humanize the stony hard edges of his character. This much is clear: neither Jacket Guy, nor the show, will ever be the same. Officers stand their ground as Jacket Guy steps carefully back over the rubble, to the awaiting sunlight.

— C L I C K —

Bo opened his eyes. The ceiling stars he'd stuck to his side of the room had almost entirely lost their ability to glow, even in the dark. They were a pasty green color, now, just barely absorbing the morning light. Through the floorboards, he felt his father's footsteps downstairs.

He was not sure which day it was. He had trouble keeping track when not in school anyway but was having more trouble now. He counted back. His grandparents had been by the day before. He and Kaz had played upstairs while the adults had talked. The day before—or maybe it had been the same day—Bo had woken to snowplows clearing the streets. He'd woken to their sound that morning and forgotten for a moment that they'd driven home from the hospital the night before.

The clouds had teased them with flurries every few hours and the streets were still cold enough to make them stick, but not enough to pack together. The frost would be gone by morning. Bo could place the snowplows in his memory better than anything else. The snowplows had come the day before his grandparents, Bo was quite sure now. Which would make today Christmas morning. He sat up, rubbing an arm across his eyes. Kaz was still asleep in his bed, arms raised haphazardly around his head, a corner of his blanket trailing the ground.

Bo rolled quietly from his blankets and went out to the second-floor landing, where the stairs wound away toward the glow of the kitchen light. He stayed still, listening. His father was on the phone; his voice could be heard in low tones curling around the stairs. Bo reached the top of the stairs and felt the last floorboard dip, giving a hissed creak when he put his weight on it. Downstairs, Hal quieted. Bo held his breath.

"Hang on," Hal said. "I'm just—give me a second. I think one of my guys is awake."

Each waited, listening. Hal stood, his footsteps fell across the kitchen to the staircase. He poked his head up. They found each other. Hal held a phone to his ear. He smiled, comfortingly, and beckoned with his hand. Bo idled, nervous, but came down the stairs. Hal had returned to his seat at the kitchen table, where a mass of papers and manila folders had taken up the available space.

"I'm sorry, let's finish this tomorrow, yeah? I'm really sorry—I don't mean to make all this work for you on Christmas . . . no, not at all. No, we're hanging in there. My Bo—"

He glanced over his shoulder as Bo reached the bottom of the stairs "—my Bo's so strong. We'll be okay . . . Yeah, talk soon—Merry Christmas."

Hal hung up. Bo watched him replace the phone among all the papers on their table. He turned around, reaching up to rake his fingers over the back of his head.

"You're up early," he said, observing with surprise. Bo shrugged, the first thing that came to mind, though he couldn't be sure it was really what he felt, or why he had found himself awake. Hal came to him, crouched low, and kissed his head. His arms were heavy.

"I love you. Merry Christmas."

"Merry Christmas, Appa."

They didn't speak much more. Hal set about clearing the table and poured Bo his cereal. The television was turned on. A morning news show ran through a sappy segment on soldier homecomings. Hal watched him eat.

"Who were you talking to on the phone?" Bo asked. Hal seemed to hear at a second's delay. He raised his chin from where he'd rested it on his crossed forearms. He had endless energy whenever around the boys. Now, he looked seconds from sleep.

"Just some hospital stuff." He'd been on the phone for hours, most every day since. Bo didn't recall anymore the sounds of his climbing up the stairs at the end of the night.

"Are we going to have a funeral?"

They turned their heads at a scream from the television. A video was playing of a dentist whose soldier son had surprised her in her office. They watched the shaky image capture two hugging bodies, the mother's arms wrapped tight around the soldier's head.

"Yes," Hal said finally, "we are. But not until after New Year's."

They were in their boxers. Bo glanced under the table, his feet swinging free off the chair, and those of his father's planted firmly on the ground. They had the same exact toes.

"Bo," Hal said, moving closer. They were just inches apart, now. Bo strained to hear noise from upstairs. "Let's have a good Christmas, yeah? I don't want you to worry right now. We'll open presents when your brother's up."

"We have presents?"

He saw Hal's face falter, slightly. His breath smelled like coffee. "Of course we do," he said.

Creaks sounded above them. Kaz's feet bounding across the floor to the door. "CHRISTMAS!" he howled, tumbling down the stairs. He sprung into Hal's arms. "Christmas, Merry Christmas, merry Christma-a-a-as—"

Hal strung them both up, one in each arm, and carried them to the tree, already lit. Bo and his brother were tossed onto the couch. Kaz was screeching something about Power Rangers, bounding up, performing a running leap off the cushion onto Hal's back. Their noises filled their quiet house anew.

— C L I C K —

"You've gone off the end, Detective," says Jacket Guy's commanding officer. "I can overlook your methods. I can shield you from the DA because you get me results, better than any other guy on my payroll. But this—this is absolute, unequivocal danger. You're telling me you can take care of a kid right now? A kid that doesn't even speak English?"

Jacket Guy is seated in his commanding officer's glass cubicle. Together, they look over the chaotically organized desks of the precinct. Moto on the edge of one, wrapped in a blanket, holding court among three officers gathered around him.

"It's temporary," Jacket Guy says, gruffly.

"There's not a chance in hell."

"Not up to you, sir," Jacket Guy says. About this, he is surprisingly coolheaded, though this would come largely as no surprise to this viewer by season 2. "I'd like to take him while we handle this shop vandalism. We find his parents, he goes back. We don't, he goes into foster care. I want access to him. He knows something about what happened."

"And you think he'll tell you a damn thing. You. For all he knows you're the cop that scared off his entire goddamn family."

Jacket Guy motions over his shoulder. Moto smiles, hands curled around a cup of—Jacket Guy turns his head—yes, it's a cup of coffee. He stands, banging his fist against the glass. "Fellas, take that away from him. What are you thinking?"

"Apologies, Daddy-o," says Douche Cop. "Little pot sticker sweet-talked us."

Jacket Guy decides against picking the fight. He waits for Douche Cop to take Moto's cup away, then sits back down. Jacket Guy's commanding officer shakes his head, slowly.

"This will come back to haunt you."

"Let it," says Jacket Guy, with finality that cannot be understated. Even Jacket Guy's commanding officer is smart enough to recognize the weight behind the words. He says nothing more. Jacket Guy gets up, taking a mess of folders of the desk between them. He finds Moto outside.

"Where we go," Moto says, looking up at him. Jacket Guy pauses. On his face, in a close-up, is a brief entertainment of the fact that the consequences of his actions today have far graver effects than he has considered before. There is nothing to suggest, logically, that he has kept this boy out of danger by doing so. But this look disappears from Jacket Guy's face within another second. Because Jacket Guy does not overthink. It is one of his best qualities and yet, in his line of work, sometimes a flaw that his enemies have sought to exploit. But something has changed in the way Jacket Guy views this boy and, by extension, himself, a change that does not announce to him its absolute enormity just yet, but will, soon enough.

"Are you hungry?"

Moto makes a face, then nods.

"Then we'll eat."

They are interrupted by the sound of a courier at the entryway. A teenage boy enters, carrying in his uneasy arms a bouquet of flowers wrapped in parchment paper.

"Mr. Raider," he calls. "Package for Mr. Raider."

Jacket Guy approaches the teen, who sets the flowers down on an available desk.

"I didn't order flowers," he said.

"Nobody orders flowers for themselves, do they?" says the teenager.

"Who sent them?"

"I deliver them, boss, I don't ask questions."

The teenager exits. Jacket Guy is left in a clear space between the desks, considering the bouquet, which has been tightly wrapped around with twine. Jacket Guy's commanding officer emerges from his office, leaning against the doorway.

"Loverboy," says Douche Cop, slapping Jacket Guy on the back. "Don't keep us waiting."

Jacket Guy shakes off the hand. The camera follows the blurry outlines of the unraveling twine, focused in the background on Moto's face, watching it happen. The paper falls away. On the desk is a bouquet of white roses. A gasp is heard, off camera. The flowers are caked with blood, red splotches on the delicate white petals. Moto looks around the precinct, unaware. Jacket Guy's commanding officer reaches them at the desk. "What the hell is going on here? Who sent you that?"

Jacket Guy doesn't answer. He reaches forward, then thinks better of it and uses the sleeve of his jacket to knock the bloodstained note off the petals. It falls open in front of them.

"Value your discretion, officer," it reads. "It is your greatest asset. One day, it may save your life."

Douche Cop attempts a show of bravado. "That's the worst love letter I've ever seen in my life."

"It's not a love letter," Jacket Guy says. "Somebody's telling me to stay away from the break-in this morning."

He faces his commanding officer.

"This isn't some wannabe drug dealer. Anybody who sends something like this to the precinct has got to have the firepower to back it up. It's a threat."

"You think it's Xi."

"Who else would it be?"

Jacket Guy's commanding officer circles the desk. He waves over an evidence team, who form a perimeter around the desk. Shouts go up: "somebody get outside, find that kid—"

"This isn't ideal," Jacket Guy's commanding officer says. "We're not in a position to pick a fight with the Demonhead. Let me call down to the 1-9. They've got better federal access—"

But Jacket Guy isn't listening. He has realized: he has unearthed something far more sinister than a small-time break-in. In an elongated tracking shot over his face as blurry bodies swirl around him in slow-motion, it is as though Jacket Guy has received a vision of sorts, that he can sense the impending arc of the next ten episodes: in which a witness to the antiques break-in will surface, leading Jacket Guy to the underground gambling den in the heart of Little China. In which Jacket Guy will learn of a smuggling operation in the McAuley shipyards contingent on the delivery of fifty million dollars' worth of counterfeit bills and a revelation of an informant within the precinct relaying Jacket Guy's movements direct to the Demonhead's network. In which a shootout one episode later orchestrated by said traitor, the very man standing next to him—tall, wretched Douche Cop—will put Jacket Guy in the hospital with bullets in his chest and stomach. In which a crime beat reporter whose name this viewer has never remembered, the only woman to appear recurrently among Jacket Guy's sexual exploits—dangled in front of this viewer's eyes as Jacket Guy's one true chance at a happy future—will inadvertently save him from certain death at the hands of assassins hired to kill him in his bed, yet end up a swollen body in the river just one episode later when she attempts to investigate the faulty shipyard and its network of handlers. An arc in which Jacket Guy's return to the precinct, motivated by vengeance, will instigate a two-episode finale that will inevitably pit one man against unerring evil, while the integrity of a neighborhood on the edge of ruin and total takeover by a violent crime syndicate hangs precariously in the balance.

Jacket Guy appears deep in thought in this moment, as though considering these hypotheticals. But, with a movement of the camera over his shoulder, the truth is revealed: he is staring, with hard concern, at Moto, who is watching the mess of officers slowly begin to bag the bouquet and note in plastic for examination and analysis. How is it that within twenty minutes, an abandoned child has come between Jacket Guy and the inimitable pursuit of justice? Is he thinking of little Hui-Ling Tao, left behind a dumpster by her father to freeze to death in season 2, episode 2, "The Mighty and the Weak," to date the only victim whose death he has failed to bring to justice? Perhaps. None can say but Jacket Guy, who doesn't say anything at all.

— C L I C K —

Hal handed Bo the first box under the tree, wrapped in foil. Bo dug his fingernails into the paper and ripped, uncovering a Game Boy Advance in silver. He nodded, quietly, over Kaz's claps and hoots. Hal winked at him.

It turned out, every gift was either for Kaz or Bo. They sat, surrounded by shreds of paper, with hauls of toys, boxed Lego, socks and mittens from their grandmother.

"Appa, where's your presents?" Kaz asked, absentmindedly. Hal was busy gathering their trimmings into a garbage bag. He glanced around, feigning surprise.

"Santa didn't bring me anything this year, Kazzie. Must've done something naughty."

"That's not true," Kaz said, standing up. "He brings you coal if you're naughty."

Hal opened his arms and Kaz leapt off the couch into them. "Let's build your kite, huh? Open the box for me and I'll help you."

Bo watched his brother haul the box he was looking for out from the bottom of a tower of Lego, sending it tumbling to the ground. He held the Game Boy in his hands. It was the color he wanted. Hal had even wrapped a value pack of batteries. There were no notes, he saw. He wondered how long it had taken Hal to unstick them all from the wrapping paper without ripping them. How many of them said things like *Love, Umma and Appa*, or other things his father didn't want him thinking about anymore? His mother could make things so warm, and it only appeared to him now just how different the tree looked, the light coming through the windows, even the sound of their voices. He closed his eyes. He wanted to do what his father had asked.

"Bo, why don't you put on an episode? I'll watch with you while I'm building."

"I *hate* that show," Kaz complained. "It's scary."

"It's about real life, Kazzie," Hal told him. "You know, police officers do a lot of the same things that superheroes do. A lot of really dangerous things. Maybe that's why your brother likes that show."

It wasn't, but Bo knew better than to make corrections. Kaz would never like Jacket Guy, no matter what he said. Kaz could never *understand* Jacket Guy like he and Hal could.

"I don't want to watch that show," Kaz repeated himself. Hal paused, bent over the kite-building instructions.

"Let's go into the kitchen, honey, follow me. Turn it on, Bo. I'll watch with you in a bit."

"I can hear it from the kitchen." Kaz clamped his hands over his ears. "That's not fair. Umma wouldn't let you watch that show, Bo."

Bo counted the spaces between his fingers while Hal herded his brother into the kitchen. It was too early for Kaz to latch genuinely onto his frustration. They were not near a meltdown in any sense, but they had all heard Kaz say it and it had stopped their flow of time. Things moved out of order now, too fast for Bo to perceive them clearly. Because of all of the ways he has been reminded of her this morning, and for the past few mornings, none had cut him exactly the way it sounded when Kaz said her name. Because it was his voice, too, that he could hear in his little brother's voice. It was the same tone the word took when he said it himself. Bo would not say it for a long time, he knew this much. He might never say it again. He crossed the room to the drawer where they kept the VHS tapes. He liked all of them. He hadn't seen the one with the shootout in the police station in a long time. It was frightening, even for him, and a lot of blood. Any that approached the end of season 2 were strangely unsettling to him, now. Especially knowing what happened at the very end. He didn't like the way it made him feel. He picked an early episode from season 1, "Head of the

Bear," in which Jacket Guy infiltrated the Russian mob at the pier-side carnival. There was a naked woman in it, a girl Jacket Guy sleeps with who later saves his life toward the end of the episode. It was that penultimate moment in which Jacket Guy finds himself tied to a chair while the big Russian strongman holds a shotgun to his shoulder. He is told what the shell would do to the muscles and bone. His arm would be taken clean off. Jacket Guy stares, defiant. The strongman is about to pull the trigger when the girlfriend sneaks in from behind and shoots him dead. The rest of the strongman's cronies kill her, quickly, then run scared as the sirens emerge and Jacket Guy's long-awaited reinforcements finally arrive. It is the last shot of the episode: Jacket Guy, in the chair, still tied up, looking over her dead body off-screen while the credits roll over his face. Bo put it on, sitting at an angle on the couch so that he could best hear into the kitchen. Over Kaz's shouts, he had to strain to hear some of the words people were saying. He sat, following Jacket Guy's conversation at the precinct, the carnival at night, the bear in the cage, the beautiful lion tamer who didn't wear pants, the warehouse shootout, and only realized once the moment that had always sent chills up his spine arrived, that long, solemn shot of Jacket Guy's face, that he'd watched the entire thing by himself.

— C L I C K —

Jacket Guy screws his eyes shut against bright white lights hitting his face. The camera wavers, blurred in the foreground in and out. Beads of sweat roll down his forehead. It is evident

Jacket Guy is in a fair bit of pain after the cliffhanger shootout at the end of season 2, episode 19, "Send in the Clowns," that left several officers dead and Jacket Guy lying in a pool of his own blood on the floor, sprawled among flying papers and stomping feet. Jacket Guy's eyes adjust to the light, wincing. The lacerations to his stomach were serious enough that he has grown a half-inch beard while unconscious in the hospital. The scruff hides his impeccably sharp jawline and gives the appearance of a man at least five years older. His eyes are sunken, circled around with intricate bruising. A half-inch cut still shows up red under a bandage on his cheek. His hospital gown hangs off one shoulder, exposing pale and bony flesh. It is Jacket Guy as this viewer has never seen before, vulnerable, an important distinction between the Jacket Guy that hangs in the balance of death, partially unclothed, and the Jacket Guy that has many times over smoked a cigarette in bed without a shirt on while his girl of the week folds his clothes. The hard shell has gone, the bruises are proof. This is a broken man.

The camera pans away from him, revealing the back of a black-haired head. Moto regards him with silence, though his eyes are quite wide. Jacket Guy swallows, painfully, attempting a sound. He glances around the hospital room for help, finding none.

"Hurts?" Moto asks him. Jacket Guy shakes his head.

"You lie."

"So what if I am?" Jacket Guy croaks, finally managing to make a sound. "Who brought you here?"

"Miss Lady," Moto supplies, jerking his head toward the window. Jacket Guy's middle-aged neighbor, a Russian widow and seamstress with two adult daughters, consults with a doctor in the hall. Her first appearance had been in the pilot episode, in which Jacket Guy, attempting to mend the gash in his jacket sustained in the first action sequence of the series, refused her stitching advice through the fire escape window where they occasionally spoke.

"She shouldn't have brought you here," Jacket Guy says, complaining. He attempts to sit up but makes a defeated moan, his stomach seizing, and capitulates, falling back against his pillows. Moto swings his legs out from under him, jumping off the chair set up in front of the motor bed.

"Almost die," he comments.

"I wasn't going to die," says Jacket Guy, massaging the back of his neck. "Get a doctor in here. I need to get back to work."

"Tommy ever learn?" Moto asks him. Jacket Guy stops moving, considering him. The boy is wearing a baggy tank top over basketball shorts that almost reach his ankles. They were Jacket Guy's clothes, even though Jacket Guy, until this very moment, has never been seen wearing anything but his jacket and a pair of slick, dark-wash jeans.

"Learn what," Jacket Guy says, glumly.

"Èmó tóu, bad man." Èmó tóu. Demonhead.

"You don't know anything." Jacket Guy lets out his breath. "I had this under control until Torrence sold us out."

Moto is silent for another moment. Then, in a burst of fury, he balls his fist and punches Jacket Guy clean in the stomach. It is an expert display of the self-defense tactics Jacket Guy had spent a short montage teaching Moto in the previous episode's cold open, and is massively effective. Jacket Guy doubles up in agony, catching Moto's next fist. "Moto! Jesus, stop it—"

"Tommy not learn!" Moto shouts. "Tommy play game with Èmó tóu. Tommy lose."

They stop moving as quickly as they started. Moto bows his head, his shoulders quaking. Jacket Guy listens, helpless, to the little boy's cries escaping his mouth.

"No one," Moto says, barely a whisper. Jacket Guy knows what this means. He is thinking, undoubtedly, of the mid-episode tantrum Moto had thrown near the end of "Mercy for the Damned," in which Jacket Guy had attempted to explain to him what had happened to his parents. Barely six months have passed between then and now. Moto's parents are still unaccounted for. Sometimes, Jacket Guy reasons, it was not so cruel to let Moto be human. He reaches out, straining the IV needle in his wrist in the process, and takes hold of the boy's shoulder.

"This was my fault," he says. "I know. Okay? I know. I'm sorry."

"What if Tommy die?"

"I'm not going to die."

"Lie."

Jacket Guy squeezes the boy's shoulder, briefly.

"I don't lie to you. Not ever."

Something strange has happened, then. As Jacket Guy opens his mouth to speak, Moto crumples, falling into his arms. There is a brief moment in which Jacket Guy reacts stiffly to the boy's arms around his neck, seemingly unable to understand while Moto cries little tears of relief into his hospital gown. It is apparent, in this moment, that Jacket Guy does not habitually show love, perhaps because he has never been shown it in the first place. It follows: an apathy intrinsic to his character has completed its transmogrification into something warm, for once, and forever. Jacket Guy puts his hand on the back of Moto's head, holding him there, prepared, he realizes, to hold him for as long as the boy asks.

— C L I C K —

Hal made them grilled cheese for dinner, peeling slices of Kraft American from the refrigerator and leaving a mess of burned butter in the pan when he was done, the smell of which permeated the entire kitchen where they sat and seemed, almost, to flavor their bites. The three of them ate while the television droned. It had been on all day.

It was the first Christmas that Bo could remember in which nobody had come over, short of several phone calls from his aunt and uncles. "Everything is going to be okay, baby," they said to him, and explained that once the snow cleared they would be on the first flight available to come help out. Bo didn't ask what his aunt meant by "help out," nor did he really hear their words. Like most of the noise, Kaz's included, he had tuned it out and watched six episodes of Jacket Guy straight through, sticking to a patch midway through season 1, while Kaz screamed about the kite that wouldn't take to the wind outside.

"Bo," Hal said, hopefully. "How about I watch with you after dinner?"

He smiled. Bo took his eyes off his food.

"I'm tired."

Hal put his lips together, but nothing more. He nodded.

"You've got a lot of schoolwork, don't you? New Year's coming up really fast."

"Yeah."

"Seriously, it makes me mad they give you so much homework. I mean, is it Christmas or not?"

"Appa," Bo said. He couldn't eat anymore. Hal had been about to continue. They looked at each other. Hal attempted a laugh, and its hollowness hung stark in the air. He picked up his glass, nearly empty.

"I'm trying here, Bo."

"Trying what?" Bo said. His face had grown hot. He would cry soon, he knew it was a matter of time and wanted to get his words out first. "What are you doing?"

Hal gave him a second. He looked so docile, holding the second triangle of his evenly divided sandwich in both hands. Kaz hadn't heard a thing, and was aiming with a pointed forefinger and curled thumb at the top of his glass of milk as though shooting a sniper rifle.

"Don't you think we should try to be having fun today?" Hal asked him.

"No," Bo said, quickly. "This doesn't make any sense. It's stupid."

"Stupid—" Kaz repeated. "Appa, can you make snowmen with me after dinner?"

"Bo, that's not how we talk."

"We don't *talk* about anything," Bo said, balling his fists under the table. "You're trying to pretend to be happy and it's not true. You're a liar."

This would have earned him a slap on the face, he knew this and still said it. Somehow he had worked himself into the kind of blind anger that resulted in things like this. Hal set his food down, a sad look on his face.

“You told me you’d try.”

“Appa, Bo’s mad,” Kaz said, grinning. “Bo’s gonna get in trouble.”

“Shut up, Kaz.”

“Bo—” Hal’s voice cut deep, suddenly low. “Knock that off, right now. Apologize to him.”

Bo stared at him, tears streaming his face. “No.”

“Tro-o-o-ouble,” Kaz sang, clapping his hands.

“I said shut *up*, Kaz.”

“You shut up—”

“Bo—”

“I want to tell the truth,” Bo said. “I want to talk about Umma.”

“Bo, I promise you,” Hal said, his eyes pleading, “We will talk about her after I figure out what to do. This isn’t—”

“Umma’s not gonna let you watch TV,” Kaz said. He raised his hand, intending to bring it down on the table for emphasis, but Bo had already grabbed it, before he realized what he was doing, and twisted it hard. Kaz screamed, almost falling off his chair, “Get off—get off—”

“Bo!”

“UMMA’S DEAD, KAZ—” Bo shouted, beating back the kicks Kaz aimed at him, “UMMA’S DEAD, UMMA’S DEAD—”

“Stop it—” Kaz shrieked, his face gone scarlet. Bo held on until his hand was ripped away. Kaz crumpled to the floor, pounding his fists. Bo was dragged out of the kitchen by his father, up the stairs, into his bedroom. Kaz’s screams reverberated through the walls. Hal slammed the door behind them. In the dark, Bo couldn't see just how angry he was but the strength of Hal's hand on his bicep was crushing him.

"Let go of me," he choked, trying and failing not to make his stuttering cries. "I hate you. I hate you—"

Hal only stopped him breaking free and caught his other hand when he tried to flail a punch. They struggled until Bo fell limp, exhausted. His limbs were on fire. He breathed gasps into the corner of his bed. After a while, Hal let him go. When Bo looked up, he saw the black silhouette of his father's head framed by moonlight, soft snow falling outside. Hal took in his breath many times over the course of a minute, each time saying nothing. They were both shaking. After another minute, Hal had regained his breath. Their silence allowed Kaz's shrieks to be heard at full volume downstairs.

There were a number of things Bo knew he deserved for his behavior, not excluding any amount of yelling and screaming in which his father wanted to indulge, from the look on his face. He wanted it, too. He wanted something other than silence. But Hal turned to leave, doubling back. He raised his hands above his head, flinging them downward.

"I can't—" he started, "I can't believe you, Bo."

He tried again to leave and stopped himself.

"You—" he choked, "you—"

At last, he opened the door, illuminating his face.

"I don't want to see you for the rest of the night."

"I don't care."

Hal looked at him a moment longer, then shut the door. Bo stood in the center of his room, alight, and heard his father's footsteps down the stairs. Kaz's crying stopped soon after. He was so angry he was beginning to shiver. He paced his room, stopping once to rip the blankets from his bed, then from Kaz's. He stopped at the window.

It came to him quickly, before he knew what he was doing. He couldn't hear anything downstairs, no voices or movement. He retrieved the hat, gloves, and jacket from his closet, and put them on. He returned to the window and dug his fingers under it. The wind buffeted him as soon as an inch was clear. He got it open to allow about ten inches, then shimmied himself through, headfirst. He came out on the side of the roof and, steadying himself, continued the way to the overlooking tree. There was a two-foot gap between the trunk and the end of the gutter. He steeled himself, planting his feet, then took a running leap and hit the tree trunk, wrapping his legs around it as though climbing a rope. His weight sagged it to the right. He scooted himself down the trunk, then let go, tumbling onto a dirty snowbank in which his legs sunk up to the knee. He stopped himself glancing over his shoulder at the windows. He would not even remember their faces. He wouldn't spend another second thinking about them and would be happy to stay true to his word as long as he lived. He dug himself out of the snow, rolling onto his back, then got up. He reached the clear patch of their driveway, then the sidewalk, then the street. Crossed the road at the stop sign, and ran against the wind until his ears burned like hot coals.

— C L I C K —

The Demonhead—staggering, holding a knife wound on his thigh closed as he runs—escapes through the backend bowels of the shipping warehouse, and Jacket Guy follows, both hands on his pistol. The torn epaulet of his jacket tatters in the wind. A large cut above his eye has bled down the side of his face. This scene, following quick and successive cuts by wide-angle cameras placed in crooked positions along the walls, progressing among the dark, stacked pallets, is the culmination—the season finale that would serve as series wrap, episode 24, "The Doorway"—of a massive twenty-minute abduction scene in which Jacket Guy had been brought to the McAuley shipyards after being black-bagged just outside the precinct. There, he had come face to face with Chien Xi, a thin man with wispy black hair, dressed in a sharp, custom-tailored suit with no tie. With several rifles aimed at his head, Jacket Guy had had no choice but to listen to a lengthy monologue concerning the whereabouts of the counterfeit bills the Demonhead was currently in the process of shipping through his network to China, where, lost in the shadowy imports system, he will escape unconfronted.

"You don't belong here," the Demonhead had said to him, drawing close enough for their faces to be six inches apart. He spoke over-enunciated English with a slight British accent, having escaped extradition to the United Kingdom the decade before. Jacket Guy glares defiantly back, his hands secured around the back of his chair. "You are a sickness. You think you have power over me. Over my businesses. There is nothing I won't do to protect my assets. You white cops are all the same, thinking you speak for us. How many of us have you slaughtered? Do you know the number?"

"I don't speak for anybody but myself," Jacket Guy had said to him.

"You're a fool," the Demonhead spat. He fingered a forearm-length knife in his hand. "You don't understand the reaches of my rage. I am a calm man, a reasonable man. But I will punish you, to the ends of the earth. Better to make an example, for the next who stumbles into my way. How shall I do it? Take your fingers off? Your nose? Start at your feet? Perhaps it doesn't matter. By the end, any which way I choose, I will be your god."

The words had fallen like shattered plates, one after the other. There have been countless moments like it, situations in which Jacket Guy faced certain death, but always—always—there had been a way out. Something this viewer had habitually missed but realized, upon rewatchings, had always been there. A suspicious call on a payphone outside. A sidearm stowed in a pant leg. Jacket Guy always had a way out. Not this time. What had fallen after these heinous words was the notion that were Jacket Guy to be killed right then, there would be nothing to stop the Demonhead from bribing more officers at the precinct, from conscripting more men and women of Little China into his shadowy business of violence, from finding the one who had escaped, Moto, and extinguishing the spark of the last living threat to his plans.

And yet, Jacket Guy had smiled at this. It was easy, with the flashlights crossing his face, to witness the ease of his charm. The music had swelled, then died, instantly. All eyes had been fixed, breath held, for him to speak. At last, he spoke.

"That's the funny thing, Mr. Xi. There is no God."

A bang and a crash had sounded through the warehouse. A

police cruiser had charged straight through the wall, over the floor, and hit Xi's two bodyguards square in the back. They had sprawled across the floor like rag dolls. Jacket Guy launched himself out of his chair, tackling Xi to the floor. There, they had struggled, the knife sinking into Xi's thigh before Jacket Guy was kicked in the head, the scene spinning for several distorted moments. As Jacket Guy's backup converged on the scene, Jacket Guy had grabbed a discarded pistol and followed Xi out the door, through cluttered boxes and containers that glistened like crystals under the swinging lamplights.

They reach the end of the warehouse, a locked door. Xi spins around, raising his hands. His face is red, livid at his failure. The doorway, the doorway that gives this finale episode its title, is closed to him. Jacket Guy raises his gun.

"Kill me," Xi says, spitting blood.

"Give me a reason and I will," Jacket Guy says, a sound that almost escapes him like the bark of a dog. He is thinking of his lover, the journalist, who lies bloated and blue lipped in the morgue. "I swear to you."

"You don't have it," Xi taunts him, as footsteps converge.

"You don't know anything about me," Jacket Guy says. "Five seconds, I could do it. I'd waste you and nobody would know a thing."

They watch each other, tense. The music is near deafening at this point. The camera lingers on a close-up of Jacket Guy's face. It appears, certainly, that he is about to pull the trigger. It is an action he has performed without question hundreds of times before. The outcome seems a near-inevitability. Yet, after one more second, Jacket Guy blinks, then lowers his gun. Police converge behind him. Two officers wrench Xi's arms behind his head, and guide him away. The two men are given enough time, as they pass each other, for something clear, an electric charge, to occur between them. It is a confrontation that has built suspense, held breath over almost twenty episodes, that has come, finally, to this moment. This viewer is waiting for the last word, something that may at last suggest the final balance of their struggle. But they exchange a look, no words, and, as quickly as the black bag had slipped over Jacket Guys eyes just twenty minutes earlier, the scene cuts to black.

— C L I C K —

Bo ran as fast as he could, squinting his eyes against the icy wind. He marked the trees that passed, the houses. The neighborhood slowly melted away, until, surrounded by darkness, he could no longer place where he was.

He slowed to a stop. He had taken several turns in the road on a whim and found himself deep within a suburb he didn't recognize. He spun on the spot, looking around him. In the distance, he thought he heard a car, but the roads were empty. Each of the houses surrounding him were dark, not even their trees lit.

— C L I C K —

Jacket Guy debriefs in his commanding officer's office. Flecked with blood, nursing a knife wound on his forearm, there is a simple finality to the scene, one in which the case has been solved, the enemy apprehended. Jacket Guy has won himself a night's rest, another season. The jungle has returned to a state of peace.

"You had a chance to kill him, didn't you," Jacket Guy's commanding officer said. Jacket Guy doesn't respond.

"Why didn't you?"

Jacket Guy raises his head, and on his face, unmistakable, is a little smile. And oddly enough, to this viewer it has always been plain. It is this moment that this viewer can pinpoint, the moment in which a terrible sense of foreboding has always invaded. The smile is too comfortable, the music too heightened.

"I'm going home," he said, getting to his feet. "Kid's probably driven Mrs. Abramova up the wall by now."

"What's that?" Jacket Guy's commanding officer frowns, looking at him. "You change your mind or something? You told her to put him to bed at your place before you left. She left a message an hour ago."

Jacket Guy's eyes stay focused, the camera closing in to follow his face. A brief, honest look of confusion. Then it dawns on them both.

"Oh, God."

— C L I C K —

The wind blew violently around him. The shadows cast by the trees looked like fingers along the asphalt. He was very, very alone. He breathed, first shorter, than harder. He doubled back, running down the street he'd come from. Something terrifying had seized in the pit of his stomach. He glanced all around him, the darkened faces of the houses. He felt a chill up his back.

— C L I C K —

Jacket Guy forces his way into the lobby of his building, bounding by two up the stairs to the fourth floor. He sees it before he reaches the landing, the door to his apartment ajar, a crack in the doorframe where the lock has been bashed open.

— C L I C K —

Bo started to cry, heaving wails that seemed to flood from his lungs. He ran, faster and faster, searching, desperate for familiar houses, a street, anything. He rounded the corner of a curb, felt the dip in the pavement too late, and caught his foot on the concrete. He was airborne, falling, collided with a nasty crack on his right hand, palm out. He rolled onto the ground, drawing in his wrist. He glanced at it. He'd landed on a twig that had embedded itself deep into his palm. He whimpered, unable to scream. When he tried to straighten his wrist, pain shot through his arm like an injection of molten steel. This time, he screamed.

— C L I C K —

Jacket Guy bounds through the broken door, into the wreckage of his apartment. His table lies overturned, cabinets rifled, the floor is strewn with broken pieces of china. "Moto!" he shouts, entering the bedroom, spotting the blankets and sheets in crumples on the floor. The window: broken open, letting in the cold night air. Jacket Guy falls to his knees. "Moto," he whispers, unable to rage, his eyes are wide, his face a mask of terror.

"No," he whispers, "no, no—"

And then he says it, Jacket Guy's last words, the last words the show ever airs. Words that live forever in this viewer's mind, synonymous with a certain kind of despair that feels, in the moment, unending. And it is not the revelation that the Demonhead's network of criminals has somehow formed a contingency plan and successfully kidnapped Moto from under Jacket Guy's watch, but rather the idea that Moto, in the moments before he was hauled, kicking and screaming out of the window, had called out for him and had not been saved, that makes Jacket Guy speak the words as the credits roll:

"There wasn't enough time. There wasn't enough time, Moto. There wasn't enough time."

10

I weighed it in my hand, counting the number of times it rang before going to voicemail. Kaz had never called me, not once, not since we'd put our dad in the nursing network four years ago. To be fair I hadn't reached out, either. We fought bitterly about our father, what he needed, what we could provide. Seeing his name used to fill me with dread. I'd be fucked up for days afterward. It surprised me that his number was still the same. Often he was moving around too much to bother using his own phone; recently, he'd been calling from friend's houses, numbers I didn't recognize: Detroit, Culver City, Menlo Park. He was working, I imagined. I didn't know for sure.

The last time I'd heard of him, genuinely, was when he'd been arrested in Austin last year. I'd been in the office when the police reached my phone, asking for the last place of residence I knew he'd maintained. I told them I didn't know. "Could I talk to him?" I asked, just about too late, and was denied anyway. Admittedly, I'd breathed a sigh of relief. It had been his first arrest that I knew of. It was a wonder he'd made it so long in the first place. The charge was petty theft. He'd said while being booked that he needed money to pay his dealer. Cocaine, or maybe marijuana. It was pussy stuff, certainly nothing to try and rob a bodega for. He wasn't exactly tweaking. In the end he'd been put on probation. I told the police I'd reach out if I heard anything concerning, but he never called. It had been the same ever since he finished school, moving around, driving wherever he pleased, I imagined, getting bored, or tired, or both, and moving on, working barista jobs and night custodian gigs. When I got curious every now and then, I found him on Facebook, which he'd stopped updating seriously around 2015 but still posted pictures on every now and then. An empty road. The tops of two sneakers, his, caked with black dirt. We were too far apart in age for me to have genuinely grown up with him, not in the way that would have let me make much sense of him. That was the strange thing about leaving. Leaving home, leaving school, never looking back, leaving him behind, and our father. When I thought of his face I saw the face of a four-year-old, still. A kid with no means to express much of anything, or rather, nothing I could really understand.

Did he think about me? He wasn't easy to talk to. There were barriers there that had in recent times begun to feel like crutches, things we couldn't function without despite the distance they created. It was sad. Of course it was. But I'd stopped feeling at fault for the way we were. It was what I told myself.

I put my phone back on the counter and hadn't even turned around before it rang again. I waited again, until it lay silent. A voicemail popped up on the screen. My kitchen was dark, still empty of light that had not quite reached over the tops of the city through my window. I turned on the lights. The place, cloaked in black and white marble, had acquired a layer of dust I hadn't noticed before. I ran a finger through it, squinting at the grey fuzz that accumulated underneath. It was quiet. I glanced at the clock, almost eight-fifteen. I was going to be late. I stepped over to the windows and looked straight down, saw the black roof of the car already there. I turned, spun on the spot, looking around this apartment, white walls, no pictures. Not a single piece of the furniture I remembered from the shoebox I'd lived in before—

Before what? Before the job. I blinked. Before the job. Before Flux. And where had I been before that? It took several seconds for the word to form: *Metropol.* Monthly arts and fashion periodical pivoted from newsmagazine in the late '80s after its acquisition by conglomerate. This month's cover star: an arthouse twink named Hadrien Haubert, wearing the ugliest shag carpet coat I'd ever seen off his shoulders and crusted shadow smeared all over his eyes like—

My phone was ringing again. I approached it, slowly, and saw it was the front desk down in the lobby calling. I picked it up.

"Hello?"

"Good morning, sir," the girl—I knew her voice, the one with the long earrings—was perking up through the speaker. "Just wanted to make sure you knew your car was waiting downstairs. I'll tell the driver you're on your way down?"

I told her yes. She hung up. An inch of sunlight had come past the clouds and was hitting me straight in the face. I blinked, screwing up my eyes, dug my palms into each socket, cocked my head left and right, forward and back, trying to work feeling into my joints. I popped my wrist several times, as though assuring myself with the noise it made. I put on my shoes, looped my belt bag around my shoulder, and headed downstairs.

The girl with the long earrings waved at me, smiling, and was about to speak when I sped past her, out the doors and onto the curb. The car's back door opened for me, and I slid inside. My driver, gazing over his shoulder at me over the top of his sunglasses, watched me fumble with my seatbelt.

"Sorry," I told him.

"Happens to the best of us."

"I didn't mean to keep you—"

"It happens to the best of us," my driver repeated himself, cutting me off. Without another word he punched the gas and sped us away from the curb. We listened to the hum of the wheels on the asphalt beneath us, the car's engine under the level of a whisper. I watched the dense portion of the city where my condo building was nestled fall away slightly as we reached the bridge and the water below it. I tried not to look when the ground around us fell away, opening out; we seemed to be climbing into the sky, the way it just vanished from underneath us like that. I opened the window, flooding the car with rushed air. We were approaching the turnoff onto the ramps. I took deep breaths, filling my lungs, but my head still spun.

"Happens to the best of us."

"Hey—" I choked, turning my driver's head. I'd never learned his name. "I'm sorry, can I get out?"

"Something wrong?"

"Nothing," I said. "Just . . . feeling kind of sick. Stomach stuff. I'll call in."

We slowed to a stop on the shoulder, near the bridge's midpoint. I wrenched away my seatbelt, dizzy, and almost ate it falling out of the car, steadying myself.

"I can drive you back," my driver offered. It was the most words we'd ever exchanged. Cars whooshed past us, some honked their horns. I shook my head. "It'll be good for me to walk," I told him, "really. Thank you."

I waited, not sure of how long or what was said afterward, but with some time the door shut again, and the car pulled away, joining the line of traffic. I hopped the divider onto the pedestrian path along the asphalt, turned the other way, walking back toward the city. The wind howled freely around here, in the open air, vibrating the bridge cables, the pavement under my feet. I walked quickly, firing my legs. There were steps leading off down to the riverside parks, populated at this hour by joggers, a couple walking their dogs. By the water, I sat on a bench, digging the heels of my hands into my thighs. It was colder than I'd imagined.

It had been a week since I'd started at Flux. Just enough time to move my things into the new apartment. The car ride was so new; I hadn't been paying attention to the last couple of times we'd crossed the bridge. This was an area of the city I didn't know very well. I looked around. Grey-green water lapped at the edges of the walkways. I remembered Io's visit to headquarters, Lev's gift, the jacket that hung in my closet. My birthday.

My birthday. That had been February. I glanced down at my phone. Under the clock, above the voicemail still untouched from my brother, I read: April 4. When had I lost my job? Three days before Christmas. "It *is* Christmas. It's three days from now. We're all supposed to be off for vacation." I was in Gil's office the morning he told me we'd all been bought out by France Corp. Francis Corp. I remembered the look on Gil's face as I'd said that to him.

Gil—I opened our last messages, expecting something. It had been radio silence for nearly four months, since the day I'd left his office, the day I'd come down to the mall and—

My phone rang. Lev was calling. I picked it up.

"Big boy," he said, there was gay electronic music blasting behind his voice, the sounds of exalted breaths moving as one: the rhythm of cultish exercise. "Can you hear me? I'm spinning. You sick? What's going on?"

"Yeah," I found myself speaking. "I'm—I'm sorry, Lev. I can't come in today. Something I ate. Feel like shit."

"That's just fine, bub, you let me know if I can do anything." He paused. "You home?"

"No, I—I was on my way in and decided to turn around. I'm walking back."

"That's what the car's for, big boy, why didn't you just ask him to drive you back?"

"I needed some air," I said. It wasn't a lie. "I'll be fine, just want to walk home and sleep."

Somewhere in the background, I heard the crowd of Lev's classmates yell as one: "I AM BEAUTIFUL. I AM WORTHY."

"I'll send another car."

"It's okay, Lev."

"Are you—"

"Do your class, Lev." I faked a laugh, my head spinning. "I'll be fine."

I hung up before he could say anything else, waited. When he didn't try to call back, I stood, pacing the little square park along the water. Where had I been? I couldn't remember anymore. Gil, the elevator, the date. I hadn't pictured the name, her face, in the longest time. Min. I was halfway downtown. South another thirty blocks and I would find myself at the boutique where I'd met her, where I'd—my hand came to rest of the leather corded strap around my shoulder, the bag she'd sold me.

I was waking up on a regular schedule. I saw the corner of my phone the clearest, poking out under my pillow. Reaching for it. Taking my shower, resting my head against the white marble, trying to work feeling into my skull. Dressing, coming downstairs. The girl in the lobby's earrings, silver with little charm trinkets on the ends. I wondered if she ever changed them out. Did she sleep in them? Did they rust in the shower? The car, the drive over the bridge, down into Flux's car park, through the revolving glass doors, my ID, swiped across the blond boy's desk, the dining concourse, the skybridges. The elevator up, to the tenth floor, across the last bridge to my office, shutting myself inside—

Inside my office. Inside my office. Like running again and again into a wall, tricking myself into believing something different there. There was nothing there. Nothing afterward each and every time. I had stopped walking, clenching my fists. "Fuck, fuck, fuck," I whispered, closing my eyes. Begging, something, there had to be something. It ended there. Every morning, there in the office, the clock strikes nine, and—and—

It came quickly to me. The strobe lights inside Dream. Ry's

voice echoed on itself, compounded by noise all around us. The bathroom. The guys blowing each other in the stall next to me. "I love you." The go-go boy's tongue forcing its way into the pocket of my cheek. The street, the waiting crowd. The helicopter. The pool, the house. The smell of Kodi's vomit on my lap, his nose pressed against the back of my neck where we lay in bed together.

I took out my phone. I had come to the alarm and what I'd read on it. *Try the one percent. Try the one percent. Try the one percent.* One in ten American households were food insecure. Marches had happened all over the country over the last year in which the words "Try the one percent" had been written on placards, chanted for hours in the street. "Try" meant something hopeful, "sue," "litigate," "prosecute." The wealthy hoarded food, land, energy itself, and it would continue to get worse. The outages would continue unless something was done. "Try the one percent" meant "take the motherfuckers to motherfucking court over this bullshit." There had been a name. A signature. I'd deleted the alarm but could see it, where I'd lain with Kodi's arms around me. Jem. I didn't know any Jems. Had it been somebody's initials? And who could've set it, if not for me?

I started walking. The wind had picked up around my legs. I was going farther uptown, toward the building. I squinted at the skyline, I could place it among the other towers and walked haphazardly. I could think, here. A loop, a closed circuit that had lain broken and was now made whole. And it had brought me back, somewhere. Back to April, four months I had spent in a removed place. Back to you. Do you remember what it was like to hold that kid in your arms the first time? Did you know? There would be only eighteen more episodes after season 2, episode 6, "Mercy for the Damned," in which you rescued him from the gutted remains of the antiques shop his family had abandoned him in. Moto would be in every single episode after that. The writers committed, this was going to be a new show; you can see it in the way they treated you afterward. You become so much of a hero that they give you a villain, the crime boss the thugs and cronies call the Demonhead, who sends the precinct those bloody roses with the note, warning you: stay out of his way or face consequences. The first thing you do isn't something cheeky, the way that I'd imagine you would have the first season. You're being sent roses by a mob boss and you'd have something dumb and slick to say about it under normal circumstances. Something awesome like "Guy hasn't even met me for dinner yet." But the show has changed. The first thing you do is look over at that little kid crumpling the paperwork on your desk because he's bored. What are you thinking about? Your commanding officer, Douche Cop, they're wondering what in fuck's name you're thinking, taking this kid out of Little China. There was no place for him here, certainly no room for him in your life, in your shitty apartment. But it doesn't escape you: Moto's parents are dead or long gone from the city, and maybe at that point it doesn't matter, because either way they will not come back for him.

What am I doing, Raider? Where did it all go? I was thinking, then, about something I remembered Lev had said, maybe the first time we met, maybe afterward. A myth about the world's energy consumption, that a system that did not work anymore had been accepted, and there seemed to be no alternative plan. Until Io, that was. There was the idea, that of the Lifetime generators, machines that could power entire buildings, city blocks. Once they cracked the technology, the world would change. It was inevitable. Something like that, you couldn't understand. We were on the cusp of something unbelievable. It involved brainwaves, and electrochemical processes between synapses. Lev had walked me through it. The images were getting foggy; even now, looking back, it was hard for me to remember, to parse through the noise in my head, and there is—was—always, so much noise.

I had come to a block that I recognized. The corner, a facade of glass and expensive concrete that jutted like a blade straight into the sky. I stepped inside, adjusting my eyes to the light. The girl at the desk was on the phone but angled her head toward me. She hung up.

"Everything okay?"

I came to the desk, the pink salt tableau behind her. She had arranged her face into one of concern, but her eyes stayed flat and still.

"Sick," I managed to say, and headed for the elevators, feeling her eyes on the back of my neck. The apartment sprang to light when I stepped inside, hanging my belt bag in its spot on my door, and slipped off my shoes. I checked the time, ten past nine. Still, Kaz's voicemail shone out onto my face. I waited, long enough for the screen to go dark, then woke it again, then waited, in a cycle after which I made the decision, pressed it, held it up to my ear. I heard static first, movement as though he were dragging his phone across Velcro.

"Um . . . hey, Bo—"

He coughed.

"I tried to reach you just now, couple times. I—I know it's early, or whatever. I haven't—I mean we haven't talked in a bit. Can we—um—"

His voice was dipping in and out of focus, as though the connection had wavered.

"Wanna talk with you, soon, if you can. I'm in the area. Let me know. It's Kaz."

It went silent, then clicked. I stayed listening a while after that, as though I'd wanted to be sure he'd really gone. I shut myself inside the bedroom and collapsed onto my mattress with my clothes on.

I'd been dreaming about my mother. I hadn't seen her face in a long time. Dad kept photos of her around the house but never talked about her again, not seriously. There would be memories, little hints of things we had forgotten, but not much more. Sometimes I wondered if he was thankful that he was beginning to forget all of it, if at some point he would eventually forget her, and not have to think about the way she died anymore. That he might even hope for it, at this point.

It was always the same in my dreams, every time, the back of her head on the curb, waiting for the bus to pass, just outside the school. Holding our lunches, Kaz's and mine, in her hand, that she'd brought from home. It wasn't like me to forget something like that. I'd brought our lunches every morning, never forgot them once on the counter until that morning.

It happened each time, almost every night I slept and dreamed, that I could reach out my hand, just barely, and touch the end of her finger, her palm, her wrist hanging at her waist.

Did I remember what she sounded like anymore? Did I recall the way she made Kaz and me watch the Korean-language version of some of the movies we had at home? The way she had made us do it because we needed to practice speaking? I'd rebelled, hadn't I? I'd said something to the effect of: I wouldn't need to speak Korean when I was older. Nobody around me spoke it, not my friends, not my teachers. There wasn't going to be a point, I'd argued, and pouted, and—in the end—obliged, just like I always had.

I closed my eyes. I wanted to see her again, wanted to reenter that old moment, her on the pavement, reaching my hand out to touch hers. Wondering if she could feel it, wondering if she could hear me call for her.

I woke. My alarm was blaring. I could see the edge of my phone half under my pillow and dug it out, silencing it. I raised myself off my sheets, turning my head in slow, careful circles. My limbs were sore. I'd wandered aimlessly, switching the television on and off, closing my eyes, drifting off for an hour, for two, then waking back up again. Lev would ask: how had I spent my sick day? I'd make up something about shitting my guts out, downing a liter of ginger ale from the convenience store. He'd make fun of me for it, and I'd laugh about it. I dressed for work, took my new jacket off the hanger and put it on, saw myself downstairs. The girl with the earrings wasn't at her usual spot, and instead of a substitute, the desk was empty. I paused there, in front of the salt sculpture, looking around. The lobby was quiet, empty. I stepped outside, the car was waiting. My driver nodded at me as I climbed inside.

"Stomach bug," he commented.

"Something like that. All gone," I said. He nodded.

He dropped me off outside the turnstiles into F1, I stepped inside. The blond kid swiped my ID, especially bored looking this morning, and waved me inside. I came up to my office. My ears rang as the door swung closed and the echo of the atrium outside was cut short. I'd made it with three minutes to spare. I set down my bag, crossed the room to the pantry, and poured myself breakfast. In the fridge, I saw my jug of whole milk, neat and full, alongside skim, one percent, and almond. My hand lingered, inches from the whole. The jugs were tempered glass, stuck with neat labels of their contents. I spent a second too long looking at them all, remembering what I'd read on my phone. Try the one percent.

Try the one percent, as in the pithy catchphrase I'd seen popping up all over Twitter, the wealth wars, billionaire presidents and congressmen. Thousands had marched on the Chamber of Commerce just a few weeks before Christmas, I'd seen the coverage on tv that night. But: try the one percent. It didn't mean . . .

I grabbed the third jug from the left, carrying it to my desk. It was a blaring difference between one percent milk and whole, an egregious difference that escapes children trying to decide between them that I'd only discovered right then and there, watching that grey milk-water fill my bowl. Absolutely disgusting. There was nothing right about one-percent milk, absolutely nothing. I laughed. What did it matter anyway? I was going to drown the entire thing with cinnamon sugar anyway. I held the jug in my hand. This was stupid. Imagine the hinging of everything I had been looking for on my choice of milk with my morning cereal. I poured. I sat down, making myself level with the windows looking out over the trees. I ate quickly, draining the bowl. Thirty seconds to nine. Twenty. From across the skybridge, I saw Lev in his office, on the phone, pacing the white rug. He saw me out of the corner of his eye, raised a hand. Ten seconds. Nine, eight.

This is what I told you about. This was where it started. I promised I'd get you there and I'm doing it, and I don't know any more whether it's because you need to know, or because I need to hear it again. I know it doesn't matter. I know you don't understand, that you're not real, that only I, by speaking, make you real, and only to me. But you're all I have. Isn't that funny? You. You.

I was staring at the clock when the second hand reached the twelve, the time became nine sharp. Thinking about you, about her, when a sledgehammer flying at light speed hit the back of my head, and the last thing I saw before it went white was her face.

— C L I C K —

I am in a waking place, between lightness and the dark, greyness around that fills corners, morphs into shapes in front of me, breaking form, interrupting their own lines: static, black and grey. I turn my head to each side, moving forward and backward, grasping fingers on empty spaces. I have fingers again. I can feel their movement through—something. Not air. Not water. I raise my arm, hold it out in front of me, the tips of my fingers sparking, shifting a frame or two to the left, then the right, up and down, then not at all. There is nothing before or after, only me. I wish, in my mind, for something to look at. The back of my head throbs from the hit I've taken. It is clear in my memory, the weight of it when it landed and sent me out of the world.

Shapes appear, sifted like particles, converging on each other, interfering waves creating matter. Clear lines, a floor, walls, a ceiling. Whiteness, greys, clears, and blacks, becoming sharper. There is a floor under my foot when I take my first step. Hard and solid, I hear the distortion my shoe makes as my heel hits the surface, then another. Two steps. Glass walls. Shapes behind them coming into focus. I am standing in the middle of my office. It is mine, I know, from the arrangement of the fridge and pantry on the other side, the wet bar, the white cushion couches and coffee table. If I look at anything long enough, its particles begin to dissociate, blending back into black and white static. I keep my eyes moving, a figure traversing quicksand, trying not to stay in one place. It's my office. I have not left my office. Above, in front of me, I see the clock, one minute past nine, second hand crossing the six at the bottom of the clock-face. Outside the glass walls, things get fuzzier. I can almost keep them in focus, when I squint hard, think cleanly of what I'm supposed to find outside. When I do, the office around me begins to dissolve. I keep moving, keep my head turning.

I remember the word Lev had used. Commute. There is something, I strain, that I've forgotten, something about that meeting that I can't picture anymore. It was a word Lev used for something that involved me, something that was supposed to happen. I turn on the spot, looking for my desk, and see it.

See him, rather. A body, hunched over, resting its head on its forearms. Cereal bowl beside, tipped over, spoon scattered inches away, flecking the remaining drops of sugary milk across the tabletop. It was—it is—me.

I am backing away, steps growing wider. My hands come up in front of my face. I want to get away from the thing in my chair as fast as possible. My mouth is open in a scream. The coffee table hits the back of my knee, I feel my upended gravity pulling me backward. I twist, trying to throw out my arms. Out of the corner of my eye I see the floor coming up to meet me become particles, white scratches of static. My hands enter it first, fall straight through. My head goes after. I am spinning in the air, trying to land, falling through nothing. Everything is white, turning and swirling around me. I want to tuck my knees in, brace for what comes. I am remembering the way the walls had phased away when I stopped picturing them. In a simple movement it clicks, it makes sense. I scramble, running through words in my head as I continue downward. Walls, floor, stop, floor, ground, st—

My knees buckle. I've stopped falling and slammed my feet into something solid. I come down onto my hands, I've nearly bashed my head open on the floor. I settle, pressing myself to the floor. I'm almost laughing. I raise my head, looking around. Out of the grey fuzz, chairs and manicured palm trees set every few yards. Storefronts, walkways, above me, the giant glass ceiling. Behind me, the elevator, doors closed. Lights strung up along the columns and palm trees. Christmas. I'm in the mall, the lobby of the conglomerate's headquarters. They start as shadows, coming out of the framework, taking shape, becoming solid. People passing as I steady myself back on my feet. Color begins to seep into the area, first garish, then more muted, the tan floors, bright flash signs and showrooms. At the other end of the atrium, the bright little boutique. I keep walking. Sounds fill in alongside me, the echoes of footsteps and conversation vaulted back by the glass roof. I keep walking, toward it, looking for her. It's almost taken shape, now, the entirety of it. The whiteness all around has leaked away and left almost everything the way I remembered. The boutique is open, soft jazz filters in through the speakers. I stop by the doors, blinking. There is another girl at the glass counters with the wallets, but it's not her. I crane my neck, looking farther inside. I hear steps behind me, turn just as I see her enter, sidestepping me on her way into the boutique. Min takes the bag slung off her shoulder and stows it behind the counter, giving a sleepy good morning to the other girl. I watch her pull the hat off her head, take her coat and bag and turn, headed for the doors to the back. She turns her head, almost catching sight of me, but I've ducked behind the wall. I continue, taking more steps, watching the world go white again. The floor is changing, becoming carpet, walls shifting closer, ceiling coming way down. Fluorescent lights above me. I've gone ten feet when the color returns. I pass a desk, on the corner the stack of the week's magazines. Hadrien Haubert's cover sits prim and neat on the topmost issue. I stop, picking it up.

"Look at you."

I freeze, turning around. I know her face, over the top of the pod dividers we used to keep in the office instead of real walls.

Lee(?) clears her throat, and I glimpse the ring on her left hand when the light hits it. Her face freezes every few seconds, her mouth moving but nothing else.

"I didn't know you changed for work," she says. "Do you do that every day? I love that jacket. Is that leather?"

I glance down at my clothes, at the jacket she's talking about. From where we stand, I can see the snow falling, still, in big clumps outside through the windows. It is the morning I—*we* all lose our jobs, three days before Christmas. I manage to laugh.

"Yeah," I say, awkwardly. "I—I'm coming from a . . . hookup. I keep a clean outfit here just in case."

Lee(?) makes an excited little noise, waving me over, "Why didn't you tell me in the elevator? This is news worth talking about, Jesus—"

I turn my head—to the end of the bank of offices, around which is Gil's office. I am in there with him, being an asshole and losing my job. My head hurts. I want a way out of this dream and I can't seem to create it. I close my eyes. I've barely heard what Lee(?) is telling me about her fiancé when it occurs: I see her clearly, after I leave Gil's office. She will ask me something about my clothes, then about the almond butter machine. I will ignore her, take my stapler out of my desk, and leave without telling her what's coming. I am only a few minutes from leaving Gil's office and coming back down this hallway. That is, if I'm lucky.

"Hey—" I tell Lee(?), rounding the end of the desks to her. "I'm sorry, I—I've got to—they're going to—"

I'm thinking, not fast enough, when I realize that the answer is in front of me. That the answer has already happened.

“I heard they’re getting rid of the almond butter machine on the third floor,” I say to her. “I’ll be back. Do you—want some?”

Lee? doesn’t let it show on her face how strange she finds me, because she smiles, and nods, and tells me no. I’m running out of time. I cross the hall, continue down toward the elevators, then double back to the other end of the floor. Five minutes pass. Then Gil’s door opens. I watch me leave, leaving the door swinging in a wide arc, stomping down the carpet. I wait for me to turn the corner, come back to the floor where Lee(?) sits. I watch Gil lean out of his office, watching me go, see the back of his head and want more than anything for him to turn around so that I can see him. But the walls are already dissolving back into static. I back away, trying to keep it all in my head, but it’s dissipating faster than I can will it back. I close my eyes, the hammer hits the back of my neck.

— C L I C K —

“FUCK!”

I’ve screamed it, seizing every muscle in my body, throwing my head back up off my desktop with force enough to knock myself over. The chair, massively heavy, managed to stay put while I windmilled my arms, leveling myself, soaked in sweat. Above me, I saw a glimpse of my clock, 9 a.m. The secondhand ticked ahead, reaching the 1. I saw across the atrium that Lev’s office was empty and dark. I breathed, yanking breaths into my lungs as fast as I could. My body felt heavy, unwieldy, as though I’d spent hours underwater and was just now surfacing. I looked down at my hands, the bowl of cereal knocked over on my desk, leaking milk into the seams on my steel-and-bolt desk, puddling onto the floor.

I gasped for air. As if by clockwork, my door opened. Two guys I'd never seen before marched inside, carrying a black box that one clipped open on my desk while the other cleaned up my spilled milk and bagged my bowl and spoon. Neither paid me any attention. The one with the black box had introduced a handful of wires hooked to a monitor. The one who had cleaned up my desk pushed me backward into the chair and started unbuttoning my shirt.

I lay there, shaking.

One of them snapped his fingers in front of my face in a diamond pattern, and instinctively, I followed his hand. The wires were stuck to my ribs, one just under my belly button, two more on each side of my neck.

"Breathe," I was told. I had just registered the words when they looked at each other.

"I'd like whatever they use to knock him out in an IV for parties," one said.

"I don't think you want this shit, brother. Looks like one out of three's a bad trip, at least."

"You'd think he'd remember by now. *Breathe*, guy. In, out."

I stared between them, then did as I was told. They went about their duties, talking intermittently to each other. After about five minutes, one stripped the sticky patches from my chest and they packed their gear. The other buttoned my shirt back up and left me sitting at my now clean desk, going the way they'd come. The door shut behind them. I sat, shaking, clenching my hands together, too afraid to look around me.

The world was solid again. I reached around my head, feeling around my skull, rubbing my eyes. My door opened again. I looked up, saw Lev take a seat at the other end of my desk on one of the chairs set up, facing me. He was looking at his phone.

"Remind me again what you've got today?" he said, vacantly. I sat, staring at him. He glanced up at me.

"Big boy," he said, a little louder. "You with us? Big week, you know. Io's visit, and all."

"What just happened?" I took little, uneasy breaths, inching myself back.

"We're going to do this every time, aren't we?" Lev said, standing up, coming around the desk to me. He cupped my face in his hands, "I was hoping you'd settle down by now. It's been months."

I jerked away, standing, "What the fuck are you doing to me?"

"Don't struggle." Lev rolled his eyes, sitting back down. "It's embarrassing. In an hour you'll be back down and won't remember a thing. Can we just get there? Do we have to trek through all this nonsense beforehand? You know, I would've hoped you'd develop a better tolerance. Irritability, disorientation. Why do I bother?"

He returned to his phone, and started typing something long, ignoring me. I sat, looking around the office, the concourse below. I counted dots, people continuing on with their work, oblivious.

"Apartment good?" Lev asked me, bored. "Getting everything you need?"

I could have broken his head over the edge of this desk. But I knew something more, something he didn't, at least I hoped. It was the same day for him, but a different day for me. I took in my breaths, coming back to zero. This was going to require skill.

"I am," I said. Lev smacked his lips, in response. "It's a great place."

"Course it is," Lev said. "You keep it a pigsty, by the way. You're okay if I step away a bit early today? I've got a spin class."

"Do whatever you want."

"I knew you'd say that," Lev smiled. "You always do. I like this jacket on you, by the way. I hoped you'd like it."

He stood. "You know, Io really did love you that day. It's hard to tell with her, but I know she did. I've asked her to pretend, of course, what with everybody watching, but I could tell. It would kill you to know how much of the crap that flies out of her mouth is crap she genuinely believes in. The Parable of the Friend at Night. Jesus Christ. Just nail me to some wood now, save me the torture of listening to that drivel for another goddamn second."

He chuckled at his own joke.

"You got a bit heated this morning, big boy," he said. "I haven't seen activity like yours in a while, probably not since your first. Anything good this time?"

Lev made snoring noises, tilting his head back in his chair.

"Do you know how grating that gets, four months later? It's every day, my guy. It doesn't seem healthy for you. I don't know anybody who fixates that deeply on their mothers, and yours isn't even alive anymore."

I sat quietly.

"What do I normally tell you about my mother?"

Lev checked his watch.

"There was a time, early on, where we thought the dreams were going to point us somewhere fruitful. Maybe somewhere we were getting at for amplified activity. Maybe if he localized to the memory center, left or right half, somewhere in there. But we've tried everything in the book, big boy. Honestly, there's nothing there. You're just a little boy, aren't you? Still hurting, still torn up. It comprises everything you do and say. That, and that fucking show. Jesus, how many times do I need to hear about this show? I've watched it, by the way. Couple months ago I rented the whole thing. Couldn't make it through more than a few hours. You're a dark little soul. Death and drugs and motel fucks. Not to mention it's the most racist fucking thing I've ever seen in my life. The nonsense people get canceled over these days; does nobody remember the kind of shit you could get away with in 1985? It doesn't suit you. I shouldn't complain. It's the focus that makes you ideal. Consistency. We wouldn't have come this far without you."

He slapped his palms down on his thighs.

"You might have just proven me wrong," he said. "You're usually off the walls by now. Could it be . . . tolerance? I won't jinx it."

He stood. "You're the most fun I have all day. I think that makes you my best friend. Sad for both of us, isn't it?"

I listened, glimpsing over his shoulder the pantry, and the refrigerator. He was about to leave, and it would be my only chance.

"Lev," I said. "Who's Jem?"

"I don't know any Jems, big boy," Lev said. "Friend you know?"

"Something like that. He gave me some advice a while ago."

"Good for you," Lev said. "I hear you don't have any other friends."

"Lev."

He had risen from his seat and stopped, across my desk, peering intently at me. We waited, looking at each other, wondering who would be the first to make their move. Then it happened.

A great groan of the ironwork around us, a whistle tone through the walls as every light blew out, the comforting hush of the air conditioning ground to a halt, silent and dark. Lev glanced out my window at the rest of F1 gone entirely dark, the streets, the buildings, the city over the water. It had all gone dark. He narrowed his eyes.

"Absolutely fascinating."

He straightened up.

"We make something to fix that," I said, catching his attention. "Don't we, Lev?"

He turned his head, noticing me, giving me a look, one that had the feel of a look he didn't usually give, an indicator of something changed. His lip curled, not a smile. He swept out of the room, closing the door behind me.

I sat still, my mind racing. I stood, paced the office a few times. The elevators were out. After a few minutes I saw him jog out of the stairwell ten floors down, leave through the doors, come out to a waiting car, and climb inside. I waited for the car to leave through the ramp, enter the traffic on the far side of the campus, watching it all through the windows. When it was gone, I bolted. I had only my jacket and didn't remember if I'd brought anything else but didn't care. I followed Lev's path down the stairwell, where a crowd was already evacuating, and let myself out on the ground floor near the trees. I crossed the empty space framed with fake landscaping to the other side of the campus. I slowed, coming to a jog, in front of a group

I recognized. Ry, two others, seated at one of the tables. There appeared to be a stark divide between those acknowledging another blackout had wiped what was likely the entire city and counties beyond, for the foreseeable future, and those who still had their lunch to finish.

"Ry—"

She saw me, her face falling. I reached them. Her two friends fell silent.

"Do you know who I am?"

"Uh, yeah," Ry said, trying to laugh. "Can we help you?"

"What day is it?"

"Tuesday."

"When's the last time I talked to you?"

Ry frowned. The joke was no longer funny.

"What's up with you?"

"Tell me," I said, forcefully. "When was the last time I talked to you?"

She shook her head, smiling, giving fleeting looks to her two friends. "Um . . . a couple weeks? What's—"

I looked around the area, then back up to the tenth floor.

"Listen to me," I said. "I need you to come to my office at 10 a.m. tomorrow. Please. Just do it. I'm up on the tenth floor. Do you know—"

"Do *you* know," Ry said, "that you look like you've put a spray can of paint up your nose? We just blacked out, do you realize? My night's ruined. Last time I didn't get my Wi-Fi back for four days."

"Jesus, just listen to me," I said, breathing fast. "Something keeps happening—I get to my office at 9 a.m., every morning, and something happens. It's like, I get shot in the head, and then everything goes white, and I can see parts of my past that have already happened, and I don't know what to do, and Lev knows what's going on and—"

Ry stood, slightly pale, raised her hand.

"Ry, please, just listen to me."

"I'm going to go," she said. Something in her face had changed in a way that had closed itself off to me. There would be no more convincing. "Please, do not talk to me anymore."

"Ry—"

"Maybe you don't get something here," she said, more forcefully, "We don't know each other. We have never known each other. And if you keep talking to me, I'm going to HR."

Her friends stood, gathering their lunches. The three of them turned, leaving me at the table. F1 was slowly emptying itself as most packed their offices and prepared for the trip home. I watched them go, their heads close together. One took a last look at me before they sped away.

I was breathing hard, soaked in sweat. I turned on the spot, revolving, looking up at the glass walls, the walkways high above me.

"Fuck." The word had escaped like a short breath of air.

I wasn't thinking anymore, just turning my head, looking for a place to go. I saw the bank of bathrooms tucked behind the food and started walking. The hollow sounds of the great atrium sunk away. I found the door; I pushed it open, expecting pitch black, but saw the sky first. The ceiling was punctuated with bright round skylights every few feet, throwing solitary beams of light onto the floor at regular intervals.

I saw her reflection in the mirror second, then the back of her head, leaned down to wash her hands in the sink. A row of stalls and urinals extended far behind us. Io Emsworth straightened her back, drying her hands with a paper towel she pulled off the dispenser.

"Quiet out there," she said, "isn't it?"

I glanced around, looking for the bodyguards. She was alone.

"What are you doing here?"

Io Emsworth snorted, a confused sort of amusement on her face.

"This is my bathroom. Every single toilet in here is mine. What are you doing in here?"

"I—" I stopped myself. "I don't know. Looking for a quiet place, I guess."

She seemed satisfied with that, coming closer.

"I wonder how long this one's going to last," she said. "It's been ten minutes already. Not a good sign."

I stared at her, with nothing to say. She didn't seem unnerved by the fact that we were in here alone.

"You look uncomfortable," Io Emsworth said.

"It's been a long day."

"Are you enjoying yourself?"

She gestured around the bathroom. "You know, our average retention used to be around three months. People didn't quite seem to get what we were doing. When you work somewhere shiny like this, everybody notices. It's easy to get a job out of here."

"Do I work here?"

"What a stupid fucking question," Io Emsworth said.

"I don't think it is," I said. "I don't think you mean anything you say."

"That's a problem of cognition that I can't help you with," Io Emsworth said, stepping toward the door.

"Are they even real?"

She glanced back at me, raising an eyebrow.

"Is any of this real?" I asked her. "Are you even . . . doing what you tell the press you're doing?"

"This company is so much bigger than you," Io Emsworth said, quietly. Evidently something in her had trained itself on me, annoyed, and was choosing its words more carefully than she normally would. "Bigger than your questions, bigger than mine. We have so much work to do."

"Have you even made . . . a single fucking battery yet, Io?"

The expression on her face had barely changed. I supposed she was used to this. She was recorded almost every minute of her life. She'd learned not to react. I would never get used to the way famous people lived their lives. Simultaneously the most open and the most distrustful people alive. There was no telling what kind of things a person like that was capable of. Io Emsworth was quiet for the longest time. In the back of my mind, I wondered if she'd ever been talked to this way, certainly not in this building, certainly not in the past five years.

"Let me ask you something: what if we haven't?" she said, finally. "What would you do then? Would you act any differently?"

"I would stop lying to myself."

"No, I don't think you would," she said. "I don't think you can accurately estimate the level of comfort you operate at. Nobody can. I think you get so . . . comfortable, that deep down, you will accept any truth they tell you that lets you keep existing the way you're accustomed to. Whether you make a single fucking battery or not. Whether you even know it."

I tried to speak, thinking of nothing. She took another step closer, bringing her face just a few inches away from mine.

"Before you do something stupid, let me tell you now," she said, quietly. "He's listening."

The door behind us opened with a bang, and two guys in suits shouldered their way into the bathroom.

"What are you doing," one asked, not even a question.

"I'm taking a shit," Io Emsworth said, frowning. "You could have found me if you really looked."

The other reached for her arm and jerked her away from me. "Copter's here."

"It's about time," Io Emsworth said, and I noticed that she hadn't yet taken her eyes off me. The bodyguard's grip on her arm remained tight. The door was opened. The three of them left without another word, leaving me there.

I didn't have anywhere else to go. Once I'd started breathing normal again, I walked back out into the atrium. Io Emsworth was gone. Down the escalators, which had stopped working, the blond kid was deep in conversation with a row of security guards overseeing the evacuation. They waved me through. The city loomed, over the water. I would have bet this could have been a sight to see if it were nighttime, the city laid out in front of me, across the water like this. You'd think it was any old establishing shot from any number of the episodes that began like this: cold winter night, cars crawling, people just trying to get home. But with the sun out, you could barely tell anything was wrong. My car was waiting, its doors opening for me.

"Crazy," he commented. "Wonder how long this one's going to be."

I sat in his backseat, numb, unable even to follow the view of our journey back over the bridge, back to the glass front of my building. I shouldered the door open, reaching the lobby, and realized then, far too late, that I'd left my belt bag hanging on my desk chair back at F1. I came to the desk, where the girl with the long earrings was sitting. The dark lobby was eerily quiet, tomblike around us.

"I left my things at work," I said. "I don't have my keycard."

"Not a problem, sir," she said, smiling. She opened a drawer behind her and rummaged around a mess of old metal keys with both hands. "Until the power's back, the locks have switched to manual. I'll send your driver back to your office to get your bag."

"It's all right," I told her. "I'll find them tomorrow."

"So you'll go back tomorrow," she said.

I looked at her, at a face that didn't seem to move any of its muscles above the mouth when speaking or listening.

"What do you mean?"

"Because . . . " She trailed off. "You have to go back. That's what you signed up for, isn't it? You've got a lot of people to answer for. A lot of people watching. Watching what you'll do next."

I didn't answer, staring at her. She smiled.

"Before I forget," she said. "Lev left a message for you. He asks that you think before you ask any more questions."

She passed me my key.

"Anything else I can do for you?"

I shook my head. Because there really was nothing more. Made my way up to the elevator bank and punched my number before realizing it would not come. I found my way around the side of the lobby to the stairs and climbed twenty flights. On my floor, I stepped into the hallway, passing the windows, high vaulted glass that looked out over the city, at the sun rising high over us, all of us. I wanted sleep. I wanted nothing. I wanted to wake up in Gil's arms again. I wanted my old job, I wanted my mother. Does it occur to you that I did everything I could? I hope it does, because it's not true. It only means I tell a good story. One in which it makes sense, what I do next, when I turn the corner to face my front door, and see—sitting in front of it with his legs crossed, hugging a ratty backpack to his chest—my brother, Kaz.

11

Here's the thing about Maxie Lang. There really is nothing, literally, to prove he *wasn't* just some shitty spoiled kid and that's why he never worked again after the show got canceled. There's nothing. There are no interviews, no citations—this was an age before social media, yes, but the fact that the kid basically disappeared off the face of the earth and only reappeared eleven or twelve years later when they found him dead doesn't give anybody much to work with. And as a result, Tran Duc Hien doesn't get talked about enough. The fact that he was born in San José to Vietnamese refugees, the fact that he attended an open call for Asian child actors between the ages of eight and ten ("older okay but scrawny," said the description). It was known that the character was a clear rip-off of Short Round, the most famous Asian kid in the world after *Temple of Doom* came out the year before. It was also known that Moto was written male or female, and therefore could be tweaked to fit two possible thematic undercurrents: a boy who would underpin Raider's development as a model for masculinity, or a girl who would humanize and reframe his chauvinistic attitudes toward women, perhaps even catalyze a change in his sense of chivalry. Either way, the cast addition made you a father. Tran booked the part; a savvy producer gave him the far more billable name Maxie Lang, and it stuck. Season 2 filmed for five months and wrapped. *Raider* was canceled by the network halfway through airing the season. Antonin Haubert made a young, hot Houdini biopic and received his first Oscar nomination at twenty-seven the next year. You know the rest.

I wondered a lot about Maxie Lang, whether he ever watched the show, if he was proud of it. I've seen the clip they played at the Emmys the year he died along with the rest of the dead folks, a scene from season 2, episode 17, "Checkmate," in which Moto rubs his hands together over a steaming bowl of noodles. Massively stereotypical, sure, but there was something true there: Moto, an orphan, a gang child whose parents left him for dead, someone to whom the worst possible things have already happened, but still—a kid.

Dad and I liked him the best, for that reason. There was humor in the way the writers treated him. He could cut deep with his words, usually just a few syllables in accented English—despite the fact that Maxie didn't even have an accent himself. There wasn't enough attention I could pay to the idea that a Vietnamese kid with more of a Bay Area twang than anything was ching-chonging his way through the role of a Chinese street urchin. It wasn't important, which was to say it was—massively—but not to me. Moto had a habit of appearing around the scene like a ghost, the camera catching only the top of his head and swinging down in a dramatic pan to his face afterward. Those shots made us laugh, the both of us. I wasn't sure I looked like him anymore. There had always been some who could guess what I was, but quite a few in my recent memory could barely tell I was Asian. What was it about those genes that made it so easy for me to grow out of them? Like shedding a husk, less and less a part of me.

Kaz didn't look like that. Kaz still had our mother's eyes, his hair was darker and his skin tanned more easily. He'd been out in the sun a while, recently. The back of his neck was brown and his eyes had sunk a bit deeper into his skull. Grown. He stood, keeping his arms around his backpack, while I reached him in front of my door. He smelled like garbage. I couldn't imagine how he'd even gotten into the lobby given the state of his shoes.

"Hey," he said, both softly and sadly. "Nice jacket. Edgy."

He stepped aside, and I let us inside with the key. We took off our shoes. He left his on top of each other by the door and wandered around my kitchen and living room in his socks. I flicked the switches in the hall for a moment before realizing the obvious. I might have been more worried if I'd had anything perishable in the fridge, or anything, really.

"This really where you live?"

Sunlight poured through onto us, blasting the filth on his clothes into clearer definition. It was just barely noon. The building had gone quiet without central air.

"It's new."

"Must be."

He set his backpack on my couch and took several seconds to canvas the view from the windows, shimmying to each end of the glass.

"What are you doing here?" I asked him.

Kaz feigned some kind of hurt, hearing me.

"What am *I* doing here?"

"How do you know my address?"

"Are you impressed?" he asked. "You like your new job?"

"It's a job, and it pays well."

"Pays really well, apparently."

"Kaz, what are you doing here?"

I was wondering, all this time, what it was going to take for me to forget what I'd just seen in my own office. Most peculiarly obvious were the tender points on my chest where the techs had ripped my electrodes off. My head pounded. Kaz wasn't supposed to be here. I wasn't in the mood for him and never would be.

"You never called me back," he said. "What else was I supposed to do?"

"A lot of things," I said, "short of showing up at my door."

"You say that like I'm not welcome."

"You aren't," I said, crossing the room, swiping his bag off my couch, leaving grey streaks on the suede. "I've had . . . I don't even know what kind of day I've had. I don't know what the fuck's going on in my life. You should've called."

Kaz put his hands up, showing me his palms, saying nothing. I dug my knuckles into the sides of my head. Right. He had, in fact, called.

"How did you even get up here?"

"Looks like the East Coast is a little preoccupied with more pressing matters, doesn't it?" Kaz jerked his head out the window. "I'd love to see this view at night, all the dark buildings. Might actually see the stars for once. If we're black for that long, God willing."

He gestured to the couch. "Can I sit?"

"You look like you've been sleeping on the street."

"I didn't have anybody to crash with here. This city is expensive. Plus five hours on a train from Illinois. You could be nicer to me."

"Tell me what you want and leave."

My brother laughed, only half serious.

"Why was I expecting you to change? You *look* different, definitely, but you're still tired of me. I'm here for Dad. Remember him?"

He pushed past me, bumping our shoulders, and poured himself a glass of water in my kitchen.

"I want to talk to you about moving him to long-term care. I found some really good places in-state. Medicaid can pay for some, but I need help selling his house."

He looked at me funny.

"Are you gonna help me, Bo?"

"Don't call me that," I said. "What are you talking about long-term care for? He's fine."

"According to you?" Kaz said. "When's the last time you talked to him?"

"Christmas. He called me."

"Yeah, I know he did. He told me you hung up on him."

"I didn't—"

"Anyway," Kaz cut me off, "maybe you can believe me instead of yourself when I tell you that he needs it. He's calling every morning and he doesn't remember what day it is.

I've been back home ten times the past month because he's left the house at night. Police stations, fire stations, hospitals. He needs to be somewhere safe. I can't keep thinking about him like this anymore."

He finished his drink and rinsed the glass in my sink. He looked at me, expectantly.

"What?" I said.

"I'm asking you for help. Do you know what help is, Bo? It's when you think about someone else when something bad happens. I need to tell Dad, I need to convince him it's going to be the best for him, I need to file fucking mountains of paperwork and email his case rep and I don't even have an address right now."

He paused, about to say more and rethinking it. And what was I thinking about? Maybe that I'd drunk the wrong milk in my office and fucking blasted myself through time, through space, all the while realizing that I've been the pawn to some twisted psychopathic science experiment for months and, for all I knew, was floating in a tube of goo somewhere dreaming all of this up in my sleep. That I was being watched, that Lev was probably looking at the two of us right now through a camera he'd installed in my toilet, under my bed, behind my own fucking eyes. How do you talk to somebody like this, Raider? How do you think?

"Look," Kaz had softened his voice. His face—was that pity? He was idling his hands together in front of him, fretting. "I know it's been a while. I know you don't want to talk to me. You don't have to talk to me. But I'm worried about him. I'd like for him to get some better meds, and see some better doctors.

They say once they start realizing they're losing it, they get angry, and they get violent. I don't want to get there and have nobody backing us up."

He'd said something like "my son's calling," the night he'd called me. I'd imagined at the time he was with a friend. He had friends, I thought. I saw him sitting alone in that house, speaking to no one, dialing the phone and thinking he wasn't. If it was in fact the springtime already, I hadn't talked to him in months.

I had closed my eyes. In the season 2 finale there was a moment like this, the split second, after you are cornered in the warehouse by thugs with guns and sat forcibly in your chair in the center of the room, you hear those footsteps the first time. Loud and sharp, the sound of expensive leather on concrete. The moment in which a man—that all signs both literal and thematic point to as the Baddie, the one you've been waiting for, the first time you've ever really seen his face, the one pulling the strings behind you all this time—enters in silhouette, and slowly reveals his face. A moment in which the Demonhead's piercing eyes light up the screen and we are all left wondering, to ourselves, what in the fuck is about to happen and whether we can take it.

It happened quickly. We heard a sharp whistle. Groans as the air came to life inside the walls and started again to cycle. The hall lights flickered to life behind us. Beyond, the sound of a hundred more whistles and groans, cogs underground that began again to turn, water that began again to boil.

"Give me a reason, Bo."

I looked straight at him, freezing to the spot. The room had gone quiet around us, the sun hiding itself behind clouds.

"What did you say to me?"

Kaz frowned. He gave a quick glance to his left. I closed the distance between us, a foot away.

"What did you say to me just now?" I asked him.

"What's up with you?"

"Tell me what you just said." I was almost shouting. I shook, from deep inside, trying to keep my focus on him. My brother's face had gone pale.

"I was just telling you—people in Dad's condition could start getting violent if they're confused enough. I was saying—"

"That's not what you said. You said something else after that."

"No, I didn't."

"Did he send you here?" I realized I was panting. I pulled at the top of my head, raking my fingers across my scalp. "Tell me the truth."

"Dad? Did Dad send me here?"

"Lev, you motherfucker, I'm talking about Lev. I'm asking you if Lev sent you here to fuck me up."

Kaz had backed away, slightly, though his face remained calm.

"I don't know what you're talking about, Bo."

"*Stop* calling me that," I spat. I think I wanted fear. I wanted to scare something out of him and was doing my best. "Nobody calls me that."

"I did," Kaz said, gravely. "Dad did."

"Fuck you," I said. "What, is this—this some kind of test? Are you out there watching me?"

I spun around, trying to find something in the corners of the walls, the seams in the paint.

“I know you’re watching!” I shouted. “I know you can see me and you’re *sick*, you’re fucking *sick*—”

I felt hands on my shoulders and almost fell, stumbling back against the section of my couch that caught the back of my knees. Kaz had put out his hands to steady me. He was looking at me funny again, the way he’d done before.

“What’s happening to you?”

I tried to answer. I really did. I could feel the words ticking away inside, could imagine the way they might tumble from me, the way he’d understand them and stop looking at me funny. I saw a way out in his face, it was clear and plain. I caught my breath. Kaz waited for me, as though waiting for the punchline, the joke I’d been withholding, cruelly, from him. I straightened up.

“Just get out of here.” Kaz didn’t move, continuing now to look at me in a way that I hated. It was like he was lording it over me, his goodness, his loyalty, everything Dad liked about him that I didn’t have. And who would it be that he called, the next time? Certainly not me. Some days I forgot I even had him. On the best days I could get myself to erase it all, I could pass hours and hours without a father, without a brother, and it would be the sweetest feeling in the world.

Kaz took his bag off the ground and looped it over one shoulder.

“You don’t”—he broke off—“you don’t even call him anymore.”

“Fuck you.”

“Who did this to you, Bo?” Kaz asked me. “Who made you such a fucking cunt?”

"I'm sure you'd all love that," I told him. "You're always winning, aren't you? You're the one Dad loves, you're the one Mom loved. You are this—this shining *light* and I can't help spewing shit all over your perfect family—"

"Nobody's saying that."

"That's what you want me to say, right?" I couldn't stop myself. "You want me to say it was my fault. Well, it was. I know it was. I know you can't stand it. I know Dad . . . Dad—"

I let it all fall to the ground. There was nothing left, nothing more I could do. Kaz put his hand out toward me, raising a finger. His eyes were wide. When he spoke, his voice was a whisper.

"She loved you," he said. "Umma loved you."

He seemed about to say more. There were times, when I looked at him, at old pictures, in my memories, in my dreams, when I could see all that it was I wanted to be. Everything he had. No job, dirtbag friends, points and parole, but he was, in fact, free. He was, in fact, good. And there, waiting for him to say more, I caught myself wanting so badly to be told what a piece of shit I was. It would be concrete, fact, and therefore, somehow, better. But it didn't come. I wanted it, but he didn't give it to me. Just turned, picked up his shoes, and was gone within the span of less than ten seconds. I found myself straining, listening for footsteps outside, on the carpet, and heard none. I stood there, breathing deeply, sweat dripping from my forehead. Your jacket was hot and sticking to the back of my neck but I didn't take it off. My phone rang. I glanced at it, reading *Dad* written on the screen. I answered it.

"Dad—"

"Bo, honey, I can't seem to find the catalogs."

I felt emptied, hearing him, pressing the screen harder to my face.

"Dad, I want to—"

"Because I had them here a minute ago, I swear," he said, his voice crackling through shoddy reception. It sounded so gruff, he'd gotten so old. "If you came here and figured this out it might help me find the catalogs."

I took in a deep breath. "What are you talking about? What catalogs?"

"Well, if I had the catalogs, I could figure out . . . " he trailed off. "No, that wouldn't be right. I couldn't ever. I couldn't figure—"

"Dad, Dad—" I could feel it coming without any means to stop it. I gritted my teeth. "Dad, just tell me what you want."

"Can you come here?"

"Come where? Home? I'm a hundred miles away—"

"Because I just need to find out how to get those—"

"APPA JUST TELL ME WHAT YOU FUCKING WANT. TELL ME WHAT YOU WANT—"

I was crying, my voice had gone out and reduced itself to a hoarse whisper by the time I'd stopped myself. He was breathing on the other line, I could hear his breaths soft and gentle through my phone. I sank onto my couch. I was heaving harder than I had in recent memory, just lying out there, letting it all go. You'd be ashamed of me, Raider, I know you would. Thinking that if anybody deserved to be beat up like this it was me and not him. We were not so alike after all.

"I'm sorry—" I managed to get out. "I'm so—I'm so sorry, Appa—"

"Bo? What's going on? Are you—"

I hung up, heard the end of his word cut just as my finger hit the button, and dropped my phone to the floor. I didn't speak anymore. Just tipped sideways and buried my head under a cushion, waiting for sleep.

I woke. Sun streamed in through the windows I'd left open. My phone was halfway under my pillow. I dug it out, sitting up, finding myself back in bed. I remembered only vaguely having slept for most of the day, getting up to pee, to drink water. There were alerts all across my screen. The blackout had lasted a total of forty-three minutes in the city, longer in the suburbs for fifty miles in every direction. I stopped reading. I was wearing all of my clothes and my jacket had dug a red line into my cheek where the lapel collar had ridden up under my face. I stood and made it to the bathroom, wetting my hair. I didn't feel rested. My muscles were leaden and sore, as though I'd been clenching them, keeping my whole body rigid for hours. I checked my phone, no messages or calls. It was nearly eight. I stumbled to the windows and looked straight down to the street, spotting my car pulled in beside the curb below.

I shut myself into my office five minutes to nine and dug around the pantry for my cereal. Out of the window, I saw Lev's office was empty, across the open expanse. I paced my office, trying to shake myself further awake. I was hungry. I paused in front of the fridge, bowl in hand. I reached out, took the one percent, and sat in front of my desk with two minutes to go. I ate quickly, as I usually did, and drained the bowl. One minute. I sat, hands folded in front of me, watching the clock, its minute hand coming to rest at 12.

— *C L I C K* —

I am standing in a snowy street, whipped by wind. Flakes fall slowly, appearing out of the air like ghosts escaping the static. I turn my head toward the light, a streetlamp on the far end of the pavement. I start walking.

12

The snow was falling heavier around him, collecting on his jacket, around his shoes. His hand stung, extending from his wrist at an angle he didn't want to look at. Bo sat up, holding his arm close to his chest, and tried to stop crying. When he looked down he saw his blood marked on the asphalt, stained in a print of his palm on the ground.

Bo had stopped moving, sat up because he had seen him coming, a pinprick on the surface of the road where he lay, cheek to the ground. The figure was taking slow, careful steps toward him. In the distance, car horns sounded, traffic miles away that carried through the air and in the streets. It was a man, Bo could see now, tall and slim, and wearing a black leather jacket. He squinted, trying to see clearer. Yes, he knew the jacket. It was perhaps the one thing he might be able to spot from a mile away, no matter how old he got. It was Jacket Guy's jacket. It had to be. The missing loop, the shiny silver buttons, the way it hung loose and boxy on the man's shoulders. It was all there. He shivered, inching farther away. But Jacket Guy kept coming, closing the distance until there were ten, nine, eight feet between them. He couldn't quite see his face, though the hair was similar, the shape of the body similar. When he spoke, it was as though the sound reached into the back corners of Bo's mind, unearthing what he knew.

"Hey, Bo."

Bo wiped his eyes, keeping his throbbing wrist locked close to his chest. He didn't move, out of fear of hurting again. The stab he'd felt was worse than anything he'd ever felt in his life. The man stopped just short of him, regarding him on the ground with his hands in his pockets.

"H-how do you know my name?" Bo asked. Jacket Guy didn't quite know how to answer this question, as though coming across it for the first time himself. He tilted his head, slowly.

"I know a lot about you," he said, "including: why you're out here all alone in the street."

"I got lost," Bo said.

Jacket Guy crouched low, so that their heads came level. Still dark, Bo could not make out the details, but the voice was there. He spent a second wondering if he were dreaming, coming across no good answers.

"I think your wrist is broken," Jacket Guy said. Bo got to his knees. His nose dripped steadily and he raised a sleeve to rub his face dry. He stood, head down, overwhelmed.

"I don't know," he whispered. His eyes ran. He wiped them, and they kept running. "I just—I—"

He didn't know where it came from, the way it took him over, swallowing his insides while the heaving breaths he took seemed the only thing that offered relief. He cried and couldn't help it, missing his father, and his brother, but mostly his mother. He wished for a way that he could tell Jacket Guy and not sound so pathetic. Although if truth were to be told, there was a part of him that knew Jacket Guy could already tell. That Jacket Guy would understand, having grown up without a mother himself, having grown up without friends, or family, or really anybody, not even regular people, strangers even, to fill the emptiness of his life. He felt Jacket Guy reach out, tip his chin back up so they could look at each other face to face.

"You know, Bo," Jacket Guy said, "I bet you've really freaked your dad out tonight. I bet he's looking all over for you. I bet he's really scared that he's lost you."

Bo nodded, the streaming tears had stopped, somewhat, more out of embarrassment, but stopped nonetheless, which he was thankful for. Jacket Guy straightened up. Together they looked down the street, now small and dim, just a street now that Bo could see clearly.

"Come on," Jacket Guy said, putting out his hand, "I'll walk you home."

Bo hesitated, glancing around, at the dark houses. On the far end, a small yard in front of the last one on the block was lit with weakly glowing lights throwing jagged shapes onto the street. Jacket Guy took back his hand. He nodded, understanding, and crouched. Bo put his arm gingerly around Jacket Guy's neck and was lifted into the air. He watched the houses pass as Jacket Guy continued down the block. They were silent for several minutes, listening only to the wind, and the faraway traffic. Jacket Guy walked slowly, trying to keep his movements smooth so as not to disturb Bo's wrist.

"Hey, Bo?"

"Yeah."

Jacket Guy took a minute to figure out how to say it, Bo could tell. The side of his neck smelled like mint, prickly with stubble. Bo inched himself deeper into Jacket Guy's arms, trying to get warm. They had reached a crossing that he recognized. They were less than ten minutes from the house. Gradually, the trees and sidewalks he knew began to take shape around them.

"What do you remember about your mom?"

Bo thought about this for a long time. There were, of course, many things he remembered, so recent as not even to be memories yet, he thought. She was wearing a white sweater that morning he had left for the bus with Kaz. Her hair had been tied up and her socks had been two different colors as she hadn't finished with the laundry downstairs. Bo himself had been wearing a pair of underpants he hadn't worn since the first grade and had been stuffed into the corner of his drawer. She had told him the usual, to have a good day, to look after his brother, to hold his hand when they got onto the bus, and Bo had told her yes, yes, and yes he would, and still Kaz had tripped and almost broken his teeth on the first stair onto the bus. His mother had watched from the door, hugging her arms to her chest in the wind, and waved as they pulled away, down the street. It had been the last time he saw her face. Hal had not allowed them inside her room in the hospital.

"Lots," Bo said, finally. "I don't know."

Jacket Guy was quiet, edging around a patch of the sidewalk covered in ice. He spoke again.

"You remember her breakfast she made you?"

"Pa-jeon," Bo said. "No shrimp. I don't like shrimp."

Jacket Guy stopped, looking at him with a curious expression on his face.

"Who says you don't like shrimp?"

"Me," Bo said, shrugging. "It smells weird."

"No, it doesn't."

"Does, too."

Jacket Guy frowned, then continued walking. They had come to the end of the block, rounding the circle on which the house stood, the tree still lit, the living room a warm yellow glow leeching out onto the snow in front of it. They lingered, looking up at the house. Jacket Guy was making a strange face, gazing up at it; Bo followed the line of his eyes to the tree, visible through the sheer curtains.

"I like our tree this year," Bo said. Snowflakes caught in his hair as they fell to earth had begun to melt and send a little drip of icy cold down past his ears, raising the hairs on his head. Jacket Guy nodded, shakily. He appeared afraid, looking up at the house.

"Your mom must've liked this one," he said.

"She did," Bo said.

They spent another minute in front of it, safe in their quiet little space, away from whatever had happened and whatever would come next, just for a minute, a moment of time that would no longer be. Then Jacket Guy climbed the snowbank, crossed the lawn, and knocked his shoes on the porch before reaching out and ringing the doorbell. They heard footsteps, the deadbolt turning. Bo saw his father's face, flushed red, his eyes wide and bright. He held the phone, evidently still on the line with somebody, in one hand. They looked at each other. Hal forced his lips shut.

"Bo."

His eyes fell on Bo's bloody wrist. Bo moved, slightly, putting his head down to look at the floor.

"Sorry, Appa."

Hal's eyes were streaming. He nodded, once, then twice. Jacket Guy set Bo down on the porch. Bo approached, carefully, cradling his arm. He had been about to speak when the breath was knocked from his lungs. Hal had thrown his arms tight around his body and was squeezing him hard. His whole body heaved. Bo felt his head pressed deep into his father's chest, smelling detergent, wool that tickled his nose. Hal sobbed, hugging him tighter, making sounds Bo had never heard him make before. He wanted to cry, if not for his own pain, for his father's, knowing now, more than ever, that the hurt between them was one of the few things left that bound them.

"Bo—" Hal whispered, "Bo . . . "

It was a while before he was let go. Hal stared, holding his shoulders, moving his lips and making no sound.

"I—" he stammered, coming to his senses. "We need to get you to the hospital. I—We have to go now."

He stood, and noticed, perhaps for the first time, Jacket Guy standing on the porch behind them.

"You," he tried, "you found my son."

Bo looked up at the two of them, at Jacket Guy giving a tense little nod. It was odd to see him suddenly uncomfortable, as though being noticed had unlocked something different in the way he stood. Jacket Guy moved his shoulders, almost like a shrug. "It wasn't any trouble," he seemed to say. He wouldn't look at Bo anymore. "I should get going. Merry Christmas."

"Merry Christmas," Hal repeated, stunned, but Jacket Guy had already come down the porch and was going back through the snow. Bo looked at the back of his head, and had almost let him reach the end of the sidewalk when he ran after, fighting to get over the snowbank before Jacket Guy retreated too far to hear.

"Wait!"

Jacket Guy stopped in the middle of the street, turning to look back at him, at Hal lingering in the doorway. He smiled, as though taking in the sight of them. Bo was panting, hard. His wrist ached but he didn't mind it anymore in the cold.

"Are you really him?" Bo asked, hearing it himself the way he seemed to plead it, wanting it to be true. "Is it really you?"

13

I am looking at this boy at the edge of the snow-coated lawn, at his father at the doorway. It is a struggle to keep it all in my mind. I can see the edges of the house, parts of the pavement, beginning to dissolve into white space all around. Lights all around us, strung up on houses, beam down from the streetlamps. My eyes are wet.

"I don't really know if it matters," I tell him, and I mean it. He is disappointed by this answer, I can see, but does not argue. I look over his shoulder at his father, who's brought Kaz to the doorway and is wrapping him in a scarf. I remember how this had gone the first time, the hospital ride, the stitches I had to have put in my hand, the three months they stayed there, the four months after that until I realized I could make my wrist pop with the sound of a little firecracker. In time I would forget who exactly had carried me home that Christmas night. I would tell myself that it was a kind stranger, a neighbor's adult son home for the holidays, something more normal, more simple than what it had turned out to be.

"Promise me something," I say, my eyes watering, "just promise me you'll take care of your dad and your brother. Okay?"

He frowns. I wonder, briefly, what had passed through my mind when I'd heard it, if I was really as unmoved as he looks right now. But he's polite, tells me he understands, turns back toward the house, cradling his limp arm. There is not quite anything to explain the way it feels, watching him disappear behind the door. As though a piece of time has been lifted away, as though the house has become just a house, the tree inside somebody else's tree. The front door is so much smaller than I remember, the driveway not nearly as spacious. It *is* somebody else's house, isn't it? Whatever is there that was once mine is no longer there. Left behind when I decided to leave it along with everything else inside it. I wipe my eyes dry.

I keep walking down the road, and by the time I turn my head to look again the street is empty, hazy. The scene around me is changing, becoming dark and light and back to dark, buildings rising up out of the ground, the slick snowy road becoming dry and glossy. Cars pass, the air becomes bright and crisp, dry wind hits the back of my head. It is light, when I reach the parking lot, the brick side of the building that I know. I come to rest at the crosswalk, ten feet from a little group of kids and parents waiting to get across the street. I watch, a mother takes her daughter's hand and gets to the other side, ushering her through the doors. The car pulls into one of the available spots close by. The door opens, she steps out, holding two bagged lunches. She turns her head, away from me, I haven't gotten a look at her face. She's wearing a white sweater, green pants, her hair sits in a loose knot at the base of her neck. She steps toward the crosswalk, coming to a halt when the crossing guard puts up his sign. In fifteen seconds, a shout will echo over the grounds of the playground, distracting them all. The guard, a man in his thirties, will step over the curb, investigating, and she will not notice, swiping her boot against the ground because it has picked up some dirty frozen slush. It will occur to her, hearing nothing, that she must have been beckoned to move forward, and she will look up, coming to rest her sight on the doors ahead, and step into the path of a school bus heading down the lane. I see the bus, coming away from the curb, her head, still pointed down at her shoes. I am feet from her, walking, delirious now. The edges of the school building have started to come undone. My hand is out, reaching for her arm. My fingers have almost reached the sleeve of her sweater. Her head is still turned. I want so desperately to see her, just to look at her. I have lived this vision a thousand times, watched my fingers make contact with the sleeve, watched her foot lift up, step out onto the road as the bus barrels nearer, watched her start at my hand, pulling her head up, turning it, inch by inch, to look back toward me. I am closer than I have ever come. I see the outline of her jaw, her nose, almost, an eyebrow. We move as though encased in water, too slow to react, to stop what is coming. Her face, turning away from the bus, coming to rest on—

"Haven't you noticed? You're already in one."

Jacket Guy never misses, not once. He is given many opportunities, perps that run, perps that jump into cars, perps that fire shots over their shoulders or through walls and doors during an ongoing stickup. Jacket Guy always nails them. And while the thought does occur that Jacket Guy may not ever miss because Jacket Guy only takes the shots he knows he can't miss, it is not dwelled upon for very long or very hard. This is, after all, a great way to live.

I woke. I could spot the edge of my phone halfway under my pillow and dug for it, checking the time. I'd become used to waking just a minute or two before my alarm and today had been no exception. Sunlight poured through the shielded windows. Sunlight poured through the shielded windows. Sunlight poured through the shielded windows.

Jacket Guy never misses, not once. Always. It was your thing, your soul and your being, you were the guy who wanted everybody in the world to give you a reason and for the most part, for most of the episodes through 1985 and 1986, they did. "Have you figured it out?" "Have I figured what out?" "Why an elevator would open when the car isn't there?" Sunlight poured through the shielded windows. "What do you have? Endless, repeated wire systems. A hydrogen bomb that keeps performing fission, keeps replenishing its source. In a word: renewable. In two: perpetual motion." "No, he acquiesces, he lends the loaves because of persistence. Now, there are genuine religious applications for this story. It's thought to be instructive to the action of prayer. Ask and ask, and ask again, and it will be given you. But more than that, it's an escape valve in an action. It has no other meaning. It's transactional." Sunlight poured through the shielded windows. Sunlight poured through the shielded windows. "You're gonna have to be brave, Bo. Okay? I need that from you. Your brother needs time to figure this out, same as us. We're all going to—going to process this in different ways. You know what process means?" "Asian representation, and all that. And maybe people say they're still just one-off, supporting characters and whatever, and yeah, by modern standards a lot of it is still pretty insensitive. But somebody had to take the first step, and it was them, and I'm proud of that. Look at me, not even Chinese, and proud." *The stars are brightly shining, it is the night of our dear savior's birth.* Sunlight poured through the shielded windows. "Goodnight. I love you." "She loved you. Umma loved you." "There wasn't enough time." "There wasn't enough time." "There wasn't enough time." "There wasn't enough time." "There wasn't enough time." "There wasn't enough time."

You couldn't understand. I don't, either. I'm doing my best, but this part's always escaped me. I've been over it again and again and again and can't seem to understand. The moment in which she turned her head, the split second before I saw her face, the instant a crack opened up in the light, in the sky and the road and the air itself like a suctioned hole tearing itself apart. I don't know how long I stayed in there, how much time passed. It was, in a way, like being dead, no thoughts, no dreams, something that doesn't take substance until you're out, which, of course, isn't supposed to happen under normal circumstances. I miss it. I want to go back.

Does this answer your question? I've tried to lay it out for you. I've tried to give you every possible reason I could think of in the hopes that one of them might just satisfy you. I've been back and forth so many times that I can barely keep track anymore. It's tough living this way, in a jar of my thoughts. I can't imagine doing this forever. The choices are: go back to the dark, or go forward, and I am still not sure which way I have decided to go.

I go between opinions when I think about that last episode, the season—and inadvertently series—finale, "The Doorway." Obviously your writers had something major planned for season three. Something that moved the entire space out of a cop procedural and into something else, a dichotomy, a struggle between good and evil. Which wasn't a bad thing. Shows were, of course, allowed to evolve. There'd be half a season or more, I'm sure, dedicated to rescuing Moto, defeating the Demonhead, rehabilitating life back to something more recognizable, surely, and then—what? Back to business? Would you stay around Little China? Would you put Moto in a school? Retire from the force? Or better yet, were you going to die? Go out with a bang, defusing a bomb or taking a bullet meant for somebody else. Was that your destiny? Would you find this fair? And more importantly, did you see it coming?

"The Doorway" might have ruined me. What did they imagine would happen to all the kids like me who'd grown up watching that show? For something as cruel and evil as that to happen and for there never to be another word on the matter. What would they do with a revival movie? Go back in right where they left off? With different actors? Bullshit. You fucked yourself with that one. There was no way to save it. In your mythos Moto is gone forever, you are kneeling in that ransacked apartment, terrified, forever. There wasn't enough time. There wasn't enough time. What you had is a crisis of opportunity. And that opportunity's gone, never again to be replaced. That's what destroyed me. That's what I have to carry around in my heart every day of my life. Knowing that you'll never see rescue. And now, thirty years later, with Antonin Haubert dead and in the ground, with *Raider* relegated to sideshow status, that "Asian cop show that was kind of racist," that's where you still are. Locked in there forever. I hate it, Raider. I hate what they did to you. Why can't I ever protect you from anything? You don't deserve this. You've never deserved it. You saved my life, man, you kept me alive. Maybe that's what I've been trying to say all along, that the reason is, more or less, you, and always has been.

I can feel pressure in my wrist, the one I haven't broken, and heaviness in my feet down below. It's as if something full-bodied is lying on top of me, pushing me farther and farther into the softness, so slowly as to be almost comforting. I'm tired. I want to sleep. I haven't moved in so long, I've almost forgotten how in this state. I'm thinking of you in the hospital after the shootout, the way you must have hung in the balance, not knowing whether you would live or die, afraid of what would happen to Moto, afraid of everybody, everything. Maybe I am the same way. Afraid of my father, and my brother. Afraid of the way I've treated them. Afraid of Lev, of my job, of a company that employs me, afraid of doing my job, afraid of losing my job, afraid of my apartment, of my phone, afraid of the fucking girl with the earrings in my lobby, of all things. Afraid of you. Afraid of myself. Would it be this easy? Would it really be so, that after all this time I could just do like you do in the episode in which we find you in your hospital room with Moto, in which you turn your head, swallow spit, and—

—open my eyes. The light is the first thing that blasts me, so unbelievably harsh that the first thing I do is close them right back up again, sinking gratefully back into the darkness, thinking to myself that I'm good, I don't need to wake up after all. But those thoughts, however good and comfortable at first, don't stay for long. This isn't what I've set out to do. I've got purpose. I've got conviction. So I open my eyes again, and see white. Hazy shapes. It's not unlike being in a commute, I have to say. Things go from blurry to nearly focused then back to blurry again based on where I decide to put my energy. I turn my head, moving against pillows that smell like antiseptic.

I lift my hand, then a gunshot claps my ears. A door has been flung open. There are voices all around me, lights being aimed straight into my eyes, hands around my ankles. I am being told to blink and open my mouth and press down with my feet and take a deep breath and try to make a noise with my mouth and make a tummy muscle and make a fist and about a hundred other things that I don't understand even though I try, and I really do try. The light feels like it's burning the back of my brain, it's so bright. After a while I stop trying to coordinate my limbs and sink back down. The voices get hazier, more unhinged. I am closing my eyes, falling back down, falling asleep, giving up. Next time, next time.

I wake. I move my eyes under my eyelids, slowly, then more urgently, and lift them, finding a white wall, a television plugged into the corner. I tilt my head down, at a paper gown under which I don't even think I have underwear on. Blankets cover my feet. Sunlight pours in through the blinds. I see her.

Same sheet of black hair, same little pink heat in her cheeks, hands folded in her lap, sitting, looking at me, staring with wide eyes as I move my head, trying to get a better view of her. Min.

She opens her mouth, reaches forward, and takes my hand. I swallow, and it's like forcing down a ball of sawdust. I toss my head around, glimpsing a cute little baggie of saline above my head, a wall of monitors and instruments above me. Min squeezes my hand.

"What do you need?" she asks me, urgently. I mouth, making the first syllable, *wa—*

"Water?"

She pulls something from behind her, a little table on wheels, and pours a paper cup for me. She puts her hand on my forehead, which feels good, and lets me drink. I drain the cup and try to ask for more. She gives it to me. When I'm done, we spend a good portion of a minute staring at each other. She keeps turning around, looking for somebody through the window to the hallway, finding none. Her hand is still warm and soft in mine. She breathes deeply, looking at me.

"Welcome back."

I feel like I've rolled my eyes or at least done something that makes her smile, and I'm happy to see it. I open my mouth again. *Where am I*, I try to say. It comes out, "W-wa-m-m-m-Ee."

I've heard it back through my ears. I try again. "Wee-mee-m-m-m."

Min's face falls, as I keep trying. Again and again. I can see it so clearly in my head. *Where am I, Where am I.* But the sounds coming from me aren't anything of the sort. My mouth isn't moving the way I want it to, my tongue seems like a dead instrument lounging lazily behind my teeth. I can barely feel anything there. I try speaking again. "Wa-mm-e-t."

Min says: "Try to relax. Okay? Deep breaths."

I'm panicking now, moving my mouth, giving breath and finding about half the time that my lungs don't even obey. I'm asking *what happened, what happened.* Eventually I'm flailing so much that the door opens. A doctor and a nurse enter. I see Min ushered to the side while the nurse puts a hand on the wrist connected to the saline. I'm being told to calm down, to breathe. I'm handed a notepad and a pen. The first attempts I make to spell end with the pen slipping from my fingers. Slowly, with the thing gripped tight in my fist, I manage to write in loopy letters: *No talk.*

The doctor, my doctor, exchanges a glance with the nurse.

“You’re right,” she begins. “What I want you to remember is you’ve been asleep for a long time. You haven’t used your body in months. We—”

She stopped herself.

“Why don’t we start from the beginning.”

My eyes go beside her to Min, off to the left. My hand is out, open. I’m looking at her, begging. She slides closer and takes my hand. The doctor takes the second chair beside me.

“I’ll try to be as precise as I can. You’ve been in a medically induced coma for the past two months as a result of a stroke that almost killed you. We’re attributing it to acute stress, some irregular heart activity. For your age, we’ve found this is rather rare. You lost oxygen flow to your brain for about twenty seconds, and in that time, your speech center sustained critical damage. It’s likely—you’ve lost the ability to speak. Permanently.”

I blink, squeezing Min’s hand harder. She’d said two months. I am almost sure she said two months. I raise my other hand to my face, finding thick scruff on my chin and neck, my hair curled past my ears. I pick up my pen. *Two?*

“That’s correct. You opened your eyes for the first time last week.”

Min is staring down at our hands, listening. I write: *Job.*

“Our family planner has been in contact with your old manager. Your stroke occurred about a week after you formally resigned your position, but he’s arranged for you to receive an extended severance package given the circumstances. Call it pension.”

I shake my head, trying again to speak. *Not one week, not one week, lying, lie.* Each time they come out as gibberish. My doctor gestures to the pad.

"I know this is a lot to take in. Our plan is to let you rest intermittently while we try to answer the questions you have."

I flail, scrambling for the pencil. *Apartment.*

"Your employer has taken care of the details. The lease on your apartment has been renewed for another year, after which you'll be able to make your own decisions. You're awake, which is an extremely good sign, but your body is still very weak. You'll need physical therapy for a time before we discharge you, and for a couple months after you leave as well."

No money, hospital.

"That's been arranged."

Dad. Where is my dad. Brother.

My doctor takes a pause. She gives another look to the nurse, then to Min.

"Perhaps we should let you rest and continue on later this afternoon, if you're feeling up to it."

I look between the three of them, pointing to the words on my pad, circling *Dad*. There seemed to be no way around it. After a very long time, Min draws close.

"I'm so sorry. He . . . it looks like, on the morning you had your . . . you know—"

I wait for her to keep talking, to tell me in clear tones that they had saved him. That he was in the next room over, maybe. That he was on his way to see me. I shake my head, silently. Min doesn't say anything more.

"It was a heart attack. Quick," says my doctor. I just keep shaking my head. It doesn't feel like I ever imagined, not like anything else does. People often exaggerate, it's their best quality. They say that things sometimes happen to change the look of the world when rarely they do, when, rather, things changed gradually without their noticing it. But not this time. This time, the words take all that's left of me. I blink tears from my eyes. I shake my head for what seems like minutes, while they stand there and watch me. Min takes tissues and dabs my face with them. I wait, scrawling on the pad *Kaz.* Min keeps rubbing my hand, it's all I can feel while she speaks.

"You're going to have to talk with the police, once they get here. There's—well, I'm not sure what exactly, but your brother's waiting for a trial right now. They're saying—some kind of armed altercation. Happened in a drugstore a few days after you went to the hospital. I don't know. That was around the time of the last blackout, long one, too. It was chaos here."

I've run out of paper. I tap at it frantically with my hand while Min turns the page for me. *Not true.* I am envisioning his face, not my brother's, hardly. I see him, the only one I know capable of pulling something like this off. To put Kaz in jail, to remind me what Io Emsworth had told me that first day I learned to commute: that he was watching, and would always be. Lev. And I think, repeating his name in my head, that he'll never talk to me again, that I'll never be able to prove it, and it will stay with me until the day I die.

"Were you close?" Min asks me.

I keep pointing at my page, though it does nothing. My doctor and the nurse seem ready to leave.

"I'd like to let you rest," she says. "We'll be back in a few hours' time to check in—"

I'm told more, but I don't hear it. I struggle, moving my shoulders, trying to make them stay, but they've already gone out into the hallway. The door closes behind them. Min hasn't yet let go of my hand. I'm allowed a second to notice her, really see her face. In the time passed, there is almost nothing that I notice has changed about her. Hair a bit longer. I find myself holding on to her as hard as I can, trying to keep breathing. She's been coming here for two months, I realize. I scribble: *how did you find me.*

Min reads my handwriting. "I didn't. They found my number in your bag."

She almost smiles.

"For a while, I was never going to see you again. I was happy."

I don't know what to say. My fingers and toes are numb. My chest feels like a vacuum, depleted, entirely empty. It's hard to take breaths. My father is dead. My brother—I close my eyes. I write: *why did you come.*

It breaks my heart to look at her. I'm sorry for what I did. I don't know how to say it to her. It crosses my mind that if in any way I still deserve her, it would be because people, in some primitive and primordial way, need at least one thing in their lives to give meaning to everything they do, and since I had none, not anymore, it would have to be her. And it is not the look she gives me, reading my note, or the feel of her hand in mine, or the vast space I feel all around me, the way in which

I've grown so small and the world around me so big, but instead the little hint of pain in her eyes that tells me, almost before she does it, what's about to happen. That somehow, what I am is no longer what I used to be, that suddenly—for the second time in my life—there is a different world I have woken up in than the one in which I was knocked asleep. That I lie here, unable to speak, unable to do anything but look while she gets up out of her chair and shows me the round curve of her stomach under her shirt.

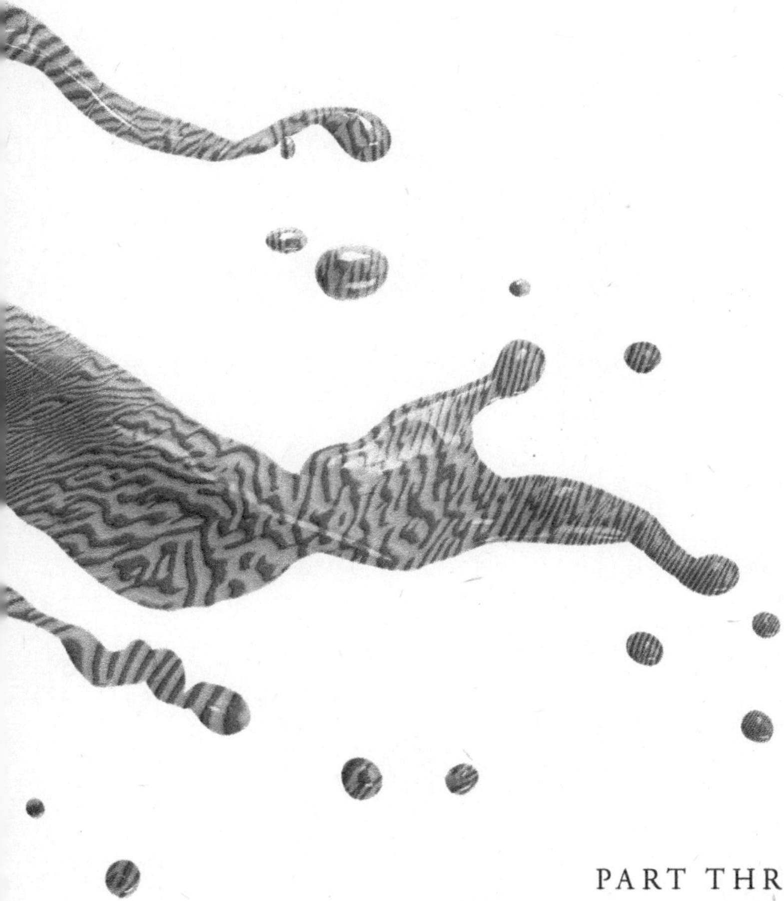

PART THREE

Pension

14

Lev fixed his eyes over the coffee table to where Blue sat, saying nothing. The city rose behind them, growing dim.

"What is it that you want to know?"

Blue looked him up and down, sitting with his ankles crossed. There was much to be said for the way he was unafraid. It had taken him a while to become so, he reasoned, not without serious trial and error. But no, he was not afraid of Lev. There was no longer any reason to be. It was, after all, why he had finally come and decided to ask the questions he had wanted to ask for years.

/ / I'd like to know from the beginning. / /

Lev waved his hand, dismissing him. "What good would that possibly do you? You know everything."

/ / I want you to tell me. / /

"And your plan is to . . . extort a truth from me under threat of death?"

/ / I never said I was going to kill you. I only said I would if you didn't stay straight with me. / /

"Can you really look at either of us and use the word 'straight'?" Lev rolled his eyes. "Are you seeing that slick producer type, by the way?"

/ / Tor? / /

"I knew he had a name like that," Lev said. "Fitting."

/ / I don't see anybody. / /

"You're not yet a misfit toy, you have time." Lev glanced down the hallway. With a limp hand, he beckoned for his cup of tea, and Blue supplied it. "Won't you ever trust me again?"

/ / It's a little late for that. / /

"No?" Lev asked. "You've got me right where you want me. You hold the chips, big boy, all of the power. You'd like me to tell you from the beginning, yes?"

/ / The generators. Were they ever going to work? Did the batteries even work? / /

"The batteries worked in the theoretical sense," Lev said. "What were we to do? Io had already lined up a board of directors, Best Buy. There had already been press out there, magazine covers. We realized: this was going to be far bigger than any of us. And it was. We lit the fires and hoped the rain would come, just in the nick of time."

/ / What did Io know about that? / /

"Io was a silly little girl. She played at a level of delusion just right for someone of her age and stature. It helped us, tremendously. The early capital wouldn't have come without her."

He smirked at this.

"I think they were going to be lithium, to be honest. Who could tell the difference? They last only marginally longer than regular batteries, the consumer thinks: inconceivable! So they really do work! They short out, or stay the same, they think: must be a dud, better buy another pack. People are exceedingly stupid. Io was very, very good at packaging ideas to exceedingly stupid people, and that's what she did. We needed bigger office space, manufacturing. Io promised us so much, there were stars in her eyes when she talked. There was valuable, cutting-edge research just on the cusp of uncovering something extraordinary, locked away in the biochemistry of brains. She didn't understand much of it, only that the research couldn't continue without more information. The first commute, it ran away from us, things were so fast after that. Nobody knew where it would lead us. Perhaps that was what made it dangerous, what would come to be at stake, the lives we'd involve on our way there."

/ / Don't pretend you care, / / Blue said, quietly. / / You've never said Ry's name, not in twenty years. / /

"And you have?" Lev asked.

He smiled after a moment. "You've always flattered yourself. For good reason, sometimes. Would I ever forget that you were once that pretty young thing they pulled out of the elevator shaft? Gorgeous. Did I embellish you to Io to get you a job? So what if I did?"

/ / I think you'd better stop trying to change the subject. / /

"You've got me there." Lev put his hands up. "I thought you knew the batteries didn't work. You were always so freshly sarcastic around me. I could only guess. We all knew, didn't we? How else does one idea birth an entire economy without being just a little bit bullshit?"

/ / Do you see it that way? Bullshit? / /

"Don't you?"

/ / It was real to a lot of innocent people. People with families. Whose lives went up in smoke in a single day when the company folded. Did you think about them? / /

"No." Lev shrugged. He paused a moment. "It was very easy not to, honestly."

Blue realized he was clenching his jaw shut, and loosened his grip. Lev looked amused by this.

"Is this what you came for? Are you here to air your gripes? I'll play the therapist. Maybe you forget all the time we spent together after your commutes. I learned a great deal about you."

/ / I thought the whole point was that I didn't remember them. / / Blue said.

"The tech was experimental. I didn't know exactly how you'd react—risks were taken."

/ / Tell me how it worked. / /

Lev gave a pitiable sigh, collapsing slightly in his seat.

"We used to have something quite pleasant, you know. You come over here, I make you coffee, I make you tea. It's different today. Why is it so—"

He paused, paying attention. Something had changed in his demeanor, making his frame smaller, frailer. He was just that, after all. A dying man. It had been so long.

"No, no, it can't be," he whispered. "There's no way."

/ / I'm not saying anything. / /

"No, you don't have to," Lev said, bewildered for the first time since they'd met, "that's just it. I've seen this coming, haven't I?"

/ / Tell me how it worked, Lev. The batteries. You owe me this. / /

Lev was still staring at him, peculiarly. It seemed, for a moment, that he would not cooperate the way Blue had wanted. Blue had never known Lev to play the way he was supposed to. But he had hoped, nonetheless. He was in the middle of this thought when Lev drank again from his cup.

"They obliterated a framework around the consciousness. A framework used by the brain, the mind, to place a person within a reality. Take, for example, the heat of a room. The feel of one's clothes on the skin. Gravity. These are things acting on us, of course, at all times, yet we don't have to concentrate on all of them at once to feel their presence, to be a conscious mind within these constraints. That was the framework. Something happened to that framework when one commuted. It fell apart. It transformed in ways we couldn't predict. Some were waking up, telling us about visions they'd had of other people, other places—"

/ / Other times. / /

Lev caught his eye.

"Who gave you that idea?"

/ / Don't play dumb with me. I was there. / /

Lev pursed his lips.

/ / What were you trying to achieve? / /

"Anything we could. We followed every route, every tailspin, every tangent. We wanted to know. And why not? The power we held. You couldn't imagine."

/ / Did it hurt, then? / /

Lev smirked at him.

"You'll have to be more specific."

// Did it hurt to be found out? I watched the news all day when the feds started taking you down. I wondered where you were. //

"You'd never let those things go, would you?" Lev said. "I suppose it was only fair you wouldn't. It was always going to fail. Scams always get found out, once money becomes involved. There was nothing we could do about that."

// Who's we? //

Lev smiled, again, and said nothing.

// Io didn't know that. // said Blue. // I know she scrambled, in those last months. Trying to save it. I know she thought there was still something to save. //

"She did, didn't she?" Lev almost laughed. "Never failed to surprise me."

// Why not tell her? //

"Darling," Lev said, calmly, "did you ever really believe that girl was in charge of anything? Anything at all? She's been in jail near twenty years. What a ridiculous thing happening now, the fandom around her. Those idiotic movies."

They had reached a pause, sitting there, staring at each other. The apartment had gone dark, and, just as the sun finally dipped away, the lights flared on above their heads, throwing Lev's face into shadowed contrasts.

// You've never apologized for putting my brother in jail. //

"I had nothing to do with that."

Blue appeared, briefly, to smile.

// We are beyond lies, aren't we? Don't I deserve that? //

"Ask me what I could've possibly gained from that. Ask me his name, even. I couldn't tell you."

It seemed, almost, that Lev had gone too far, but the shred of doubt that had lit briefly in his face was buried away just as quickly.

"I do regret the dead ones," he said. "What was her name, the one you tried to warn? Lacey? Samantha?"

/ / Her name was Ry. / /

"So it was," Lev nodded. "You know, big boy, you blame yourself too much for what happened to her, to those friends who'd heard the two of you. You were difficult to keep track of, sometimes. The monitoring wasn't easy. Seeing that if they hadn't been dealt with, the feds would've never investigated. We have you to thank for it all."

He said it gravely, as though already expecting a response. Blue tried to picture what he felt, then. In the hospital, the five more months he spent in physical therapy, the day he saw her face on the news, the two others, the ones he'd spoken to that day in the concourse, the first ones, the only ones, he had ever told about the commutes. It was perhaps the way it had happened, almost without notice, without consequence, that had broken him worst of all. Three innocent people who had heard something they shouldn't have and paid for it with their lives.

/ / They didn't have to die. / /

"You don't know a thing. It makes you vastly amusing," said Lev. He cleared his throat, uninterested.

"Have you decided, then?"

/ / Decided what? / /

He could barely see Lev's eyes, but guessed at the look on his face, reminding him of the control he did not have, and perhaps never did.

"Whether you're going to kill me or not?"

Blue got off at the stop he'd been told to and ducked through the snow into the liquor store whose window he could see vaguely through the grey haze. He read an exorbitant amount stamped onto the side of a bottle of cognac and swiped his wrist over the counter to pay for it. The apartment was just another block up the street, his in-ears notified him. While he walked, he clenched his fists, trying to stay warm. The tremor in his chest had not quite gone down and was still reverberating, oddly, inside his head at irregular intervals. His joints ached.

He found the door, rang the button for the right number, and was buzzed inside. He climbed three flights of stairs, stopping at each landing, and came to the door just as she opened it. His daughter was holding a spatula and dressed warmly. Her eyes lit up, falling on his face, opening her arms wide.

"I was beginning to think you'd bailed," she said, holding him close. Blue closed his eyes, feeling her in his arms, summoning, as he always did, what it had felt like to hold her for the first time, a memory that arrived now without invitation whenever he saw her. Both joy and sadness mixed inside it, as he breathed in the cooking fumes from her hallway and said / / Merry Christmas, Jem. / /

15

She ushered him inside and took his coat. Wafts of conversations mingled with television noises floated from beyond the hallway. Jem was asking him if the subways were crowded, if the weather was warm enough. He nodded and gave his answers, wanting to see her clearly. It had been at least a year since they'd seen each other; she was so busy in school. History, he knew, classics, but she might have changed her mind in the time that had elapsed. She never liked speaking for long about these sorts of things and he could never tell if it was because she didn't want to share or because she feared he didn't really want to know.

"Mom's cooking," she said to him. She paused. "Are you going to be okay?"

/ / This? Still? / /

"I'm just making sure, Jesus." Jem rolled her eyes. She was still looking at him. "This voice of yours, Dad. It's . . . something."

She had said it sadly, almost, in a way that he noticed blaringly whether she'd intended him to or not. He followed her down the hall, winding a path through walls that almost touched their shoulders as they passed. Min had bought the apartment shortly after the divorce, around the time Jem had started kindergarten. Small and cramped but within the bounds of the city, which is what she had always liked. She had never asked his opinion, not that he had expected her to. They spilled out into the square kitchen, and he saw her back. She was washing plates and cutlery in the sink while the television blared. He watched her turn her head and spot him over her shoulder. She looked good, still; she always looked good. She came over and put a kiss on his cheek, dampening his shoulders with her wet hands. Her lips were there and gone a moment later.

"Dad brought us cognac," Jem said over his shoulder.

"That's certainly interesting, considering you've never tried it before," Min told her, eyeing him. "You and I'll share it, yes?"

You don't like cognac, Blue signed.

"You never bought it for me," she said. "What's this? I thought you'd gone and gotten a new voice box put in. We've been hearing about it all afternoon."

Jem had brought over a square-looking boy that towered above them all, the one who had asked for the cognac.

"Dad, this is—" She said something very Russian or maybe Romanian that Blue didn't catch. He shook the kid's hand, firmly. It didn't matter; he would call him Square. Jem filled in the blanks. They had met in their Latin class and had been together since the fall. It was inconceivably early to have brought him home for Christmas. Min was still waiting for an answer. He shrugged.

It's hard to get used to. Easier this way.

"Did it hurt?"

Jem had briefly frowned at him from behind Square's arm but said nothing. Blue shook his head. He showed her the little pink dot on his neck where the implant had gone in. Min touched it gently with her fingertips.

"It looks like it hurt."

It didn't.

Min smirked at him. "What did you go and do this for, anyway?"

The television behind him, which had been blaring the news, had begun featuring the clip that had been running for the past few days. Jem and Square took their seats on the couch, talking among themselves. The man called L'Aspirant had caused equal parts outrage and acclaim for his comments of the previous week in which he'd argued in a candid and improvised moment near the end of a press junket that Io Emsworth deserved "little to no blame" for the deaths of the three Flux employees she'd been imprisoned for in an offhand post-interview debrief. In an ash-grey suit, his hair slicked back over the thinning area along the crown of his head, L'Aspirant did not make it known whether the question had been planned. Surely there were greater problems warranting consideration by the man most expected would be president by the next January. Blue had seen the clip in various spurts on televisions, on his heads-up display, and elsewhere. It had not yet ceased to floor him: the way L'Aspirant looked, a marked difference from the way he had portrayed himself even just half a decade earlier, before he had announced his candidacy. In the span of a few years, he had quit his acting career, married, welcomed two beautiful blond-haired children, and begun to lend his support publicly toward various wealthy and influential liberal meetinghouses. Blue remembered a time in which the man—now a suit wearer, now a family-first public servant—painted his nails black, wore dresses on the covers of fashion magazines. He had played rock stars, sex addicts, policemen, murderers, aliens, billionaires (he now was one in real life), and the like. He had argued, a year earlier, that the world, despite knowing his face, did not know his personhood.

A question had been framed early after the announcement of his candidacy for president that referenced a film he'd made in his thirties in which he—in the role of a serial rapist and philanderer—had brutally beaten his wife to death. "People need to separate the art from the life," he had said. "The film was a film, the role was a role. I trust the people of this country to know the difference. They are smart people."

It had been a primetime interview Blue had watched in his living room with the lights off, not wanting to but unable to stop. L'Aspirant was sitting in a spacious and handsome living room set with a live fire, across a coffee table from one of the new investigative correspondents for the network, a young woman whose bright lipstick looked so perfect that it might as well have been lasered onto her face. "Let me ask you this, Hadrien," she'd said. "Do the allegations that surfaced against your father when you were in your twenties—just starting your career—justify a response from you in this new, political context?"

L'Aspirant, who had been given said name by a digital newsmagazine in a profile that highlighted his French ancestry and numerous grand- and great-grandparents' military service, had nodded, firmly and pensively, while receiving this question. He had appeared to think about it for a long time, drawing his eyes downward to his hands and interlaced fingers in his lap.

"My father was an imperfect man," he had said, at last, "a man with numerous vices, who hurt almost everybody around him in a cycle of violence that—both tragically and inevitably—ended in his death. If you're telling me that I as a political candidate as opposed to a private citizen need to orient myself differently around him now that the stakes, the surrounding environment, is different, I'd say to you: I was just as known then as now, if not for my career, but for my last name. The consequences were just as dire should I speak. I don't believe there's anything more that I can say about my father. I'm interested in the wills and welfare of the American people."

Blue had liked the phrase "wills and welfare," even though he didn't quite understand what L'Aspirant had meant. It was a beautiful phrase, educated and glossed, that had done its job. It was a phrase L'Aspirant began to repeat at his speaking engagements and campaign appearances. It was as yet unclear what might become of the Emsworth soundbite. Some critics were indignant, accusing L'Aspirant of exercising his staggering privilege with stunning amounts of indiscretion, others began analyzing his inherently capitalist opinion as indicative of legislation that was sure to come within his future administration. L'Aspirant had yet to comment on the backlash surrounding the interview, and it was unlikely he would, at least not for a couple days, after which it would no longer be news people cared about.

Jem was looking at the screen, curling her arm around the crook of Square's elbow.

"He's still very, very hot. I'm disappointed in myself. Am I just going to vote for him because he's hot?"

Min had come around with banchan and was setting up the coffee table around the couch with four place settings. Blue could smell the sharp kick of sesame oil coming from the stove. Min could cook Korean so much better than he could. She sat, across from him on the other end of the couch sectional, ordering them to eat. They broke chopsticks and ate. Square was staying in the country rather than going home to family on account of some late finals. Jem described for them the hell of the train station the previous day.

"My friends and I were watching his show last week, the miniseries," she said after a while. "I don't know, it's weird. Maybe we just all need to stop watching his movies. I mean, Reagan was an actor. Mom, what was that like?"

"That's very funny," Min said, dangerously. "Call me eighty years old one more time."

"Well, you've heard of that show. It's pretty good, considering all that story behind it. You can tell what was going on in the writers' room when they were mapping it out. The way they take the cop and the precinct and turn it all around into this majorly corrupt empire. It's depressing."

"But largely true," said Square. "It's the one thing of his I respect."

He had said it as though expecting gasps, applause. Blue ate, silently. He had not brought it on himself to speak about L'Aspirant's last project before his retirement from acting. What was there to say about *Moto*, anyway? A young Vietnamese orphan is raised by a white police officer with political aspirations and paraded to the public as a grateful ward while the officer climbs the ladder to police chief, then mayor, then governor. The child, played by three different actresses, eventually grows suspicious in her young adulthood to the circumstances of her kidnapping from her immigrant family, and eventually sees through his fall from grace, gaining in herself: a voice. It seemed exceedingly dark. L'Aspirant played the police officer, a being of pure malice who regularly lied, embezzled, assaulted, and eventually killed in search of satiating his hunger for power.

Min had seen something on his face and spoke.

"TV off, Jem. Let's talk to each other like human beings."

It was not unclear to Blue: the show's topical commentary, cheap shots, all in all. The corrupt officer's name was even Thomas Raider. It had been partly written, produced, and for three episodes directed by L'Aspirant himself. A title card before the final episode, in which Moto plans to kill her adoptive father but is beaten to it by the mother of a dead child whose case had languished in the courts, read: "To Fathers, Everywhere." The message was blunt, inelegant. They had at least gotten the jacket right, same color and make. Blue didn't want to think about whether that was a point toward, or against, its favor.

"So"—Min had addressed Square—"you're studying with our Jem? What's your concentration?"

"Byzantine," said Square, "it's a fascinating era and people. We've been to the ancient history museum uptown. It's one of my favorite places on earth."

"I'll take you, Mom," Jem said, excitedly. "The revamped wing is unbelievable."

"I was just telling Jem," said Square, "we'll have time to go back there after New Year's, I'm sure, before the semester starts."

Min smiled appreciatively at him. Blue almost laughed. He knew that face. He was stunningly familiar with that face of hers.

"What were we talking about?" Jem asked. "Oh yeah, L'Aspirant, new president. Mom? Yes or no?"

"Who can tell." Min waved her hands. "I don't expect much from him. Famous people will never stop being so attractive to us. If it won't change, maybe he'll rise to the occasion."

"I think it's pretty sick," said Square. "It's like we're forcing ourselves to tiptoe around the most inconceivably disadvantageous political situation, the only reason being that it's the one available to us. He's such an asshole in his interviews. He's never seen hardship. He acts *better* in, like, every way."

"He *is* better," Jem said, "he's famous."

"We are so, so screwed."

"And they thought we were pessimistic," Min said.

"I think the country is resigned to somebody like him being in power," Square said, "It's convenient and shiny, so they don't complain."

They had nothing to say to this, despite Jem's glances in their direction. Min had served her pot on an oven mitt in the center of the table, short rib and root vegetables that had almost all gone but was still robed in steam wafting from the table. Blue had not had anything like it in at least a decade.

How long did it take you to make this?

"Relax," Min said. "I wanted to."

"What do you call it?" said Square.

"Galbi jjim," Jem said. "It's beef, soy sauce, and sugar, stewed for hours. Mom, you haven't made this in so long."

"Why is everybody so surprised today?" Min poured herself and Blue a glass each of cold wine from the fridge. "It's Christmas. Might as well."

"Sir," Square said, "Jem told me you've done a lot of magazine work. What was that like? Print work, I mean. I don't know of any left out there."

"There aren't," Jem translated, watching Blue's hands. "Magazines were dying for decades before I started. Even then, the work was not very—sexy."

She groaned. "Please don't ever make me say that again."

"It was a little sexy," Min said. "Those big offices. You were with at least a dozen firms while Jem was growing up. There was always somewhere new to go. We told everyone he held a record: most laid-off employee in America. What is it really, anymore? Just some social feeds. In-ear audiocasts, newspots. Magazines made kings, fifty years ago."

You're embarrassing me.

"Your father is indignant," Min said. "Luckily, we aren't married."

"Is that American Sign Language or Korean?" asked Square.

"It's American. They never taught me Korean," Jem said.

"What? Really?"

Jem shrugged. "We didn't speak it at home."

"But," said Square, eyes wide, "you never wanted to learn it on your own?"

"Have we never talked about this before?"

How could they, Blue thought. They'd been together for four days.

"I'm sorry—" Square looked between them. "It's just, my parents taught me Czech because they wanted me to be able to speak to my family back home. I don't know what I'd do without it."

"We have the genes," Min said, laughing awkwardly, "but we're Americans. Everybody, eat."

"Was that a conscious decision?"

Blue hunched himself over his bowl, preferring to count grains of rice rather than answer. Jem had gone quiet.

"It was," Min said, with finality.

"Why?"

/ / We didn't want her to confuse herself with a fob. / / said Blue quietly. He wasn't sure just how far he'd meant it as a joke, though his intentions were pure, but the look Min gave him was hint enough.

"There's a lot of literature on cultural assimilation that argues parents erase identity by cherry-picking heritage," said Square. "It's—well—I don't want to say irresponsible—"

He paled, saying it. Blue got the sense he had awoken from a trance, aware now that he was not among some stoner friends at a beat-up kitchen table. Jem was staring intently at the side of his face.

/ / You make a fair bit of sense. / / said Blue, frowning a moment. He didn't know where the implant had dug out "a fair bit." It certainly hadn't been him, but he wasn't complaining. / / We'll remember for the next kid. / /

"Dad—" Jem said, quietly.

"I didn't mean any disrespect, sir," said Square.

/ / None at all. / / said Blue, setting his bowl down. / / Except, you might be saying, none of us is really Asian. Is that what you mean? / /

"No, not at—"

/ / The assumption there being, we don't know how to operate in this country. How to be Asian and American. How to . . . what? Raise our kids? / /

Square had gone entirely colorless, a feat for his prodigious blood flow, Blue thought, given the boy was already white as chalk. He kept opening his mouth to speak but was silenced each time by Jem's hand on his leg.

"I didn't mean any disrespect," he said again.

They had arrived at a point familiar to Blue, and, he suspected, to Jem and to Min as well. And for what? He wouldn't even remember Square a month from now, he was mostly sure, and neither would Jem. He always did this, attacked, dug his fingers in, when he could have—should have—let go. Why had it surprised him? He had not quite forgotten the shouting, before the divorce, before Min had bought the apartment and taken Jem. Kaz, before that. He tried to think on it, finding nothing. He tried not to go there whenever Kaz popped into his mind. But that was the thing about memory. It often obeyed the capriciousness of a mind trying to hide from guilt, but one, always, had to live with the deceit.

"I think we all need to calm down." Min was first to break the silence, swirling her glass. She had stopped looking at him.

It was peculiar, to look at them both, Min and Jem, the way they'd appeared to brace themselves. They expected more from him and were resigned to the fact that they could not stop him. He looked down at his hands, flat on his lap, and there was nothing more to be done. Soon, the stew lay before them, cold, frozen over with a layer of white fat.

Jem was rummaging through a closet in her old bedroom down the hall, he could hear through the door when he knocked. He listened to the noises stop, the light little footsteps across the carpet, the door swinging inward. The light fell on her face; she had tied her hair behind her and leaned against the frame with her weight on one foot.

I'm going, he told her. She nodded, smiling. They waited, briefly, each for the other to speak.

I didn't mean to get upset.

She glanced down the hall, where Min was serving Square a slice of cake on the couch.

I know. They signed when they needed privacy. He thought of the many afternoons, the community soccer league she'd begged to join at eight. *What's for dinner*, she'd signed to him from the field, and he'd laughed so hard the other parents had given him dirty looks. It was one of the last times.

Where are you headed tonight? he asked her.

Mom's taking us to Joe and Allen's, and they invited their cousins. I think we're going caroling.

He didn't know who Joe or Allen were. He nodded, appreciatively.

I missed you.

She told him that she missed him, too, quickly, and he saw, where her eyes flitted, that she was looking over his shoulder down the hallway. He put out his arms, and she hugged him.

"Where are you going?"

They pulled apart. He shrugged. "Come with us?" Jem said. He shook his head.

I don't want to make things awkward.

She didn't argue. It wasn't what he wanted, an argument, but he didn't go so far as not to let himself feel disappointed. It was the thing that surprised him the most, the abrupt end to the fighting, the silence. A silence in which he wondered: who was it, really, who had accepted the other? In less than a week she would be gone again, back to school, away from him, and he would only watch, and wish for something different. He leaned in and put two kisses on her cheeks.

/ / Merry Christmas. / /

She seemed almost to wince at the cut of his voice, and he regretted it. He turned back down the hallway. When he looked back, he saw her back turned, not surveying the clothes she'd laid out on her bed but looking straight down, at her feet, or her hands, he couldn't tell. She was very still.

In the kitchen, Min washed cutlery. She saw him over her shoulder, saying nothing, and shrugged, just a little movement of her shoulders that he knew well and, at the same time, didn't know how to place anymore. They were once his girls. Once. He didn't know what they were anymore, or his place in their lives. Square was absorbed, proactively, in the television, now back on. The snow had started to fall harder outside. Blue made his exit, quickly, closing the door shut behind him.

16

He was up before the sun, pulling the blanket around his mattress tight against the bed frame, tucking the ends in with his fingers. It was the day after Christmas morning, which he'd spent on the couch, watching the snow. The heater had broken in the night and left him shivering in bed, so he wore, now, two pairs of pants and a parka pulled tight over his protruding stomach. He spotted his in-ears on the counter next to his toaster. He didn't feel like checking, though he knew his mailbox would be empty. Jem had been the only one to send him a short text on Christmas morning.

He didn't regret living off his own dollar instead of Lev's. The pension he earned, still populating in his account each quarter, funneled directly into a trust that paid Jem's tuition. He had forfeited the entirety of it in his will. The condo had a bedroom, a small bathroom with stand-up shower, and laundry. He did his own cleaning. He liked today, Sunday, for this reason, though he would be busy today. After lingering by his couch, he picked up the white pearls and replaced them in his ears. News alerts scrolled along the floor where he looked, but he had no interest. No calls. He found himself pulling up a search and typed the name "L'Aspirant" into the air with his fingers. The video he had seen at Min's apartment featured in the first hundred results, along with a message his official social platforms had posted the day before on Christmas. L'Aspirant appeared, before a fire, in a handsomely upholstered couch, with his wife and second baby. Blue let it play.

"Friends," L'Aspirant pronounced, delicately, "this, as it always has been, is a time for reflection. Among family and loved ones, we find ourselves, often, able to wipe away some of the banalities of our lives as best we can."

/ / Jesus. / / Blue said.

"It is here, during the holidays, in which the things we value most are seen to shake loose from the noise, and make themselves best known. For me, that thing is you, the great people of this great country that I hope to gain the right to serve come November of next year—"

Blue swiped the video away with his hand. He recalled a film from ten years ago in which L'Aspirant had used somewhat of the same line. He played an investment banker who falls in love with his rival vice president, played by an actress the world had forgotten after only a few more dud films. It was one of his only romantic comedies, and had enough notability and producer ingenuity to result in several high-stakes awards that season. It was a scene, near the end, taking place on the trading floor, in which L'Aspirant begs the woman not to accept reassignment to Hong Kong. "You've made me think I am valueless," she tells him, tear filled, while papers and bodies fly around them at high speed, the day's trading just begun. The camera closes in on L'Aspirant's face, highlighting the adequate curve of his cheekbone while he licked his lips. He had grown so much stockier than that slim-bodied boy he used to be, putting on muscle and grit for Western roles, a superhero franchise among them. His eyes are lit—already aware that what he is about to say will win him both the girl and a hefty promotion—and he says, "Value is traded, bought and sold. But there is a good outside the market. A thing unable to be assigned value, a thing that is priceless. That thing is you." Blue wondered if he had hired the same writer for his campaign. Other than equating women to objects in the most well-intentioned misogynistic fashion, the line was received well. In another two years, he'd film *Moto* and claim a humanitarian award from the United Coalition Against Domestic Abuse, which he would dedicate, onstage, to the memory of his mother, and to Maxie Lang. It was the first and last time anybody had mentioned that name in more than twenty years.

Blue paused, on the contacts that had swooped into the air above him on his homepage. His first thought was that it would not be worth another try. It had been ten years of the same, sending messages and emails into the air with no response. Blue knew that he was married, that his probation had ended two years ago. He did not know to whom, or where. And perhaps that was the worst of it, the fact that the very last time they'd seen each other, Blue hadn't cared—not even a little bit—what happened between them. The look on Kaz's face in that apartment twenty years ago: hurt, yes, but more than that, doubt. Doubtful that they had ever had much in common. Doubtful that they would ever be more than the distant strangers they had proven themselves to be. Perhaps there was something L'Aspirant was right about, that it was this time of the year that made him weak, susceptible. He had not slept much the night before. He supposed it didn't matter, not anymore. He toggled the name, found the number, dialed a voice call. It rang for thirty seconds, then beeped twice. He opened his mouth, then closed it. The voice would only scare him, he was certain. He opened a textbox.

Hoping you're okay. Just wanted to tell you Merry Christmas.

He sent it, then had another thought.

Please.

He let his cursor hover over the word, then deleted it. The sent message had opened the chain between them, a single message for each of the past five years, this day, to be exact. He read over each iteration, scrolling further. He arrived at what he wanted to see, a single message, the last one Kaz ever sent, dated seven years ago, just a few hours after Blue had sent his that year.

Do not ever contact me again.

Still, Kaz had never blocked his number. Each year, the message had gone through. It would not be different today. He closed out. A ping came in from Tor: *Lobby.*

He patted himself down, finding his wallet and keys. On his dresser, he found the letter he'd written the night before. He looked it over once, then again, found an envelope in his bookshelf, and sealed it. With a pen, he wrote the name on the front, *Jem*, and placed it gently on his couch, propped against the cushions, facing the door. He sent a quick reply to Tor, letting him know he was on his way downstairs, and left the apartment without looking back.

The car that drove them across the river hummed pleasantly under their seats. Tor was reading something in the air, not looking at him. Out of Blue's window, he saw the steelwork of the bridge crisscross in front of him, forming arcs and shapes as they sped by.

"You're due in makeup, quick run-through of the route. Once we have the thumbs-up, we'll start filming," Tor told him. He glanced at him from across the seat. "Don't talk until we roll, not a word. If you remember something, make a note, come back to it. Did you eat?"

/ / I'm not hungry. / /

Tor snorted at this, but didn't comment further. The water was choppy and grey where they rode over it. Blue could feel a tremor in his hands and held them right over his knees where he sat. It would be a straight shot over, then the second merge lane, down the parkway another mile, and it would be there. He had taken the trip so many times. For twenty years he had avoided the route, but it was coming back to him so cleanly that he thought he might have never even left.

"Different?" Tor asked him, gesturing to the window. He was in a calmer mood today, Blue thought. Reasonable. He was on the cusp of a promotion, most likely, for landing the television spot.

/ / Exactly the same as I remember. / /

They entered through a chain-link fence set up along the road. Two guards approached the car, rifles hung from their backs. They checked the driver's ID, then Tor's, then his, and waved them through. Another five minutes, down the ramp into the underground entrance. The film team met them in the car park, now empty. Half of it had been demolished, the rest would be once the snow had melted, Tor told him. The glass-clad building in front of them was dusty, yellowed, many of the panes had been battered, sprouting cracks all over, but still stood. Bulletproof, Blue remembered. Everywhere, trees grew, digging their roots, extending out, covering the concrete with canopies.

Artists got to work on Blue's face. His shirt was deemed inappropriate and switched out for a neutral color. Tor took another call. A kid approached him in the chair, holding a tablet.

"I'm here about your implant, Mr. Blue. Any discomfort?" He was not the same one who had installed it in his neck.

/ / Are they recruiting all of you out of high school? / / he asked. The kid forced a laugh. Blue didn't like this one as much. He handed the tablet to him, pointing at a box at the end of a lengthy waiver. Blue swiped his wrist in front of it without reading.

/ / Where's the other one? / / he asked. / / The one I met the first time? / /

"We work in shifts," the kid said, shrugging, and said no more.

He was photographed, then filmed on test roll, and allowed toward the glass entryway where Tor waited, holding two hard hats.

"At all times," Tor told him. Blue nodded. He put his on and was steered through the revolving doors. He stepped inside.

The place they had once called F1 was quiet, not unlike what he remembered. That he noticed first. Despite its openness, the office constantly ran interference speakers in the floor and from the ceiling to insulate the sound of chatter throughout the atrium. These, of course, were gone, ripped from the floors along with almost everything else, but the quiet remained. Sunlight poured in from a hole twenty feet wide in the ceiling. The manicured trees encircling the atrium had been allowed free reign, at least twice as tall now. The marble around their foundations was cracked, pushed aside as the roots grew deeper.

"We'll circle in here, get some wide shots. There's the abandoned commissary with some tables left over that we'll be using for the sit-down portion," Tor said, angling his head upward. "What a shithole."

/ / It was clean, once. / / Blue looked back toward the entryway where the van waited. They were assembling the cameras, milling around the open circle where the cars used to come swinging by. / / Are we going upstairs? / /

"Nonnarrative. Why?"

/ / It's where my office used to be. / /

Tor looked at him, blankly.

/ / Thought we might film something in there. I met Io Emsworth the first time in an office up there. / /

"Office . . . " Tor repeated. Blue could see the wheels turning. "That's—that's really good. That's—"

/ / Narrative? / / Blue supplied. Tor had walked several paces ahead of him.

"We do the interview in your office. Two chairs, lights, nothing else. We go in, post-pro, re-create the space. That's—wow. Fuck yeah."

He looked hungry now. "Show me."

The elevators were long trashed. They took the stairs, rising higher. On the third landing, the van and crew outside were behind a wall in the foundations, blocking them from view.

"Did Io work on this floor?"

/ / She didn't have an office. / /

They reached the tenth floor, out onto the steel landing overlooking the atrium. The skybridge hung ahead, suspended by beams. Several of its glass floor panels had shattered and fallen away. Tor stopped in front of it.

"What? You mean across this fucking thing?"

/ / It's right there. / /

Tor leaned over the edge of the walkway, peering down at the floor.

"Not a fucking chance. We'll get a crane in here."

/ / We don't have time to wait for a crane. / /

Tor looked at him, scowling.

"We're done here." He pushed past and went for the stairs. "I'm about to—"

Blue never heard what Tor was about to do. The intake of his air had halted, ending in a gasp when Blue lunged for him, pressing his forearm into Tor's neck, forcing him back around. Their hard hats tumbled to the floor, making noise. Tor struggled, scrabbling his hands, but wasn't very strong.

/ / Don't fight me. / /

Blue inched them toward the walkway, pushing with his chest, his hand over Tor's mouth. He made their first step. Tor gave a muffled whimper through his fingers. The walkway teetered, making creaking sounds as they crossed, halfway, two-thirds. Blue heard only the noise of the bolts groaning when they stepped onto harder ground. Blue turned his head back to the van, the workers who were still sitting around the driveway.

/ / This way. / /

He pushed Tor to the right, down the hall. Two doors, he counted, then the third. He wrestled them both inside. With his free hand, he took Tor's in-ears out and stomped them under his feet. Then he locked the door, releasing him. Tor fell onto his hands and knees, breathing sharply. He flicked his head around, looking wildly.

"Help! Help—"

/ / Soundproof. / / Blue said, circling the room. His desk, bolted to the floor, was still there, though the couch and carpet had been taken. Ugly brown stains on the white carpet. The air smelled of dust.

"What the *fuck* do you think you're doing." Tor's face was red, getting to his feet, "You're fucking dead, when we get out of here. There isn't a place you can't—"

/ / I'm not going to hurt you. / / Blue said. / / I'm sorry. I needed to get in here. / /

"What are you talking about?" Tor looked much smaller now, gasping for breath. Sweat had already started to seep in under the arms of his suit. "There's nothing in here. Feds came and took everything a year ago, before we even met."

Blue wasn't listening. He had come to the other end of the office, where the white paneling of the pantry had not altogether faded. The handles had been taken off their screws. He felt with his fingers around the one he wanted, the refrigerator. It would be here. He held his breath, and, with some decent prying, pulled it open. He peered inside.

On the shelf was a bowl, in the bowl was a little pile of cinnamon cereal. And beside it, the jug. He reached inside and took them both. The jug, still ice cold, fogged over around his hands. Tor watched him, incredulous, take it to his desk.

"What the fuck are you doing?"

Blue could barely hear him. He poured his milk, glancing around.

/ / There's got to be— / /

He pulled open the desk drawer and saw it, the single spoon flush with the corner. He held it, loosely, in one hand. He started to eat.

"You're about to tell me what the *fuck* is going on here—"

Tor's face had hardened to a deeper shade of red. He had begun hyperventilating. He looked wildly around, saw the steel leg of a chair swept against the wall, and picked it up.

"You give me some *fucking* answers," he shrieked. "Right now."

Blue swallowed his last bite. He looked up, at Tor wielding the chair leg like a baseball bat. Then he saw it, down by Tor's leg, their view from the office was an unobstructed panorama of the atrium, into which a girl from the film crew had just stepped. Tor saw her at the same time, and ran to the window.

"Help—" he screamed, slashing the glass with his weapon, making dull sounds and scratch marks. The girl looked up. Blue saw her connect her thoughts, one second, then two, then stagger backward, run for the doors. He put down his spoon. It crossed his mind for the first time that morning that it was wrong, that it was all wrong and that he had blown his chance because he hadn't understood it correctly. He looked down at himself, his empty bowl, closing his eyes.

/ / Come on, come on— / /

Tor was bellowing now, hacking at the glass with reinvigorated strength.

What was he missing? What hadn't he done? He paced the office, quietly, clenching his fists. Any minute, the gate guards would be inside the building. There would be nothing to stop Tor from telling them everything. He might even go to jail. But one thing was for sure, he would never set foot back here again.

/ / What's wrong? / / he said, gritting his teeth. / / What's not working— / /

He waited, pacing, five minutes, ten minutes. Tor had collapsed against the window, his handiwork a lattice of scratches and cracks in the glass. Two trucks had pulled up in front of the car park. Men in black combo gear had broken in through the glass doors. They pointed up at the office, spreading out over the area. Blue put himself in front of his desk, trying every angle, every orientation he could think of. / / Fuck, FUCK. / /

A team of four had come out from the stairway on the other side of the warehouse. Two of them carried a black pillar with handles in their arms. He watched them step, gingerly, over the skybridge, reaching them. He was breathing hard, now, beads of sweat had come over his brow and stung his eyes.

/ / What am I doing wrong— / /

His in-ears chirped. In the corner of his vision, Jem's face appeared. The officers had reached the door. They were yelling something, he could tell by the way they moved their mouths, but he couldn't hear. He saw the latter two orient themselves in front of the door with the battering ram. He saw Jem's face, again. He picked up.

/ / Jem. / /

"Dad," her voice was tense. "What are you doing right now?"

/ / I'll call you back— / /

"Don't lie," Jem said, "some producer for the news just called Mom. Explain what's going on. Right now."

They heard a crash as the ram connected with the door, shaking the ground. Tor pushed himself to the other end of the room, his eyes flitting fearfully from them to Blue.

/ / I wouldn't lie to you. / /

"They said they've called the police," Jem said. "That you're doing some . . . some TV thing. What the fuck is happening? Did you hurt someone?"

/ / No, never. / /

"Dad," Jem's voice broke. "What's going on, just tell me what's going on, please. I can't—"

/ / Jem, please, hang up. / /

"No."

/ / Please. / /

Another *BOOM*. The cracks in the glass had slid all the way up to the doorframe.

"I don't know you," Jem was crying. "I don't even know who you are. You're a liar. You've been lying this entire—"

/ / It went wrong. / / Blue said, speaking fast. His eyes were wet. / / All of it, it's all wrong. I don't—I don't know how it happened but it's all wrong and I don't know how to fix it. / /

"What are you talking about?"

/ / EVERYTHING! / / Blue roared, making Tor jump and shrink, cowering into the corner of the office. / / My entire fucking life, Jem! Every day it's been one goddamn piece of shit thing after another just building and building and building into—I don't want it anymore. I'm trying to fix it. I need to fix it. I need to go back to where it started and fix it or else I—I— / /

He sunk, hitting his knees on the carpet. *BOOM!*

/ / I don't want this life. / / he sobbed. / / I don't want any of it. It's wrong, it's all wrong. / /

The glass was about to give. A panel of it had separated, an inch, two inches. The ram retreated, winding back. The next one would break through.

"Are you saying me, too, Dad?" Jem said, shakily. "Am I wrong, too?"

Blue stared at her face, smiling at him from the corner of his sight, just beyond it the doorway, the shattered glass breaking, giving way just as—

— C L I C K —

He gets to his feet, surveying all around him the pillowy white smoke that seems to engulf the area, the door, halfway blowing open, Tor, closing his eyes against the impact. He knows where he wants to go, but a thought stops him. Her face, still in the corner of his eyesight. He digs his in-ears out, with no need for them, and peels the contact lens off his eye, letting them drop to the floor. He is thinking about Jem, her broken heart. He tells himself there was no other way. Decides it is only the weakest man who lets his child fall through the dark like that.

It occurs to him. The last mystery. The techniques are old and rusted but he catches on quickly again, as though naturally. Shapes reorient around him, the office disappears, dissolving into light. The world becomes dark, crowded. Music reverbs through the floor. Urinals, stalls covered over with graffiti, flickering lights, the men's bathroom at Dream in which, near the end of the stalls, two boys are breathing heavy, making noise. Yes, it is here, Blue thinks. It is right here that it happens, there is no more opportune moment. Blue walks to the sinks, starts up the water, washes his hands. The first stall door opens. Blue hears footsteps, squeaks of rubber soles on the wet tiles. He comes into view out of the corner of Blue's eye, and Blue, distracted, resisting the urge to turn his head, finds himself listing his body sideways. The couple in the farthest stall finish, taking loud breaths. Blue waits a moment, then another. The stall crashes open, the two boys stumble out, on cue. Amid the noise, the movement of bodies, Blue turns his head, contemplates for a moment the unlined face, his own, the slenderer shoulders. It is a gift, he supposes, to see himself like this, after so long. He slips his hand into the jacket and removes the phone, all in a second. The music slows to a halt around him, the boys halfway out the door, to the pulsing crowd frozen in blue light. Blue unlocks the phone, configures a new alarm set for midnight that night. He labels it, types *TRY THE ONE PERCENT*. And he understands, then, what it means. It is a name that Min told him she had already named the baby while he regained the use of his legs in his physical therapy. It is a name, *the* name, the only one that, when the time came, would tell him, the next Blue, the next and the next, what he needed to do, would tell him that it was *he* who sent the message, and would send it, in every loop, the future writing to the past. He types —*JEM.*

— *C L I C K* —

"Have you decided, then?"

/ / Decided what? / /

"Whether you're going to kill me or not?"

Blue gazed across the table at Lev, at his spindly frame and knees knocked together under the hem of his robe.

/ / Tell me if it's true. / /

Lev smiled.

/ / Tell me it does what I think it does. / /

Lev leaned back in his chair.

"You really are going to do what I think you're going to do, aren't you?"

Blue stayed silent. A display on his right corner told him his hour was close to up.

"When?" Lev asked him. "When did you decide?"

/ / I don't remember. / /

Lev nodded. He stood, limped over to a cupboard, and got on his knees to remove a black plank of wood from the bottom of a drawer. Blue's eyes darted toward the door, but it remained closed. Lev replaced the plank and returned with a sheet of paper. He looked it over, wistfully, then passed it across the coffee table. Blue turned it over. It was a page, yellowed now, scribbled over in pen. It read a date of twenty-three years earlier, three days before Christmas, that Christmas he'd fallen down the elevator shaft and received a job offer in return. A single name written on it: his.

Lev spread his arms, wide.

"You've learned my secret."

/ / What are you talking about? / /

"You wanted to know what it does," Lev said. "I think you already knew. You were the only one we hired. I saw you, I saw myself meeting you, giving you that heinous bag back, I saw myself waiting for you, getting coffee, offering you the job. I saw you accepting it."

/ / You saw the future. / /

"Are you following me?" Lev frowned. "Have we been talking about the same thing?"

/ / That's not possible. I've never—I've never been able to go forward / / Blue said, / / only back. / /

Lev was looking at him, curiously.

"You never could keep much in your mind at once. Big boy, you never went forward because you never looked."

He stretched his arms high above his head.

"Or rather, in better terms, the reason you can't go forward is because what you're about to do has already happened, and will happen, again and again. Prescribed, already, within history itself. Are you confused?"

Blue clenched his jaw tight, sitting there.

/ / If it's already happened, it means I don't have a choice, do I? / /

Lev laughed for the first time in a long time, and doing it, Blue noticed, seemed to make him just a bit older, as though parting with the sound, with the air, was erasing him slowly from the world.

"Don't make yourself upset. I've lost a lot more than my choice."

— C L I C K —

The house is quiet. Blue is inside, watching the snow fall through the windows. It is easy to see, having been away for so long, the way that the paint has chipped, the floorboards splintered away from the molding in places. He rounds the corner of the living room, glancing up the stairs. Light from the foremost room spilling down the steps. He climbs, hears a voice.

"—I had them here a minute ago, I swear. If you came here and figured this out it might help me find the catalogs—"

More silence. Blue climbs the stairs, placing his feet on the far ends of the wood so they won't make their creaking noises. He has almost reached the door, places his hand on it.

"Well, if I had the catalogs, I could figure out . . . No, that wouldn't be right. I couldn't ever. I couldn't figure—"

Blue can hear it from here, the way he screams, clipping the audio.

"Bo? What's going on? Are you there? Are you there, Bo?"

There follows a pause in which Blue can hear his father trying, straining to listen, to hear.

"Bo?"

He says it one last time, hopefully. There is no answer. The line is already dead. Blue removes his hand from the knob. There is no sense in what he does but he does it anyway. Opens the door, sees his father sitting there on the edge of his bed in his pajamas, slippers on the wrong feet. Hal lifts his head up to him, widening his eyes just a degree.

"Who are you?"

They stare at each other. Blue tries to make himself step inside but can't. His father's hair is grey. It's the first thing he notices. He wonders when the change happened, he can't place it in his mind. Wrinkles around the eyes, the corners of the mouth. His shoulders are so small. Hal lifts one foot up off the ground. "Can you help me?"

Blue comes to the bed, at last, settling onto one knee. He takes Hal's slippers off, arranging them by the foot of the bed.

"You're not the usual," Hal says.

/ / Late shift. / / Blue manages to choke out. Hal puts his hand on his forearm. Together, they stand. He helps his father into bed, drawing the covers out, then back in, up to the shoulders.

"You have kids?"

Blue glances at the doorway, the darkened hall outside. He sighs.

/ / Yeah. / /

Hal is staring up at the ceiling, folding his hands together on his chest.

"My son. He's just a bit angry with me right now."

Outside, the view out of the window grows hazy. Blue closes his eyes, willing it to remain solid. He stands, about to leave, finds again that he can't move. His eyes fall on the chair in the corner of the room. After a moment, he brings it to the side of Hal's bed and takes his seat.

/ / Is that who you were talking to on the phone? / /

"He's always been a bit moody," Hal says. "I don't blame him. He had to grow up very fast. I think it bothers him when I call, but . . . "

He angles his head, looking Blue in the face.

"It was the funniest thing," he says, "the way, when his mother died, she took everything she brought with her. He stopped talking about her, he stopped speaking her language. He stopped looking like her, even. I know it wasn't his fault. I can't stop him being angry with me."

Blue shakes his head, slowly. Hal frowns at him.

"Are you okay?"

He nods.

/ / I don't think he appreciated you very much. / /

"No, no," Hal says, waving his hand. "He loves me, and his brother. And I know he still loves his mother. There's nothing wrong with being angry. I wish I'd told him that sooner. I think it's too late, now."

He notices the look on Blue's face. "Really, are you okay?"

/ / He's sorry. / / says Blue.

"I know, I know." Hal rubs his thumbs together in an absentminded way. "If I could tell him over and over again how sorry I am, it wouldn't be enough. I tried my best, alone with the two of them. I know it wasn't enough. Now, I don't know where he is. I don't know if he eats well, if he's warm at night. I don't—"

He turns his face away, slightly. "I don't even know if he's happy."

It is the shame in his eyes, angled down to a corner of the room, that Blue can't stop seeing. That in only a few hours Hal will die, without ever seeing either him or Kaz again, that none of them, after so many years, remember Korean anymore, that if the hands of time had turned backward and brought them back to this house, back to the snow and Christmas, it is doubtful they would recognize everything in its place. Blue's face is wet, his shoulders heaving, when he shakes his head and takes Hal's hand.

/ / Your son's really happy, Hal. / / he said. / / You know, I've spoken with him recently, and he told me, he's found a girl, and they're about to have a baby. A daughter. / /

Hal blinks, wide-eyed at him.

"A daughter?"

Blue nods. / / She's due in a couple months. / /

Hal opens his mouth, then closes it. His breaths come in ragged and quick. His eyes are filled with tears.

"A daughter, a daughter," he whispered. "I'm—I don't believe this. My—my son. I never—I never—"

He tilts his head back, wiping his eyes.

"I can't believe this. I can't believe this."

His breaths slow to deep, peaceful intakes. His hand loosens its grip, and Blue lays it back down over the blankets. When he is sure his father won't wake, he gets to his feet, surveying the room. It's his old room, the one he shared with Kaz. He leaves the door ajar and the lights on when he goes, the walls ripple around him, lengthening, turning blue. Moonlight hits. It is three days before Christmas morning when his first step down lands on the center stair, sounding its wooden creak, then another. He stops, looking over his shoulder, back at the door off the first landing behind him, now adorned with paper stars glued and tossed in silver glitter sprinkles. The room in which eight-year-old Bo sits up in bed, hearing the sounds of somebody on the stairs, waiting, wanting it to be somebody he knows. Blue already knows he won't get out of his bed to look, nor call out for his father, who has left him there and gone to bed. He will sit there, for another minute or two, straining to hear more, but will only pick up the sounds of the wind. He steps carefully off to the side, continuing the rest of the way down in silence. The house's first floor, the bright pink glow of the tree lights, morphs into view in front of him as he reaches the bottom of the stairs. Blue takes one last look around, absorbing it, trying to set it securely in his mind. After another minute or two, he heads for the door, eases it open, and steps out into the cold.

— C L I C K —

/ / What do I need to do, when I get there? / /

"I've told you, what you're about to do is already prescribed. It will happen exactly the way it will happen."

/ / Why did you try to stop me the first time? / / Blue said. / / Why did you tell me not to talk to Ry, not to ask questions— / /

"I did what I was always going to do, just the same as you," Lev said. "It didn't matter how it happened, only that it happened at all."

They were silent for a while.

"Are you afraid?" Lev asked him.

/ / Of? / /

"Of what's going to happen when you do it?"

Blue thought about this question, realizing he did not quite know the answer. He put his hands to rest in his lap.

/ / I haven't decided. / /

Their eyes met. / / Do you know? / /

Lev shrugged. "If I knew, we wouldn't be here. That's the way it goes, isn't it? You can't know the answer and still be able to ask the question in the first place. Nobody has ever closed the loop, that's for sure. When you do, you'll be the loneliest man in the world. And nobody, not you, not me, not anyone, can change that."

— C L I C K —

The pavement grows lighter, the moon reverses its course high above the sky, retreating back across the night while he walks. He has neared the crosswalk that leads onto the school grounds, taking careful, deliberate steps over the asphalt. The sky burns red, the sun reenters from its place in the trees.

— C L I C K —

/ / Will I know what happens to you? To my daughter? / /

Lev gazed at him for a few seconds.

"When you close the loop, you eliminate the precedent that

allowed the commute to occur in the first place. You're talking about two points on a line, except that the difference here is that one point not only led to the other, it is responsible for the second point's existence through direct action. What happens when you sever that link? One goes on, one doesn't? Both go on? Neither? Read every book ever written with some hokey plotline like that, they'll never agree. What you're dealing with is an exercise of the imagination."

— *C L I C K* —

He rounds the first walkway toward the buildings, past the parking lot. The sun is high and bright above his head, beating down. The wind is still cold and biting around his legs, on his hands. He has come to the last crosswalk just in front of the yellow double doors. White static draws in on all sides, condensing into cars, shrubs. Lines and pixels gather, forming the ground, the asphalt. She waits, in front of the stop sign, holding two brown bags in her hand, stomping her feet to keep herself warm against the biting wind. He sees the bus turning the corner of the drop-off lane, sees her head dip downward at the half-frozen slush caught on her shoe. Sees her lift her foot up, picking it away, and, satisfied, step out into the road.

— *C L I C K* —

Blue stood, wiping his hands, considerably sweaty, on the front of his pants. Lev watched him, curiously.

"Have you decided what you're going to do with me?"

/ / I will, after you answer one last question. / / said Blue. / / Why are you helping me? / /

He expected that smile, that one he knew so well, but it did not come this time. Lev attempted to get to his feet, but his arms failed him. He collapsed against his cushions, pitiably. He seemed to linger on this moment, unaware of himself, or Blue standing there, or the apartment around them. As though he disappeared, for the briefest time, and reappeared so quickly that, had nobody been watching, it would have looked no different.

"We could've solved so much," he said, "if they'd only worked. If we'd only found a way."

Blue waited, assured he was about to hear more, but again it did not come. He straightened his back and left Lev on the couch, moving to the door. Just as he reached it, he heard Lev cough into his sleeve, a noise that rang through the silent apartment, echoing off the marble. Heard the words, the very last words before his hand closed on the knob and he pulled the door open, headed for the elevator, the street, the subway, headed for a woman he still loved, headed for his daughter, the words: "There wasn't enough time."

— C L I C K —

Blue reaches out his hand, taking the last few steps up to the crosswalk, closes it around her wrist, and, with a jerk of his arm, pulls her back onto the pavement just as the bus swings past. It misses her head by inches. It is so timely and perfect that it cannot be said to have happened so seamlessly without some fault, but it happens. He steadies her, and the lunch bags drop to the ground. Her head is turned, staring at the retreating end of the bus as it rounds the corner and slows to a stop in front of the next crosswalk. He braces himself. He tells himself it will feel like nothing, that by the time it occurs to him, he won't even be able to notice, that he has experienced death like this once before, that he remembered how peaceful it had been, how subtle and kind and quiet to lay, unfeeling, in the hospital with Min at his side. He is holding his breath when at last she turns her head, he finds her face, her brown eyes, his own nose, Kaz's nose. They look at each other for the first time.

17

Her hands were still tight around his forearms, braced and tense. Her eyes, widened from the sudden movement, acclimated to her surroundings. He let her go.

She turned around, saw the bus again, pulling away down the road, then returned to him.

"Oh my God."

He was shaken, still seeing her, still hearing her, but couldn't speak.

"That could've really hurt me," she said, breathless. "How—you—I—"

She was at a loss for words.

"You saw that coming, didn't you?"

The air hung still over them. Then she laughed.

"I can't believe that just happened," she said, stooping to pick up the brown bags. "I can't believe you—you just—"

She looked at him again, folding the tops of the paper shut. "I can't believe that just happened," she said again. "Thank you.

Thank you so much. You—wow. I don't . . . I'd buy you a coffee but—"

She laughed again. Blue found himself smiling. He cleared his throat. More cars had pulled in behind them. The bell had rung.

/ / Glad I was here. / / he said.

"Very glad," she said, "more than glad."

She noticed the bags in her hands. "I was just here to bring my kids their lunch. I'd left it right on the counter and—"

She stopped herself.

"I—thank you," she said again. She looked both ways, crossing the street. She turned around again. "You know, you look just like my—"

She stammered, trying again to laugh. She gave up.

"Thank you."

She was gone.

Blue nodded, watching her retreat inside. The doors shut closed on her back. The sun beat down hard on the back of his neck. He looked around himself. The static had gone. As far as he could see, the way was clear, its borders defined and sharp. He tried again, picturing the house, his condo, somewhere, anywhere. None of it materialized in front of him. He patted himself down. The commute had broken.

It appeared full-bodied and violently into his mind. Jem. He raised a finger, trying to call her, and realized that his in-ears were gone. He spun, slowly on the spot, looking at the little parking lot filling in with late parents and children. He was breathing hard, fearful, when he remembered it. He brought his hand to his chest, feeling with his fingers through his shirt, his heart beating steadily and securely inside him. He is—he was—alive. Still here. And if he was alive, did it not follow that Jem, Min, Kaz, that they were as well? He thought that it did. He would never be sure, but it was the bet he'd made, with Lev, with himself. He knew only one thing: he would not stay here any longer. He looked back across the pavement to the window, where he could spy the tops of little heads bent over their desks. The door at the corner of the room opened. She poked her head through. The top inch of one black-haired little boy moved, scurrying across the room. She passed him his lunch, smiling, and shut the door. She would cross the building to Kaz's classroom next, then come back out, to the waiting car. He started walking, passed the stop sign, continued on along the pavement, and after a while had left the schoolyard, the park, the streets he knew, behind.

He was not afraid. Curious, yes, he thought he was. But not afraid. He was sweating. With a smooth roll of his shoulders he took off the jacket, holding it tenderly in his hands for a moment. He spotted a trashcan on the corner of the street, took a few furtive steps toward it, then changed his mind, swinging it over one shoulder and continuing on. Naturally, the question occurred, as natural to him as though it had been inside him all along, although he knew it never had been. A question that, if he answered it, might just prove it all, might just allow him a chance at something he never had. As he walked away from a life he was not a part of and no longer could be, just one question: what was going to happen next?

ACKNOWLEDGEMENTS

This book is the product of a large amount of labor, luck and the help of others. I am indebted to my editor, Carl Bromley, and the indispensable team at Melville House: Beste Miray Doğan, Maya Bradford, Ariel Palmer-Collins, Molly Donovan, Mike Lindgren, Janet Joy Wilson, Valerie Merians and Dennis Johnson, for giving me a beautiful end product to hold in my hands and see on my bookshelf.

I owe every good thing has happened to me since I decided to try and write novels to my agent, Danielle Bukowski, who saw the very best in my work, reached out via Squarespace contact form and changed my life.

I would like to thank the many classmates at Columbia who read this novel in its various stages of life: Gauraa Shekhar, Elliot Alpern, Al Jacobs, Kage Dipale-Amani, Abhigna Mooraka, Laura Venita Green, Cameron Menchel, Lin King, Patrick Ford-Matz, Jemimah Wei, Sam Feldman, Madeline Garfinkle and Sam Granoff. I am grateful as well for my cohort at the Tin House Winter Workshop: Timea Sipos, Andrea

Bishop, April Sopkin, Tanya Zilinskas, Megan Kakimoto, Camille Jacobson, Reena Shah and our ingenious instructor, Kimberly King Parsons.

To the many generous mentors, teachers, and friends who lent their words and support to this book as it made its way, thank you: Alexander Chee, Sam Lipsyte, Gary Shteyngart, Elaine Hsieh Chou, Lincoln Michel, Manuel Gonzales, Julia Fine and Rob Hart.

To my *One Story* colleagues: I feel often like a very small, very lucky observer in a room full to bursting with your brilliance. To Laura Spence-Ash, Kerry Cullen, Karen Friedman, Will Allison, Lena Valencia, Maribeth Batcha and Hannah Tinti, working with you all is the privilege of a lifetime. Lastly, thank you to Patrick Ryan, for your weekly masterclass in editing and for your friendship.

I would like to thank my professors at Columbia: Lauren Grodstein, Binnie Kirshenbaum, Lynn Xu, Ross Simonini, Nalini Jones, Lara Vapnyar, Rob Spillman, Corinna Barsan, Joshua Furst, Erroll McDonald and Heidi Julavits. I would like to recognize the Undergraduate English Department of Georgetown University, where I wrote my first story, and my professors there: Jee Yoon Lee, Libbie Rifkin, Jennifer Natalya Fink, Nathan Hensley and my thesis advisor Christine So, who imparted to me for the first time in my life a list of essential Asian American writers, and whose guidance I recall every time I sit down at my desk. I am grateful, also, for the kindness and direction of the very first teachers in my life: John Sullivan, Courtney Crane and Susan Murphy of the Princeton High School English Department.

I would like to thank the friends I've known the longest: Lizzie Jones, Richa Rai, Emily Rowe, Katherine Richardson, Danny Smith, Megan Duffy, Danny O'Brien, Ben Germano, Josh Ben-Ami, Lilyan Tay, Arielle Thomas, Kristen Fedor, Jess Kelham-Hohler and Enushé Khan.

To my partner, Bram McGinnis, my brother, Jingu Chong, my mother, Ellen Park and my father, Saeho Chong: among a lifetime of joys, I think, first and always, of you.

The acclaimed winner of numerous "book of the year" awards, including from *Esquire, HuffPost, GQ, Cosmopolitan, Shondaland, Goodreads, Locus Magazine, Best Books by Korean Americans, Nylon, CrimeReads,* and others

A dazzling, time-bending neo-noir about a young Korean American man whose reality unravels when he suspects the mysterious corporation he works for may have inadvertently discovered time travel . . .

"The narrative pleasures of *Flux* lie less in the big reveals than in watching Chong knit together genre tropes from sci-fi movies, speculative fiction, and thrillers to tell a story about how what we remember can imprison us . . . An imaginative exploration of how cultural memory and grief interact."
—***Washington Post***

"Offers a healthy dose of brain-bending pleasure without making it the whole point . . . a deep dive into the good, the bad, and the ugly of self-serving corporate culture; and no shortage of 'wait, what the heck just happened?' thrills."
—***New York Times Book Review***

"Mind-bending."
—***Publishers Weekly,*** starred review

"Engrossing." —***Vanity Fair***

"A lavish mystery that's hanging-off-the-edge-of-your-seat good." —***Cosmopolitan***

"A genre-bending brain teaser." —***USA Today***

"*Flux* is brisk, stylish, and sexy, a high-stakes noir thriller that makes room for big philosophical ideas." —***Philadelphia Inquirer***

"Compelling and utterly new."
—***Bloomberg Businessweek***

"A dizzying, dazzling debut." —***Boing Boing***

"*Flux* adds to a growing canon of terrific ...eculative novels . . . that explore the ...nsion between Western and Asian culture ...om a second-generation perspective."
...***Locus Magazine***

...rilliant." —***Pittsburgh Post-Gazette***

FICTION
MELVILLE HOUSE PUBLISHING
www.mhpbooks.com
Cover design by Beste M. Doğan

£12.99
9 781685 891930